THE RIPTIDE RIDER

Volume one

CHRONICLES OF ABIGAIL WATCHER

Damien M. Cross

HAVANA BOOK GROUP LLC.
HAVANABOOKGROUP.COM

HAVANA BOOK GROUP LLC
2173 SALK AVE, SUITE 250
CARLSBAD, CA. 92008

COPYRIGHT 2021 All rights reserved.
ISBN: 979898919182-6

Acknowledgements

This series, Chronicles of Abigail Watcher,

-started as a birthday gift for my youngest daughter, Abby.

(How many people can say their dad wrote a book for them for their birthday?!?)

The storyline of The Riptide Rider was inspired by my father.

Thanks dad, for the gift. (the leather journal)

First and foremost, thank you, sweet wife, for making this possible.

Special thanks to the following.

-Ben, from Suspicious Observers-

-Bear, from Grindstone Ministries, and the chief shill for Refuge Medical-

And most importantly of all.

Kalebhouse.org

If nothing else on this page stands out or sticks in your brain, let me say it again...

"Kaleb house dot org"

N
W
4
E
S

Table of Contents

Introduction 7

Chapter 1. Abigail Meets Sasha 27

Chapter 2. Riptide Wreckage 47

Chapter 3. Bingo 65

Chapter 4. Captain's Log 77

Chapter 5. A True Fixer Upper 87

Chapter 6. The Heart of The Rider 101

Chapter 7. An Order Not a Suggestion 115

Chapter 8. Godspeed 131

Chapter 9. Fly By Night 145

Chapter 10. The Renegade 161

Chapter 11. Atoll 175

Chapter 12. Getting The Band Back Together 197

Chapter 13. Run Like Smoke and Oakum 213

Chapter 14. Radiation, Turrets, And A Mad Scientist 235

Chapter 15. Natives Amongst Us 245

Chapter 16. Reception 265

Chapter 17. The First Dawn 289

Chapter 18. Brought Up to Speed 311

Chapter 19. Unexpected Gift 337

Chapter 20. The Mission 351

Chapter 21. Warlock, Nero, and Alvarez 365

Chapter 22. What Dreams May Come 379

Chapter 23. Slipstream 393

Chapter 24. Shadow Puppets 407

~ Captain Abigail Watcher ~ Final Moments ~

Captain Watcher clenched her teeth as she pulled the broken cutlass blade from her side, grunting softly from the pain. The last few inches of cold unforgiving metal stubbornly pulled free, and an involuntary cry escaped her lips. Her torso and legs clenched uncontrollably during the final burst of pain.

Abigail's enraged and burning gaze fell on the dead Imperial operative lying on the deck in front of her. She saw the hilt of the broken cutlass still clenched in his fist. With tears flowing from her eyes, she kicked him repeatedly in the side. Cursing him loudly with each impact,

"Stupid! Stinking! Sneaking! Son of a..."

She stopped kicking and just hated him with her eyes for a moment, the pain quickly reminding her of the hole running through her side. She heard Norgren groaning loudly somewhere near the center mast. She heard steel ringing against steel,

Moriarty! He's still fighting...

Captain Watcher heard the rapidly approaching, very distinctive whine of a failing antigravity drive. She looked up and over her shoulder just in time to see it hit.

The Imperial ship crashed onto the edge of the bay off her port bow. A loud deep WHUMP was felt throughout the area as the burning ship slammed into the rising bedrock that surrounded the waters of Freeport Harbor. Fire and smoke flowed like bloody champagne from the crashed ship.

She watched as the groaning hull of the ship, tipped slowly toward the water. The wreckage fell over and slammed into the waters of the bay, crushing a galleon and a fishing ship as it came to rest in the harbor. Salty brine sprayed across her face. The impact created rippling waves that rocked The Riptide Rider beneath her.

Captain Watcher blinked several times then shook her head, trying to clear the fog of war and snap out of her rage induced tunnel vision. She grumbled in her head,

Never a single stupid moment of rest. You'd think getting run through with a stupid sword would buy me ten freaking seconds to catch my breath. Stupid Imperials probably broke my coffee cup, with my stupid luck...

One hand gripping the railing behind her, the injured and exhausted captain of The Rider worked her way back to her feet.

Abigail tossed the broken piece of bloody steel overboard and looked up at the Imperial ships still fighting above her. Hundreds of automated satellites were hammering the Imperial fleet with laser fire. The satellites looked like a blanket of flashing lights, spanning from one horizon to the other,

The Empire's swarm in and overwhelm me tactic didn't quite pan

out as well as they must have thought it would.

Earlier that evening, Captain Watcher sailed The Rider into Freeport Harbor in camouflage mode. She anchored the ship among hundreds of other wooden-hulled fishing and sailing ships that were scattered around the city of Freeport's bay area.

When the Imperial fleet jumped into the temporal bottleneck, they found two-hundred and forty-eight possible targets to choose from.

Sitting in the ocean with her technological systems hidden, The Riptide Rider was indistinguishable from the primitive ships around her. If it weren't for the covert ops team that got lucky and jumped in directly above her, Captain Watcher and her crew might have escaped completely unscathed.

Visibly struggling, huffing and puffing with pain, Norgren pulled himself to his feet with the help of the mainmast, shouting,

"It's too late! We have to abandon ship! Now, before they take her!"

Captain Watcher growled and looked toward the quarterdeck, where she heard the song of blades being played by a master composer. Moriarty had a tritanium gladius in each hand and an Imperial dagger buried deep in his thigh. He was holding off the last two Imperials that were trying to access The Riders control consoles.

She heard Norgren call out again, as he stumbled toward the forward stairwell,

"He can handle himself, Captain! We have to go! Right now!"

Abigail shook her head as she pressed one hand over the wound in her side. She knew her soul would soon depart her body as she felt her own warm blood flowing quickly and freely down her side,

Norgren's right, it's too late and we're out of time. We're all out of time.

Captain Watcher forced her body to start walking, staggering, fighting hard for each of those first steps. She clenched her jaw and embraced the pain. Reaching up with both hands cost her dearly, but the pain focused and cleared her mind. She tugged the leather cord holding back her long grey hair, a little tighter.

Growling and cursing under her breath, she caught up to the limping Norgren. Abigail ducked under his arm, grabbed him, and pushed him to move just a little faster,

"Pick up the pace, old man! I haven't got all day to wait on yer lollygagging!"

On the way to the stairwell, they passed Sasha's lifeless body. Abigail's tears suddenly hurt worse than the hole in her side. Sasha had a pistol clutched tightly in each hand, and a ten-inch hole blown through his chest.

His lifeless eyes were open and staring distantly toward

the sky, as if taking one last look toward the stars. She saw just a hint of a smile on his calm and slightly wrinkled face.

A thin green laser cut into The Rider from an Imperial ship high above. They both heard a small explosion from somewhere below deck. Norgren cursed and groaned,

"Probably hit a high energy conduit! Electromagnetic discharge might draw attention!"

Captain Watcher glanced up, shaking her head just slightly,

"It's more likely that the Imps working sensors are focused on the satellites. Weapons officers are running wild, their fire looks panicked and random. I see individual ships targeting different satellites. The Imps won't survive this fight."

Abigail paused to look up and take stock of the battle, as Norgren struggled with the damaged hatch.

The first wave of Imperial ships had been engaged very quickly, with many destroyed. Some were lucky enough to quickly jump back out, the ones who still had enough reserve power to jump again immediately.

Three quarters of the Imperial fleet died or fled in the first few minutes.

The Imperials jumped in a battleship, about the same time that the Special Ops boarding party dropped onto The Rider. The battleship was a desperate attempt by the Empire, to salvage the botched mission to reclaim or destroy The Riptide Rider.

The battleship dominated the sky, larger than the entire harbor and the city of Freeport with its one million residents. Captain Watcher glared up at the massive ship,

An expensive suicide mission. There's no chance that battleship lasts the days it needs to recharge its jump drive.

A hundred satellites were actively coordinating their fire on the battleship. But there were plenty of others still firing on the smaller ships, forcing them to channel their power into their shields or run.

The massive, highly advanced, automated satellites were left over from an ancient and long forgotten war. They inadvertently saved The Rider and her crew. Unhindered by laser fire, the Imperials could have simply taken their time and vaporized every ship in the harbor. With the satellites hammering them, they couldn't spare the power.

Norgren started down the stairwell toward engineering. Captain Watcher looked back across the ship. Moriarty's blades continued to sing their song as he danced with the Imperials. He was the only other living member of her crew, besides Norgren.

Soul crushing shame ripped a scar across her already ragged heart. She was about to leave him alone and outnumbered on the quarterdeck. She heard a memory of his poetic voice,

Envy the righteous blade who dies in battle, not the tortured crown that sent them to it.

Captain Watcher smiled at the memory. Moriarty was always offering his wisdom,

How right you were. Goodbye, my friend.

As fate would have it. In the brief moment that she looked back, she saw Moriarty run through by the blades of both of the Imperial operatives. Moriarty roared loudly in defiance. He dropped his blades and lunged forward, grabbing both Imperials by the throat and pushing them back.

His sudden rushing advance prevented them from using their blades further. Burning with adrenaline, Moriarty leapt forward and dragged both men over the side with him.

Abigail closed her eyes from the stinging tears. She knew that abandoning ship meant that every single one of them were going to die anyway, but seeing it happen was the hardest thing she ever had to do.

It was down to her and Norgren. She pulled the hatch closed behind her and dropped the locking bar into place,

The Imps won't get through The Rider's defenses any time soon.

Captain Watcher made her way down through the crew quarters and galley level. She stumbled down the metal steps into engineering and staggered through the heavy steel pressure door into the engine room.

She saw Norgren quickly rigging a remote detonator to an anti-matter grenade strapped to the engine. Abigail tugged at her blood-soaked leather vest and put her hand on the leather journal tucked in her belt.

She lowered her head, exhausted,

"I can't believe we're doing this."

Norgren shook his head, vehemently,

"There's no other way, Captain. This is our only possible fourth chance, like they done before. The crew before us didn't make it, and we didn't make it!

Norgren looked at her. She was drifting and fading from blood loss. He slapped Captain Watcher across the face. She turned her head back toward him, her face twitching angrily,

"Thanks."

Norgren pointed to the anti-matter grenade,

"There's nothing more we can do, Captain. Remember, you have to blow the engine immediately after you trigger the jump. It's the only way to hide The Rider's wake along the riptides."

He handed her the detonator,

"All we can do is hope she lands in the right time and place, again."

Captain Watcher held the detonator in one hand and lifted up the jump drive key in the other. She grimaced one last time at Norgren's tired old familiar face,

"Any last words of wisdom, old man?"

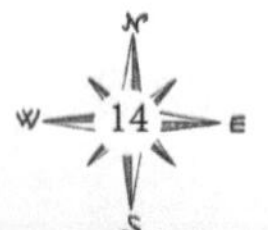

Norgren cocked his head thoughtfully,

"Well, actually..."

Captain Watcher activated The Riptide Riders jump drive and immediately triggered the detonator.

- The Next Captain Abigail Watcher - Final Moments -

Captain Abby put her hand over the broken end of the cutlass blade sticking through her side. She activated the electromagnetic palm plate in her glove and the broken piece of steel shot out from her back and stuck in the railing behind her.

Her eyes went wide from the brief flaring of intense pain,

"That'll wake you up in the morning!"

Heavy rain and hurricane winds hammered The Riptide Rider. Abby laughed loudly and spun the wheel, turning the ship just in time. The Rider's bow lifted on the high waves and turned aside, as another harpoon fired past them from the enemy ship trailing behind.

She felt her enchanted leather vest sealing up the hole in her side.

The gusting winds shifted and battered the ship, swinging Captain Abby's single braid of long raven black hair behind her like a lazy lion's tail,

"Norgren! Bring me the Peacemaker!"

Clinging to the console railings on each side of their captain, Norgren and Sasha looked at each other with wide eyes. Norgren shook his head, then hopped over a dead body from the earlier battle. He ran off toward the forward stairwell,

"AYE CAPTAIN!"

Sasha looked up from the hooded and covered scanning display,

"There's another one closing in! Starboard side!"

Captain Abby laughed,

"Of course there is!"

She spun the wheel the other direction,

"If we don't ditch these pirates with their stolen high-tech weapons, the Empire's going to get a fix on us!"

Lightning flashed through the roiling black storm clouds overhead. Abby tackled Sasha to the deck just in time to avoid a half dozen pencil-thin red lasers fired from the deck of the old wooden sailing ship pursuing them.

She pushed herself up just enough to look back. The pirates quickly stashed their weapons out of sight again. Abby glanced up at the storm, then grinned at Sasha,

"The energetic discharge from the lightning hides their laser fire from the satellites! I had a feeling that was coming!"

Captain Abby jumped to her feet, grabbing the wheel. Sasha groaned and stayed down low. Norgren reemerged from below deck with Kat in tow, the short and slender "Peacemaker" clinging tightly to Norgren's thick arm.

The insane winds battering the ship threatened to blow the slight woman right off the deck.

Abby spotted them and glanced back at the ship behind with an evil grin,

"Hope you boys can swim!"

Norgren helped Kat up to the quarterdeck and over to the control consoles. He grabbed the support railing with one hand and kept one arm around her tiny waist. Kat was holding her hair back out of her face and glaring at Abby through eyes pinched tight against the rain. Kat's displeasure and discomfort were obvious on her face.

Abby laughed,

"Don't take it out on me! The men on that ship behind us, this is their fault!"

Kat turned her glare to the ship behind them. Abby pointed back at them,

"They're packing laser rifles, from a tech-level twelve or thirteen world! Somewhere in that range anyway! Their weapons are stashed out of sight!"

Kat nodded and said something, but Abby could barely make out her soft reply over the storm. Captain Abby leaned closer to the small woman and asked,

"You see what? The power cells?"

Kat nodded, yes, and Abby smiled broadly,

"Perfect! Use the storm's electrical charge and overload the cells! The satellites will detect them and send the pirates to

the bottom of the ocean! We have a chance to just slide right past the Empire's radar!"

Kat nodded and concentrated on the ship behind them. A few moments later, Abby saw a member of the enemy crew freak out and start shouting. He tried to toss something overboard, but he was too late.

The satellites detected the energy signature of the laser rifle's power cell overloading.

A highly charged beam of radiant green microwave energy shot down from the sky and sliced across the front of the enemy ship. The glowing cloud of superheated particles that were left behind quickly dissipated in the storm. The rear half of the enemy ship ran for the safety of the ocean floor.

Abby grinned and spun the wheel away from the other enemy ship bearing down on them. She shouted over the wind,

"Rinse and repeat, Kat!"

A few moments later, The Riptide Rider was pulling away from the second sinking ship. Captain Abby thrust one fist into the air, shouting,

"That's how it's done!"

She glanced to her right and noticed that Norgren didn't share in her excitement. He was looking at the dark clouds above through narrowed eyes,

"We got a problem, Captain!"

Abby shielded her eyes from the wind and rain and looked up. Lightning flickered through the clouds, revealing the giant black shadow of an Imperial battleship in the heart of the storm. Her smile melted into regret and sadness, then slowly hardened into a deep resolve.

The captain of The Rider sighed deeply at the shadow of her death sentence and looked down at the deck. She shook her head and wondered,

How did they find us? Not one run-in with Imps since we arrived. Not once have we revealed The Rider's advanced systems.

Captain Abby pulled off one glove and used her bare hand to grab ahold of the leather journal that was tucked in her belt. She concentrated and focused her thoughts,

The Eternal Empire has found us. I have to abandon ship immediately. Imperial troops will be all over us very soon.

She turned away from the others and looked up at the dark clouds overhead. Abby reached up with her free hand and shielded her eyes from the storm, her thoughts on the killer machines orbiting the planet. She squeezed the journal tightly,

The answer has to lie with the vast network of intelligent satellites that exists in the bottleneck. They must have some kind of central backup or data archive hidden somewhere on the planet. Something recoverable must survive the cataclysm and carry on into the age of the builders. There's no other possible explanation.

Abby looked down at the ship around her,

Even camouflaged, the empire found us after the satellites fired on

pirate ships that were near us. It appears that any focused attention from the satellites that gets recorded and documented will end in failure. The Rider has to pass through unseen.

Abby turned back and put her free hand on the console. She looked down at the deck, as if she could see The Rider's jump drive several decks below. Her eyes narrowed and she continued gripping the journal tightly,

The only option we have now is to abandon ship and send The Rider back to start the long cycle all over again. We can't possibly jump away from their fleet undetected. Maybe it's somehow possible for Norgren to tweak the jump drive and hide The Rider's interdimensional wake, without blowing the engine? I don't know, but that's all I've got for you, girl.

Abby pulled her glove back on and looked up at the others. They were watching her through sad and knowing eyes. She forced a weak smile and shouted at Norgren,

"The three of you are going to need that diving gear we stashed away!"

Norgren nodded. He grimaced and shook his head. Abby put a hand on his shoulder and looked him in the eyes,

"The next crew has a solid chance, old friend! Thanks to the changes and upgrades you've made!"

Norgren nodded again. Abby put a hand on Sasha's shoulder,

"The future Captain of The Rider is going to have something none of us ever had on any attempt before! The two best men on my crew, my dearest friends, to help her cast off!"

Norgren smiled. He left the quarterdeck, went down the stairs and ducked into her cabin to retrieve the diving gear. Sasha was crying. Captain Abby wrapped her arms around him and hugged him tight, shouting over the storm,

"I couldn't have done even half of it without you!"

Sasha bawled like a baby. Abby chuckled,

He's such a drama queen.

Kat stepped close. Abby looked at her, then held out an arm,

"Most importantly, she'll have you! Come on, get in here, we're running out of time!"

Kat put an arm around Abby and Sasha, her eyes wet with tears.

Norgren came running up the stairs, shouting,

"Alright, knock it off! They'll be here any minute!"

Kat stepped away and moved toward the aft railing. Sasha grabbed two of the diving masks and joined Kat, getting them ready to go.

Captain Abby pulled off her hat and jammed it into Norgren's hands. She looked at him with cold, hard eyes,

"If you don't get Kat back where she belongs, none of this is going to matter!"

Norgren nodded, glancing over at Kat,

"According to the back channels, this was a first, Captain! They've never gone after her before! What do you think changed?"

Abby shook her head. She didn't know why the Empire decided to target Kat. Maybe they hoped to catch The Rider during the rescue. She grinned and shrugged,

"Who knows, maybe they watched The Terminator!"

Captain Abby gave Norgren a quick fierce hug, then held out her hand,

"You have my backup plan?"

Norgren wiped away the tears and handed her the detonator.

Abby tucked the detonator into her pocket,

"Get her home safe, old friend!"

Norgren nodded and walked over to Sasha and Kat, pulling on his diving mask and air supply. The three of them tightened their gear and prepared to jump. Norgren pulled out a short-range directional transmitter and pointed it toward the water behind them, calling the escape submarine closer to the surface.

Captain Abby shouted over the storm one last time,

"With any luck, the next crew will be The Rider's last!"

Norgren and Sasha both looked back with smiling, tear-filled eyes. Norgren nodded, then the three of them jumped into the raging ocean.

Abby hooked a loop of rope over one of the handles on the wheel, locking it in place. She walked to the forward hatch shielding her eyes from the wind and rain, carefully watching the sky above. She pulled the hatch closed behind her and dropped the locking bar into place,

The Imps won't get through The Rider's defenses any time soon.

Captain Abby took her time getting to engineering, giving the others time to get to the sub and get away.

In the engine room she found a large, improvised explosive rigged to The Rider's engine. Abby dropped her gloves and grabbed the journal one last time, concentrating,

Looking back over the years, I can barely remember what The Rider looked like, when I found her in the woods behind my home. She was lost and alone, she was wrecked and broken in hull and heart...

Captain Abby tugged her belt tighter and wiped away her tears with the back of her hand. She looked at the engine and thought about her years aboard The Rider,

"I'm so sorry we failed you. But the next one won't. I promise."

She held up the jump drive key and the detonator, smiling broadly beneath her streaming tears,

"Good luck, girl."

Abigail Meets Sasha

-Current Day-

Kat scooted her chair up to her desk and started typing into her diary...

This version of the future Captain Abigail Watcher is a very unique kind of child. She would argue of course, that at fifteen almost sixteen years old, she is more of a young woman than a child.

She is incredibly independent and stubborn. When she sinks her teeth in, she never gives up. I've made sure of that, over these early critical years. Although I'm sure that being the only child of a single mother who's been a widow for eight years now has had a lot to do with her development as well.

I've done my best to nudge her in certain directions. I've left her mostly to her own devices, raised her in a large house that's tucked away deep in the woods on a very expansive rural property. It takes nearly ten minutes to drive down to the gate, where the drive intersects a very rarely traveled, back country road.

My hope was that a solitary childhood would foster an independent and curious nature, leading to a desire for exploration and the eager embrace of a life of adventure. Deprived of distractions like friends, computers, and electronic games, she's been forced to read her way through

my extensive library...

~ ~

Abby scooted her chair up to her desk and started typing into her diary...

My "world-famous author" of a mother, has rarely left her study since the death of my father. Now, she is insisting that I start keeping a diary or a journal of some kind. Apparently, she wants me to follow in her footsteps of being a reclusive hermit who never leaves her room or ever sees the real world.

A thousand times she's told me that her books about the adventures of Captain Katherine the Fierce have sold millions and millions of copies. That's her rationale for her obsessive pecking at a keyboard. Like I care how many books her worshippers have bought!

To make it even worse, stupid Hollywood even made an entire stupid series of movies based on the stupid adventures of Captain Katherine! A bunch of nauseating drivel that I flip right past during my weekly two hours of television.

That's what mother does, she writes. That's all she ever does!

Since the death of my father, Justin, I've watched mom sink deeper and deeper into the imaginary worlds she writes about. She leaves the computer in her study only when she absolutely has to. She must eat and sleep, since she's still alive. She even occasionally checks on her daughter, on those rare occasions that she remembers she has one!

One of these days, mom. Things are going to change! My world is going to change!

~ ~

Kat finished her diary entry,

One of these days, things are going to change. Abby's whole world is going to change. Or, more accurately, it's going to go sideways... on the interdimensional riptides.

Kat shut down her computer and went to bed.

~ ~

Abby woke up the next morning and grinned,

Mom was right, I do feel better. Venting my frustrations into an electronic diary really helped.

She got up with a yawn, and zombie shuffled in her pajamas into the bathroom. She splashed some water on her cheeks and made funny faces at herself in the mirror.

Abby reached for the silver chain around her neck and pulled the mounted crystal out from under her pajama shirt. It was her most precious possession. A crystal necklace that her father gave her many years ago. Playing with the odd necklace and thinking about her father was as much a part of her morning routine as getting out of bed.

Climbing up on the sturdy bathroom countertop, Abby sat down with her feet in the sink and her knees pulled up close to her chest. She leaned to the side against the mirror and imagined that her reflection in the mirror was her father. It was his shoulder that she was leaning against.

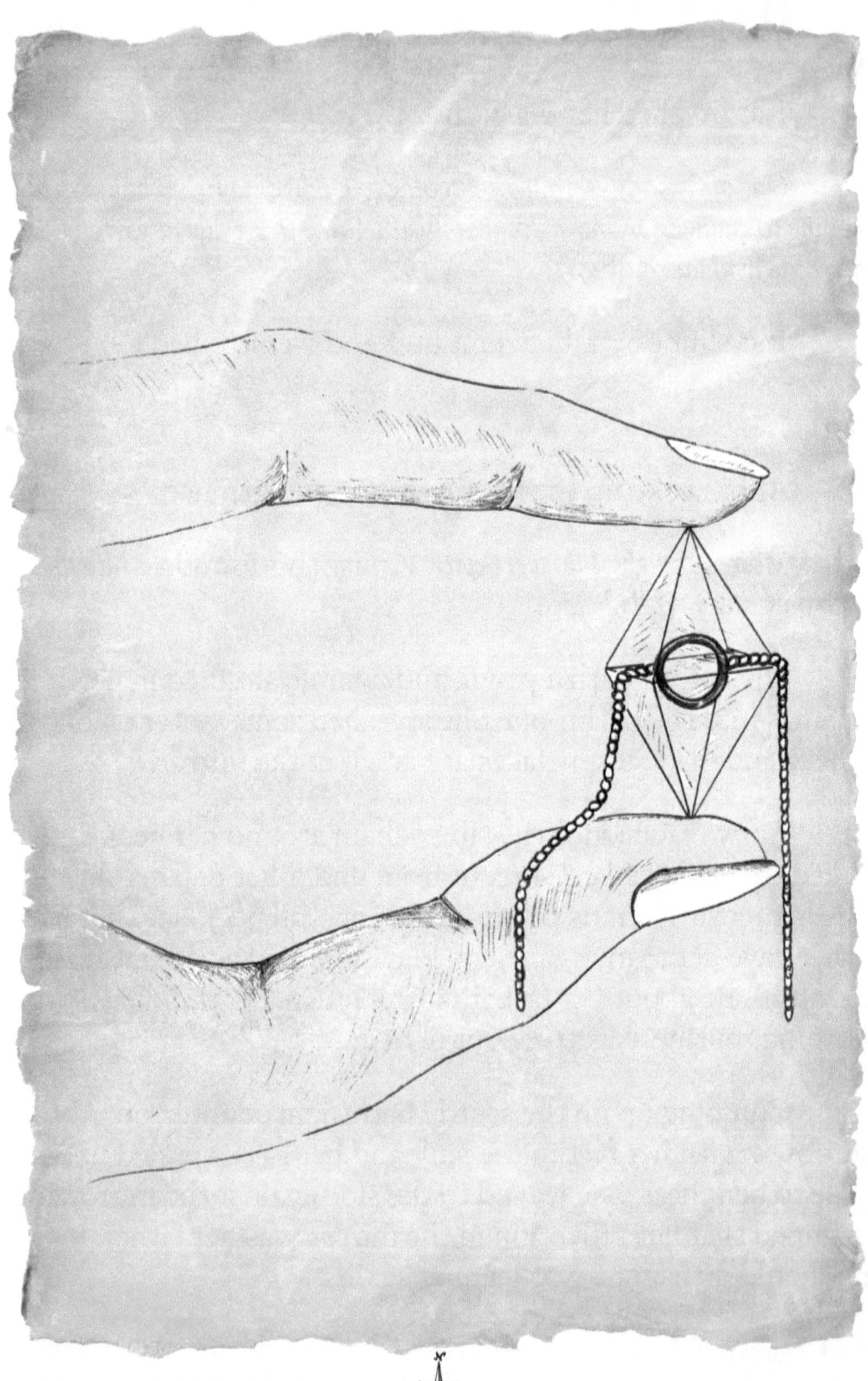

She leaned her head against the mirror. But in her mind, she leaned her head against his. She held up the crystal, wrists resting on her knees. She stared at the cloudy transparent blue stone, and imagined talking to the phantom of her father as she leaned against him,

You know, in the beginning, I did this because I was just a child. A sad little child, who missed her daddy. I did it because you gave this to me the day before we lost you. I remember holding it, just like this, every single day since your funeral.

A tear chased several others down her cheek, leaving a hint of salty essence on the corner of her lips,

I remember holding this thing so tightly at times that it nearly cut into my skin. I stood there staring at myself in this mirror, crying my eyes out and begging you to just come home.

Abby imagined his gentle hand on her shoulder, as he reached over and hugged her. She heard the sound of his remembered voice,

Now you do it to remember me and spend time with me. That's precious to me. This time with you means the world to me, little miss. You always say good morning or tell me about your adventures the day before. I remember you once saying, 'I saw mom yesterday'. That tore my heart out baby girl.

Abby smiled briefly under her tears. She held the stone up to the light,

It still amazes me, even after all these years. I can't figure out how it was made. The way the chain comes together inside the stone. Where did

you even find this thing?

She imagined that she heard her father chuckle,

You told me that it looked like someone melted two pyramids of blue crystal together over the silver ring in the center. It is an amazing stone capable of incredible things. One day, you'll see just how special it really is.

In her mind, Abby felt him turn toward her. He gave her a gentle kiss on the side of her head, and she envisioned him whispering intensely in her ear,

Never give up on me sweetheart! Never let go, never mourn my death. One day soon, you'll discover the secret of the stone, and then you'll come find me.

Abby smiled at the necklace as tears poured down her cheeks. The phantom memory of her father faded away as she tucked the necklace back into her shirt. She wiped at her tears, her burning eyes squeezed tightly shut.

She wrapped her arms around herself and choked out the words,

"Good morning, daddy."

Sobbing loudly, she added,

"I miss you."

After a time, she got up from her seat on the countertop. She looked in the mirror and wiped away the last of her tears. It was time to emotionally reset. It was time to start the rest of her day. Like she did every morning, she reached down deep

and shut off the pain. Like flipping a light switch, she stopped being sad and she smiled.

Abby pulled a warm fluffy bathrobe over her pajamas and made her way out through her room and into the hall. She crouched, looking around for pretend enemy operatives. They were always lurking in the shadows. Abby crept along the second-floor balcony, approaching her mother's door at the top of the stairs like a cute fuzzy ninja.

Quietly and carefully, she pushed open her mother's door and peaked inside. The bed was messed up and empty. Grinning, Abby went in and straightened the blankets. She imagined her mother later in the day, searching for maid fairies living in the walls.

Abby walked down the stairs, her fluffy slippers making barely a whisper on the thick, soft carpeting. At the base of the stairs, she looked carefully around the large living room.

The long, lonely leather couch had every pillow exactly in its proper place, begging for company. The fireplace sat moping, cold and forgotten. Abby looked toward the far wall, where tall, massive, side by side windows showed the dark woods north of the house. The very tops of the trees were just now being brushed with color by the faint light of the rising sun.

Abby smiled at the trees. They were always there for her. If the wind were blowing, they even waved at her. The trees, the birds, the squirrels, they never ignored her. When Abby walked the paths through the woods north of the house, the squirrels always ran off to tell their friends about seeing her.

That's when she suddenly noticed a light shining into the dining room from behind the central load-bearing wall. Abby crept toward the fireplace at the dining room end of the large wall that separated the living room from the kitchen.

She heard movement and shuffling around in the kitchen. Her eyes grew wide. Her mother wasn't in her study typing. She was in the kitchen! Abby took several careful steps toward the kitchen. She didn't want to spook her and send her running for the safety of her study and her computer.

About halfway across the living room, Abby heard a man's soft tenor voice say,

"Oh, this is positively dreadful."

Abby stopped and stood there with wide eyes, a confused look on her face. She had absolutely no idea who he was. She had never heard the man's voice before. Abby glanced toward the closed doors at the other end of the central wall, that led to her mother's study. The study doors were closed, and the lights were on.

She stood as still as possible and listened, unsure what to do. She heard more shuffling around, then what sounded like a skillet being placed on the stove top?

Was a burglar making breakfast?

Very slowly, Abby crept closer to the fireplace end of the central wall. She heard the rapid click of the gas igniter and the gentle 'FOOF' of the gas burner igniting. She heard the unknown man's voice again,

"Do you like eggs?"

Again, Abby stopped and stood perfectly still, wondering,

Is some strange man making my mom breakfast?

She listened to hear if her mother responded. The silence stretched for several moments. Then the man responsible for the strange voice poked his head around the corner and looked at her expectantly.

Abby just stared up at him in shock. The tall slender stranger, with brown eyes and short, well combed black hair made a puzzled, slightly frustrated face. He walked around the wall and stood right in front of her. He put his hands on his hips and looked at her expectantly.

Looking down, Abby saw black dress pants and shiny shoes. She noted his white button up shirt. She looked for any scars or distinctive features. She wanted to be ready if she had to describe him to law enforcement later.

The strange man shook his head at her,

"She said you were a special child, but she never mentioned that you were mute and catatonic at this age."

Abby cocked her head at him, confused,

"I'm sorry, what? She who? Who are you?"

His eyebrows rose and he gave her an exaggerated smile. He leaned slightly forward and said,

"It's a miracle! She speaks!"

Chuckling, he shook his head and walked back into the kitchen. Abby heard him opening the fridge and moving things around. Again, he asked,

"Do you like eggs?"

Abby crept forward, moving around the fireplace. She looked into the kitchen. The stranger was standing by the large stone island. He was holding an egg and staring at her expectantly. Her mother was not in the kitchen.

She glared at him suspiciously,

"Where's my mom?"

The strange man looked down at the egg in his hand. He shifted it from side to side, looking at it from different angles. Then he held it up again and looked at her incredulously,

"You can see this, right? It's not invisible?"

Abby narrowed her eyes and repeated her question,

"Where is my MOM?"

He shook his head and rolled his eyes, obviously exasperated. After a moment, he looked down at the grocery bags on the island countertop and appeared to be considering something.

Finally, he turned and picked up a black shoulder bag from the floor and placed it on the island. He opened the bag

and pulled out a tablet. He quickly smiled at her and nodded, then held the tablet up in front of himself and began slowly turning in a circle, saying,

"Scanning... scanning..."

Abby watched him with the most confused look on her face,

Is he an escaped mental patient?

Next, he tapped the blank screen a few times while making beeping sounds with his mouth and then set the tablet down. He looked back at her sadly and shook his head,

"I'm sorry miss, it appears the tracking device I placed on your mother just isn't working."

Abby narrowed her eyes and stomped a fuzzy slipper at him,

"I'm not five years old!"

He gave her a mock look of shock and surprise. He gestured at her outfit, agitated,

"Pajamas, fuzzy slippers, bathrobe, I never would have guessed you weren't a five-year-old! But whether or not you like eggs? It appears that mystery might never be solved!"

Abby glared at him angrily. Turning around, she stormed off to her mother's study and opened the door, barging in. As always, Kat was typing away on her computer. Abby asked harshly,

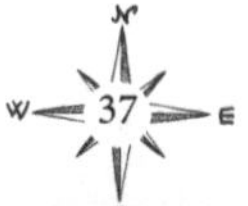

"MOM! Who's the irritating weirdo in the kitchen?"

Without stopping or turning around to look at her, Kat said,

"I don't know sweetheart. Are you in the kitchen holding a mirror?"

"MOM!"

Abby's mother absently waved a hand off to the side. It was a gesture Abby had seen a thousand times. It generally translated into, "I'm working dear, go play in traffic." Abby silently stomped a fuzzy slipper at her,

"Fine! I'll just go have breakfast with some strange man I've never met before!"

Kat stopped typing and cocked her head, she asked,

"If you've never met him, how could you know he's strange? We call that a continuity issue in the writing world. Logically, you have to meet someone before you can deduce that they are strange. Or get a really good look at them, at the very least. Did you view the stranger from a safe distance, sweetheart?"

Abby stormed out and slammed the door. She balled up her fists and shook them at her mom through the wall. She stalked back into the kitchen and saw the strange man standing in the same place by the island. He was still holding the egg.

Lifting it higher, he flashed her a huge smile,

"Loooook... an egg. You like?"

Abby put her fists on her hips, and squared her shoulders,

"Who are you?"

His face shifted dramatically and suddenly he looked absolutely exhausted. He staggered forward, barely catching himself with one arm on the large stone island. He seemed to be vibrating with the effort of remaining on his feet. His other arm struggled to hold the egg up in the air and he pleaded desperately,

"For the love of all things holy... please... just... answer the question."

Abby stood her ground,

"You, first!"

He stood up and took a deep breath. He very slowly set the egg on the island, then he sighed,

"At long last. Fair enough, I accept your terms. My name is Sasha. I'm the steward to the former captain of the interdimensional pirate ship, The Riptide Rider. At your service."

He swept one hand across himself in front of his waist as he gracefully bowed to her and then stood back up. He smiled broadly at her skeptical frown,

"Your turn, young miss. Eggs?"

Abby turned away and stomped through the living room, yelling,

"MOOOOOM!"

She got to the doors of the study as Kat walked out. Abby followed her around the near end of the wall, heading into the kitchen from the laundry room side. Kat said,

"Fine, I'll make you break…"

Abby followed her into the kitchen, then leaned around her to look in as Kat came to a sudden stop mid-sentence. The strange man was gone. The grocery bags were gone. There was a single broken egg on the floor by the island.

Kat turned around to look at her,

"What is going on with you this morning?"

Abby moved around her mother, looking around the kitchen franticly. He was gone. The bags, everything, just gone. It wasn't possible. Was she dreaming? Was she sleepwalking?

Abby ran over to the sliding glass doors on the opposite side of the island counter from the fireplace. She looked out onto the screened in porch. Nothing. When she looked back, Kat was cleaning up the broken egg with paper towels and a sanitizing wipe.

Eyes wide, mouth hanging open in shocked confusion, Abby just stood by the door looking around.

Kat walked over and gave her a hug,

"Honestly Abigail, are you just trying to get my attention? I know I've been distant lately, but I have a deadline, a novel to finish, and a book signing."

Abby shook her head, her voice low and haunted,

"No mom. He was here. He was right here in the kitchen. He was holding that egg. I saw him. I talked to him."

Kat leaned back, holding her daughter at arm's length. She gave her a sympathetic smile and said,

"Jericho, system status?"

A deep male voice answered from a speaker mounted in the ceiling. Jericho sounded just enough like a computer that it wasn't creepy like an actual person hiding in their ceiling,

"All access points secured and locked. System is armed. No incidents to report."

Kat gave her a look, like 'now what'?

Abby shook her head, no,

"That thing is BROKEN!"

Abby turned around and flipped up the lock on the sliding glass door. She pulled it open before Kat could stop her. Jericho's voice came over the speaker blaring,

"BURGLAR! BURGLAR! LEAVE IMMEDIATELY!

ALERTING AUTHORITIES!"

Abby covered her ears while Kat walked over to the control panel and entered the code to deactivate the system. She had a less than happy look on her face as she walked over and waited by the phone.

Abby smiled sheepishly and made a 'my bad' kind of expression.

A few moments later the phone rang. Kat answered it,

"Hello."

"No, just a false alarm sheriff. Everything's fine."

"No, no problem, I understand completely. Yes, password is 'Riptide'."

Abby's eyes went wide. Her mom just said Riptide. What was going on? What did that man say? She couldn't remember.

Kat hung up the phone,

"Abigail. I need these antics to stop. The book signing is the day after tomorrow. You're just days from turning sixteen sweetheart, please tell me you're going to be ok while I'm gone."

What? She was still going?

"Wait! You're leaving me here? With some weirdo in the area?"

Kat grinned at her,

"I told you weeks ago about the book signing. Like I said, you're welcome to come. I can call Janet and have her contact the airline? Book you a ticket?"

Abby's face went pale, her eyes grew haunted,

"Whoa. WHAT? You're flying?"

Kat smiled sympathetically and nodded, yes,

"Unless you have some other way that I can get to London in less than forty-eight hours?"

Abby's breathing changed, her heart was racing,

"Mom! Seriously! You have to cancel. You can't leave me here alone with that Sasha dude popping in and out of our kitchen."

Kat's eyes widened, she had a pleasantly surprised look on her face,

"You little liar pants! You said you don't read my books."

Read her books? What was she talking about?

"What books? What do you mean?"

Kat narrowed her eyes playfully for a moment. She then rolled her eyes and shrugged,

"Oh nothing, I mean it's no big deal, I might have written a couple books. Nothing you would have seen. I don't know

what made me think…"

"MOM!"

Kat spread her hands, looking incredulous,

"That Sasha dude? Abigail! Sasha's the captain's steward in an entire series of my books. Don't pretend you didn't know that."

Kat started laughing and turned away. She opened the fridge and leaned forward, searching the shelves. It came flooding back to Abby, she heard his gentle and articulate voice in her memory,

My name is Sasha. I'm the steward to the former captain of the interdimensional pirate ship, The Riptide Rider. At your service.

Abby felt like she was going to be sick. She put a hand on her stomach and shook her head,

This can't be happening. Sasha's a character from a book?

Kat looked over at her and immediately grew concerned. Her smile faded as she walked over and put a hand on Abby's forehead,

"Are you ok, sweetheart? You look like you just saw a ghost."

Abby nodded and mumbled,

"A ghost would have been so much better."

Kat took her hand away and went to the 'medical junk' drawer. Abby looked at the floor and scrunched up her face, feeling nauseated,

Am I dreaming? Did I imagine all of that?

Kat made a frustrated sound and closed the drawer. She walked over by the phone and added 'thermometer' to her shopping list. Abby leaned against the island counter and spoke quietly,

"Maybe I'm just worried about you getting on one of those flying deathtraps with wings..."

Kat walked over and wrapped her daughter in a comforting hug. Abby's eyes suddenly filled with tears, and she cried on her mom's shoulder. Kat stroked her hair and whispered,

"My sweet girl, I completely forgot what day this is. I miss him too, baby."

Abby gently pulled away from the hug, wiping her eyes. She walked toward the stairs,

"I think I need more sleep. I might just start this day over."

Kat shook her head and went back to her study.

Abby went back upstairs, kicked off her slippers, and draped her robe over the back of her chair. She climbed back into bed, pulled the soft puffy comforter over her and closed her eyes. She very much wanted to wake up from this crazy dream.

Riptide Wreckage

Abby was sure she had just closed her eyes, when she woke up to the sound of knocking on her door. She growled from under the comforter,

"Whaaaaat? I'm sleeping."

"I'm going to town for some, um groceries, and other stuff. Just some odds and ends, for while I'm gone. Do you want to come with me?"

Abby groaned back at her. Kat laughed and trailed off as she went down the stairs,

"I offered. You had your cha..."

Abby tried to fall back asleep but couldn't get comfortable. Eventually she tossed off the covers and sat up, yawning and rubbing her eyes. She sat there for a bit, thinking about Sasha in the kitchen,

Was he real, or just a hallucination?

Her eyes widened a bit as she suddenly realized she didn't know which option would be worse. Abby closed her eyes and shook her head, confused. Then a third option popped into her mind.

She grinned suddenly and nodded. She looked over at her little stuffed 'Zelda' doll and picked it up. She smiled at Zelda and said,

"That was just a dream!"

Zelda nodded in agreement as Abby's hands moved,

"That's right. That was a dream, and this is a brand-new day. And you know what? It's going to be a good day!"

Zelda nodded vigorously in agreement.

Abby tossed Zelda onto her pillow and crawled out of bed, smiling. She knew it wasn't just a dream, but she decided that's how she was going to think about it. Maybe, just maybe, if she believed it was all just a dream hard enough, she could avoid a straight-jacket and a padded cell.

She got up and put on some rugged clothes. She needed to get out of the house and spend some time in the woods. She picked out jeans, a long sleeve flannel shirt, and her hiking boots. She looked in the mirror and nodded. She decided her outfit wasn't just perfect for an afternoon trek through the woods, she also looked freaking awesome.

Abby clipped the lanyard of a folding knife to her belt and carried her daypack down to the kitchen. She tossed the pack onto the large square stone island and walked over to the pantry. She opened the wide double doors and looked inside at the obsessively packed shelves, shaking her head.

A small grocery store of food and snacks stood ready for

deployment on the shelves. Her mom said she was going into town to get groceries?

Yeah right. I couldn't eat all of this food in a year. Where was she really going? What was she really doing?

Abby put both questions on a mental whiteboard like sticky notes. She'd have to remember to keep an eye out for those answers.

She loaded up her pack with various snacks and a couple of water bottles. Abby picked it up and swung it onto her shoulders. She noticed there was a writing pad on the island. She hadn't seen it when she tossed her pack on top of it.

It must have been left behind by her mom. She thought to herself,

Ugh... Chore list.

A strong breeze suddenly blew in through the open sliding glass door next to her. Abby put one hand up next to her face and watched as the wind blew the pages of the writing pad up and over themselves until eventually, it flipped the whole thing over. The breeze stopped just as suddenly as it had started.

Underneath the writing pad, was a very old-looking piece of tattered parchment paper. Abby picked it up. It looked like a map drawn in pencil,

Did mom leave this for me?

Abby looked at it closely. She recognized the outline of

the back of her house and the edge of the woods beyond the back yard.

The map only took up about the middle third of the paper. The top and bottom thirds of the page were blank. She saw a trail of tiny dash marks leading from the back door of the screened porch into the woods behind the house.

It was strange, the map didn't look complete. Abby looked out the kitchen window toward the woods. She looked back down at the map. The trail and the trees were detailed on the map about as far as she could see. The writing pad had been sitting directly on top of the map.

Mom left this for me to find. There's no other logical possibility.

It was like a surprise treasure hunt. Her mom must have thought that she would either pretend not to see the chore list and miss out on the map. Or she would decide to be good and pick up the list and find the map.

Abby grinned and war-gamed it out in her mind,

So, mom leaves this weird treasure map to cheer me up after the rough morning. Well, the jokes on you mom, that was yesterday to me. So, ha. But she doesn't want to just give me the map. She also wants to mom it up with a lesson that deciding to do the right thing sometimes pays off in ways you didn't expect.

That's two jokes on you mom, the wind handed me the prize that I probably would have missed.

Abby laughed and nodded to herself. Sounded right to her. She tugged the shoulder straps of her pack a little tighter

and headed out through the sliding glass door. She was looking at the map and walked right into the closed door, bumping her nose painfully against the glass.

She backed up and blinked in confusion. The sliding glass door was closed. But it had just been open. The breeze blew in. Abby glanced at the island and saw the upside-down writing pad lying where the wind blew it over.

She took a step back from the door,

"Jericho, system status?"

Jericho's slightly machine-like voice responded,

"All access points secured and locked. System is armed. No incidents to report."

Abby looked at the sliding glass door and shook her head. This day just refused to be normal. She wasn't going to let it win. She walked over and disarmed the system. Then she reset it and headed out, closing the door behind herself before the system rearmed.

She stopped on the porch and closed her eyes, taking a deep breath and slowly letting it back out. She opened her eyes and smiled. This was going to be a good day. She had already decided that. The day was just going to have to get onboard.

Abby headed out the back door of the porch and walked across the back yard. She vaulted herself over the short black metal fence. Once on the other side, she looked back down at the map. Her eyes went wide. It was different. The drawing changed.

With raised eyebrows, she slowly turned the single sheet of old paper over. She was absently looking for some kind of hidden electronics that obviously weren't there.

She stood there stunned, just staring at the paper,

This isn't possible. Pencil drawings on paper don't just change themselves.

She shook her head and looked around. Everything looked real. She was pretty sure she wasn't dreaming.

Looking back at the map, she saw that most of the house had disappeared into the blank part at the bottom of the page. The trail was longer and now showed more of the woods ahead.

Abby shook her head and laughed. Possible or not, this was really happening. She grinned and narrowed her eyes at the map,

"You're not freaking me out! If I'm meant to spend this day in a dream, it's going to be a good freaking dream!"

Abby looked up at the path ahead, then looked down and double checked the trail on the map. It appeared to follow along the path that she knew very well. She had been hiking through these woods for years.

She shook her head again then just laughed and started heading down the path. She couldn't even begin to imagine how all of this was possible.

Another sticky note went up on her mental white board,

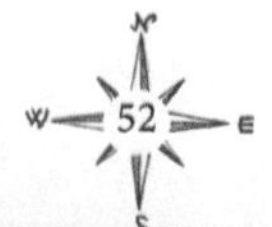

Probably wasn't mom that left the magic map for me to find. Freaky Sasha dude strikes again.

Abby followed the path, occasionally checking her progress on the strange magical map. It followed the path for about a mile, then suddenly diverted off into the woods. Abby looked at the map closely.

Whatever it was leading her to, was nearby. She didn't like leaving the path as a general rule, but she knew these woods and she was only about a mile from home.

Abby looked around and saw a squirrel staring at her. She glared at him,

"There is no possibility of me getting lost here! Ok?"

She heard the squirrel thinking,

Unless you suddenly get caught in a pop-up thunderstorm, and you become disoriented. That is possible.

Abby laughed and shook her head, no. The sun was up. She could see just fine. She decided the mystery was worth the risk. Plus, based on the map, the end was just over the hill in front of her.

She looked up and down the path one last time. She reassured herself that she knew exactly where she was. Then she turned and headed off into the woods and started up the gentle hill in front of her.

As she got closer to the top of the hill, the trail was getting shorter. The picture on the map was getting bigger. No,

not bigger, closer. The closer she got to the end, the more the map was zooming in. She could make out individual trees on the paper now.

She looked up, shook her head at the crazy map, and walked to the top of the hill. From this vantage point, Abby could see down the far side. There was a smaller, much steeper hill near the bottom, where a creek emerged from an underground spring.

Abby grinned. This is exactly where she thought she was. She played in that creek and hunted crawdads with her dad when he was still alive.

She remembered him holding one up for her to look at. It looked exactly like a tiny little lobster. She remembered following him to this very spot, where he told her that the creek emerged from a magical spring under the small hill.

Abby walked the rest of the way down the long gentle slope and sat down next to the creek. She looked at the map. There was just a large X in the center of the paper now.

She set the map down next to her and pulled off her pack, placing it between her feet. Abby dug out a protein bar, looked around, and smiled. She spent some time snacking and remembering back to when she was very young.

More and more memories kept coming to her. Hunting crawdads, finding pretty rocks in the stream. She remembered lots of laughter and smiles, while spending time with her dad. He spoke softly, he was so funny. She finished the snack bar and drank some water.

It felt like the day was trying to make it up to her, for giving her such a crazy morning. Abby smiled and looked down at the map. It still had a big X in the center of the page. Fair enough.

No secret buried pirate treasure that she could sell and then blow the money following her favorite band around the world on tour. Just a crazy map leading her to some wonderful memories of her father. Abby smiled and decided to head back and see if her mom was back from the store.

A sudden strong wind swiped the map right off the ground. It flew up and away, toward the steep little hill where the creek emerged. Abby reached out and tried to catch it, but the wind was too fast.

The map flew up into the air and fluttered around, laughing at her. Then it whisked away toward three tall, oddly straight trees coming up out of the brush on top of the low hill.

The map landed against the side of the center tree for just a moment. Abby looked at the tree and saw wooden boards under the vines and leaves. The map whipped away around the tree and vanished. What was she seeing?

She looked closely at the tree. It was perfectly straight, like a telephone pole. She looked at the other two trees on the hill, one on each side. They were also perfectly tall and straight. Abby narrowed her eyes and cocked her head,

What is going on here?

Brushing off the crumbs from the protein bar, Abby

climbed to her feet and swung the pack back up onto her shoulders. There was something clearly manmade beneath the leafy vines and brush surrounding the small hill.

Abby walked closer, approaching a steep wall of vines. Her heart quickened with realization. The trees were masts of a ship! The boards she saw were the bulging crow's nest on the center mast.

She stepped back, staggering in shock, looking around wildly. She realized suddenly that the hill wasn't a hill. It was a ship. A very old ship, overgrown with brush and covered in vines with big green leaves,

Wait a minute! This is an OCEAN sailing ship! Hundreds of miles from the ocean! The insanity of this day is back with a vengeance!

Surrounded and covered with dense overgrowth. It was too steep for her to get closer to the masts. She would need a ladder or something to get up onto the deck. Abby walked around, studying the thick vines and the brush, looking for some way through.

Eventually, she came all the way back around to where the creek emerged from the low hill. The low hill, that was actually a ship. She walked to the place where the creek started and looked closer, pulling aside some of the overgrowth.

The water wasn't coming up out of the ground. It was actually gushing out of a wide crack at the bottom of the ship's hull. Moving a little higher, she pulled aside more of the overgrowth. The crack in the hull narrowed as it ran up the side of the ship. Something had split the hull open, and now

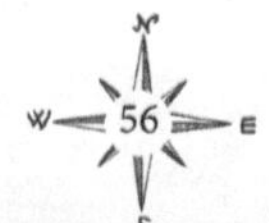

water was gushing out from the bottom.

Abby put one hand on the ship and turned back around to look behind her. The creek was flowing. She looked down to where the water flowed out of the opening. It was like the ship ran over a fire hydrant. It was a lot of water.

She squatted down and tried to see through the opening. It was too dark. The opening was too narrow. She couldn't see in. She had no choice. She was going to have to climb.

Abby tightened the straps on her pack, then she reached up and grabbed a vine. The leaves crackled in her grip, but the vine felt solid. She placed a foot carefully and pulled herself up. The vines were holding her weight. Reaching as high as she could, she climbed.

About five minutes later, she pulled herself up and over the railing at the top. She rolled forward onto the brush covered deck and lay on her back, laughing. She was slightly crushing some of her snacks and breathing hard from exertion.

Looking around in amazement, she got to her feet. From up here on the deck, it was much more obvious that the short hill was actually a ship. She was fairly certain that she was near the front end.

At the other end, beyond the three masts, she saw a raised area with a door and some rickety-looking stairs going up on each side. It was covered with growth, but it was definitely a door. She carefully made her way over to it.

In between the second and third masts, she had to avoid

a large weak-looking area that seemed to take up a large part of the center of the deck.

Reaching the door, it took her a while to clear away enough of the vines and other growth holding it closed. With considerable effort, she pulled the door open just enough to squeeze inside.

The smell reminded her of a damp cave that never got any sunlight. Inside, there were gloomy shapes and outlines. She saw what might be a bookcase, a desk, a large chest on the floor. There was a table and several chairs.

Abby reached down into the pocket on her thigh and pulled out one of her chemical lights. She bent the plastic casing and heard the snapping of the glass tube cracking inside. The first faint light revealed cobwebs and drifting particles of dust. She shook the chemical light. It brightened and revealed the captain's cabin.

With the glowing light in hand, Abby moved farther in, looking around. Everything was covered in either dust or cobwebs. She walked closer to the desk. On it, she saw a shiny brass object with tiny mirrors and small moving parts. Several books were stacked to one side. Then something caught her attention.

In the center of the desk, she saw a clean leather journal. It was closed and wrapped with a long leather cord. Abby picked it up and ran her thumb across the cover. Not a single speck of dust or a hint of a cobweb.

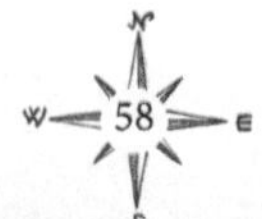

Bringing the light closer, she saw a detailed compass rose pressed into the thick leather of the front cover. She lifted the journal and saw a small golden wheel tied to the end of the leather cord that was wrapped around it. It looked like a tiny golden helm, about the size of a quarter.

Abby put the light between her teeth and lifted the small golden wheel between her fingertips. She rubbed her thumb across the intricate and complex center of the small disc. She heard a voice behind her,

"...not to be toyed with..."

She dropped the wheel, snatched the light out of her mouth, and spun around. The voice sounded like the weird guy in her kitchen. The one that kept trying to grill her about eggs. The one who called himself Sasha, the steward.

Abby didn't see anyone else in the cabin. She held the glowstick up high and looked carefully. She appeared to be alone. After looking around one more time, Abby guessed she had just heard the wind and imagined the voice.

She took the journal with her and walked back outside. She wanted to get a better look at the golden wheel. Once outside, she held the journal up in the light and caught the tiny wheel in between her fingers.

Looking closer, she noticed it was even more intricate than she had realized at first. It wasn't finely carved. The center of the wheel had tiny complex clockwork parts and gears beneath the openings in the center disc.

Abby put her thumb on the center disc and turned it slightly counterclockwise. Looking very closely, she saw the tiny gears beginning to spin underneath.

Wind slammed into the side of the ship. She had to shift her feet as it pushed hard against her. The wooden hull groaned loudly under the pressure. The masts shifted. Abby felt the deck moving beneath her feet. Despite the roar of the wind, Abby heard a rough harsh voice shouting from above and behind her,

"CAREFUL NOW! THE RIDER'S IN NO CONDITION TO SAIL!"

Abby didn't have a chance to look behind her. In a panic, she accidentally pushed down on the small disc in the center of the wheel. She felt it 'CLICK', into place.

So many things happened so fast, to Abby they seemed to all happen at once.

She felt the whole ship shift to the side under her feet. She heard a loud electromagnetic whine quickly spinning up, rapidly getting louder. The sky flickered back and forth between light and dark. The ear-piercing whine pulsed with a deafening, low frequency warbling discharge and instantly everything was different.

Abby suddenly found herself back on the side of the ship, still climbing up. But only her feet were in the footholds. She wasn't holding onto the vines. She still had the leather journal and the tiny golden wheel in her hands.

Panicked and falling backward, Abby let go of the tiny wheel, and reached for the vines. At the last possible second, she caught hold of a vine. The long dead and dried out section of vine snapped away from the rest. Her weight carried her backward and down.

She saw the vine-covered side of the ship rapidly moving up and away from her. Her last thought was that she had it backwards. She was the one moving, falling away from the ship, and down. Everything went black.

BINGO

Abby slowly opened her eyes as pain pulled her back to consciousness. It was dark. She was cold. She looked up and saw the outline of the ship looming large in front of her. She saw the shadowy shapes of trees all around her against the dark sky above.

She heard someone shouting her name from somewhere far away. Abby tried to sit up and cried out in pain. Her right arm felt like it was broken. Her back and head suddenly hurt also. Her whole body began screaming for attention.

Her eyes squeezed shut as tears began running down her face. She felt thick strong arms lift her from the ground. The stranger carried her quickly up the hill toward the path, jostling her painfully. At the top, they set her back down just as quickly.

It was all incredibly painful. As her body hit the ground, Abby cried out in pain again. Forcing her eyes open, she saw a large dark shape moving quickly away from her, back down the hill toward the ship.

~ ~

Sheriff Baker found Abby on the hilltop near the path. He

checked her over quickly and decided she was well enough for travel. He knew Kat was at home, worried sick. She wanted to be out combing the woods. He insisted she stay at home in case Abby came home on her own.

Kat must have seen him carrying Abby out of the woods, limp in his arms. He heard her scream and then she exploded off the back porch, running toward him,

"Easy now, Kat! Easy. She's just passed out. I think she might have a broken arm, but she's going to be just fine."

~ ~

Kat clenched her teeth. She gently touched Abby's hair, nodding rapidly. Of course she was ok. She had to be ok. Kat had tears running down both sides of her face. She had been crying for hours, devastated by worry and tortured by the cruelty of her vivid imagination.

Sheriff Baker gave her a sympathetic look and nodded toward the driveway,

"Let's take my truck. I can get us there a lot faster than you can."

She snapped a fierce look at him. The Sheriff chuckled and corrected himself,

"You need to hold her while I drive, is what I meant to say. Come on, let's go. Get the door and climb in, I'll pass her to you."

~ ~

When Abby woke up, she was lying in her bed at home. The lights were turned down low and it was quiet. She felt something odd and looked over. Her right arm was in a soft inflatable cast. Abby heard her mom's voice come from her other side and turned her head to look,

"You scared me near to death, Little Miss."

Abby hadn't heard anyone call her that in a very long time. Little Miss was her father's nickname for her, it made her smile,

Mom looks wrecked, totally exhausted.

Abby blinked and lifted her head just slightly,

"What happened?"

Kat stood up and stretched, then she came over and sat down on the bed. She stroked Abby's hair,

"When you didn't come home, I called the sheriff. He came out with two of his deputies. By the time they all got here, I was starting to really freak out. It was way past dark."

Kat laughed and shook her head,

"I didn't handle myself well. I shouted a bit. I screamed a bit. I cried a lot. But then there you were. Sheriff Baker came walking out of the woods carrying you."

Kat reached across and checked the cast,

"The sheriff thought you might have a broken arm. It's

bruised up really bad under that cast. But the doctor said it's just a bad sprain and contusions. No lasting damage. Your turn, young lady. What exactly happened out there, Abigail Watcher?"

Oh no... Mom just full named me, she must be serious.

Abby answered a little hesitantly at first,

"I... uh... I was climbing. I reached for a vine, and it broke. I fell. I don't remember anything after that."

Kat slowly shook her head. After a moment, she smiled and leaned down and kissed her on the forehead. She looked at the cast on Abby's arm. She took a deep breath and let it out slowly,

"I'm going to cancel my trip. I'm going to cancel the book signing in London."

Abby looked over her mother's shoulder and suddenly saw Sasha standing behind her mom, in a fancy black suit. His dark hair was combed back to perfection. He held up both hands in a pleading gesture. He looked scared and desperate, shaking his head quickly, NO.

Sasha gave Abby a serious stare and intensely shook his head no, again. Then he touched his left wrist under his jacket sleeve and vanished. He just disappeared, as if he had never been there.

Abby looked back at her, as Kat started to stand up. On impulse, she blurted out,

"NO!"

Kat looked confused. She sat back down,

"It's ok. I'll tell my fans I had a family emergency come up. I can reschedule. People will understand. It's just a book signing sweetheart."

Abby shook her head, no,

"No, mom, no. You can't. You can't cancel."

Kat started to say something, but Abby wasn't finished. She struggled to come up with the right words,

"You can't... do that... to me. You can't put that stress on me. That will be all I'll be able to think about, how I ruined your trip to London."

Abby held up her right arm, showing the air cast,

"It's just a sprain. That's what you just said. I just fell mom. It happens. I'm ok. Please don't cancel. Not because of this, I'll never forgive myself."

Kat smiled at her. She had a strange look on her face, strained yet thoughtful. A tear rolled down her cheek,

"My little girl is growing up. I'm so proud of you. Your dad would be so very proud of you. It's like you snuck up and became a young woman while I wasn't looking."

Kat stood up and put her hands on her hips. She looked down at the floor for a moment, then looked up into Abby's

eyes,

"Are you sure? You'll be, ok?"

Abby smiled and nodded her head,

"I got this."

Kat turned to walk out,

"Get some more rest sweetheart. I'll wake you up for breakfast in a few hours."

Abby watched her leave and close the door. She looked around her room. Sasha was gone. What had she seen? Was that a vision? A hallucination? She suddenly remembered the leather journal with the long winding strap and the tiny golden wheel.

Abby froze and stared distantly at nothing, remembering the intricate wheel with the tiny central disc and the clockwork gears turning inside. The gears that had altered wind and reality.

She remembered the ship shifting under her feet. The sky flickering between light and dark. That insane noise. And then, what? She had traveled back in time? She was suddenly back to where she had been, climbing the side of the ship. None of it made any sense.

Abby got up out of bed and turned up the lights. She looked around and found her daypack by the foot of her bed. She opened the zippered pockets and searched for it. It wasn't there.

She found the flannel and boots she was wearing earlier, in a plastic bag that the hospital must have sent home with her mom. Nothing. Where was the journal?

She had a moment of panic. She remembered it had been in her hand when she fell. When she fell back toward the creek. Or rather fell back toward the water that was gushing out of a crack in the hull of the ship. If the journal fell into the water, it might be completely ruined.

~ ~

Kat got out of bed a couple hours later. She was exhausted from all the stress and lack of sleep the night before. She went down the hall and found Abby's room empty. She walked downstairs and found Abby in the kitchen making breakfast.

Kat smiled pleasantly, despite the smoke in the air. She walked into the kitchen,

"This is a wonderful surprise."

Abby grinned, setting plates and forks on the table. Kat eyed the blackened and burnt meat on the stove suspiciously. She couldn't be positive what it once was before Abby burnt it to death.

Kat turned on the exhaust hood over the stove before the smoke detectors got annoyed. Her daughter wanted to make her breakfast, and it was the thought that counted.

She walked over to Abby and gave her a big hug,

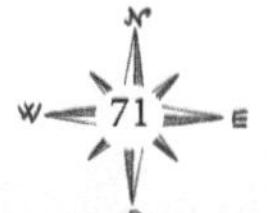

"How's the arm?"

Abby shrugged and shook her arm a little,

"If it weren't for this cast, I'd probably have forgotten all about it."

Kat nodded and smiled,

"That's good. Hey, I have an idea."

Abby stopped setting the table and turned around to listen. Kat walked back to the stove and turned off the burner. Then she moved the smoking skillet off to the side. She turned back to her daughter,

"Since this is my last meal on the ground, how about we take Sheriff Baker out to breakfast as a thank you? I mean, he was the one who found you and then carried you almost a mile back to the house after all."

Abby gestured toward the stove,

"But I made you breakfast."

Kat gave her a sympathetic look and shook her head, no. She gestured to the skillet,

"We'll chalk this up as a learning experience sweetheart. Because, when it looks like this, it was done at least thirty minutes ago."

Abby rolled her eyes,

"Maybe you just don't appreciate my cooking style."

~ ~

An hour later, they sat down for breakfast with Sheriff Baker. He was older than her mom. In his sixties maybe, Abby wasn't sure. He had a bit of a belly, but he was also very strong looking with a big thick chest and arms. Which explained how he was able to carry her all the way back to the house.

Abby poked at her food, eating occasional bites here and there. She was only half listening to them talk. Mostly, she was going over recent events in her mind. Sasha was in her kitchen, that was real. He was standing behind her mom last night,

A character from mom's books?

He even left the broken egg behind on the floor. She watched her mom clean it up,

That happened. That wasn't a hallucination.

The moment she told her mom about him he vanished, all of his bags of groceries and everything.

Kat interrupted Abby's thoughts,

"Wasn't there something that you wanted to say to the sheriff, Abby?"

Abby gave her a confused look, then looked over at the sheriff. Then it dawned on her. She sat up straighter,

"YES! Actually, yes. Thank you, sir. Thank you for finding

me and for carrying me home.”

Sheriff Baker smiled and nodded,

“You’re most welcome, of course. Your father Justin, God rest his soul, was a good man. He’d have been there for me if the need arose. I couldn’t do any less. It’s just a good thing you were able to get to the top of that hill, or I’d never have seen you.”

Abby furrowed her brow

Top of the hill? What is he talking about?,

“I don’t understand. I fell near the bottom of the hill, down by the creek.”

Sheriff Baker cocked his head, thinking,

“Well, doc said you might have had a bit of a concussion. It’s possible you crawled or scampered up someway and don’t remember. When I looked around with my flashlight, I could tell there were tracks of a sort leading up to where I found you.”

Then she remembered. The big thick arms that lifted her up, down by the creek. The large dark shape moving away from her back down the hill. The sheriff wouldn’t have picked her up, moved her, set her back down, then picked her up and carried her home.

Someone else picked her up. She suddenly remembered the harsh, rough voice shouting from above and behind her,

CAREFUL NOW! THE RIDERS IN NO CONDITION TO SAIL!

Whoever he was, he didn't want anyone to see him. He moved her to the top of the hill so that the sheriff would see her from the path. Sasha didn't want her mom to see him.

A lightbulb turned on over Abby's head.

The server moved quietly and slowly. He refilled the sheriff's coffee and then Kat's water. He came around the table and leaned down next to Abby just in time to hear her quietly say to herself,

"I'm not supposed to tell anyone about any of this."

In response, the server whispered,

"Bingo, Captain."

Abby looked up at him in shock. Sasha, in a server's outfit, smiled at her.

She thought,

Captain? What the...

Captain's Log

Sasha refilled her water glass as she stared at him with her jaw hanging open. She couldn't believe it. Sasha was serving them breakfast. He examined Abby's plate closely, studying the few scraps of sausage and pancake left behind.

He sighed deeply, then gave Abby an irritated look,

"That doesn't tell me anything. Now does it?"

Abby heard him make an exasperated noise as he walked away. As the minutes crept by, Abby kept looking around, but Sasha never came back.

Kat looked at her watch and became slightly alarmed,

"Oh dear! Sheriff, I'm sorry to rush off, but I seem to have lost track of time. My bags are already in the car, but I'm barely going to have enough time to get Abby back home and still make the airport in time. We have to get moving."

Sheriff Baker waved his hand dismissively,

"Don't even stress about it, Kat. I can run Abby home. That'll give you plenty of time to make your flight."

Kat smiled,

"You just keep running to our rescue. Thank you, Matt. I appreciate it."

Kat stood up and walked around the table. She pulled Abby to her feet and gave her the biggest hug ever. She looked her daughter in the eyes,

"You ARE going to be ok, yes?"

Abby smiled and nodded,

"I got this mom. Go to London and scribble on some books for your sycophants."

Kat laughed briefly,

"That's unkind to my fans sweetheart, but I love that you know that word."

Kat walked around the table as Sheriff Baker stood up. She gave him a hug also and thanked him again for everything he had done for them.

The sheriff just smiled and waved it off,

"My pleasure to help out. And don't worry, I'll keep an eye out while you're gone and make sure no strangers are lurking about. You just come home safe."

Abby smiled. She liked Sheriff Baker. He was a good man with a huge heart. She remembered hearing her mom say that everyone liked him. Now she could see why. Abby waved goodbye to Kat when she looked back before going out the door.

Turning to look at Sheriff Baker, Abby saw him adding a few more dollars to the tip her mom left for the waitress.

Abby gave him a big smile when he looked up and realized she had caught him adding more money to the tip. He gave her a sheepish look and shrugged. He put his wallet away,

"The wife used to work for tips, I'm biased."

Abby grinned,

"Uh huh, you big softy."

The sheriff rolled his eyes then put on his sunglasses and gave her his best 'cop look',

"You just get in the truck miss, before I arrest you for loiterin, ya hear?"

Abby laughed and followed him out to his Suburban. They climbed in and he drove her back to her house. On the way, Abby looked over at him,

"You're going to make sure there are no strangers lurking about?"

The sheriff gave half a shrug from his seat,

"Single mom flying out of the country and a young girl home alone for the first time, I just didn't want Kat to worry about you."

Abby gave him an accusing look,

"She told you I saw a man in our kitchen, didn't she?"

He took a deep breath before responding,

"She's just worried about you, Abby."

Abby didn't let up,

"She came to you yesterday and asked you to keep an eye on me, didn't she?"

The sheriff chuckled,

"You're pretty sharp for a girl your age, did you know that?"

Abby turned and looked back out the windshield,

"My best friends for the past decade have been the thousands of books in my mom's library."

Sheriff Baker nodded,

"That explains it. Most kids your age have been hypnotized into a stupor on them computer phones."

Abby laughed,

"Computer phones?"

The sheriff nodded,

"Folks call em smart phones, but that ain't what they make a person. Turn kids into zombies. You know when math skills went straight downhill? When they gave everybody

calculators.”

Abby rolled her eyes,

“You’re such a grownup.”

The sheriff grinned,

“Thanks.”

Sheriff Baker dropped Abby off by her front door and
gave her a card with his cellphone number on it,

“Don’t hesitate to call, and try to keep your feet on the
ground, maybe?”

Abby looked back as she headed up to the door. She gave
him a jokingly evil grin,

“No promises. Thanks for the ride.”

She gave him a genuine smile and waved as he laughed
and drove away. Abby went inside and turned off the alarm
system. She watched through the window as his Suburban
made its way down the drive.

As soon as his truck disappeared from view, she ran
up to her room and switched from her sneakers to her hiking
boots. She grabbed her folding knife and hooked it to her belt.
Then she threw on a new flannel shirt, grabbed her daypack,
and checked the contents. Tossing one strap over her shoulder,
she headed down to the kitchen and tossed the pack on the
kitchen island.

She still had plenty of water and snacks, but her father had always been the type to carry three times what he needed, just in case he met two people who didn't have enough. She tossed a couple more water bottles, trail mix, and a handful of protein bars into her pack. She put the pack straps over her shoulders and tugged them tighter.

She set the alarm and headed out the back door. Abby leapt over the short black fence and went running down the path. After a while, she was beginning to worry she might have gone too far and passed the spot where the creek started. Abby turned west into the woods and headed away from the path.

Very soon she ran into the creek running south.

Abby grinned broadly. She hadn't missed it. She just hadn't gone far enough. She turned north and followed the creek up to where it started. She walked around a bend in the stream and came into view of the ship. Her eyes went wide.

Most of the vines and brush had been dislodged from the ship. It was now, very obviously, an old, wooden, ocean sailing vessel. She shook her head. She had found a ship, deep in the woods, hundreds of miles from the ocean.

As she walked closer, she saw piles of brush, broken vines, and broken tree limbs all in a huge cluster around the base. It all must have shaken loose when she did whatever it was that she did, when she fiddled with the tiny golden wheel that was attached to the journal,

The journal!

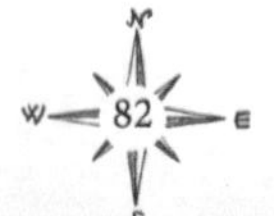

Abby ran for the head of the creek next to the hull and started searching the area franticly,

It isn't here!

She checked under the same pile of sticks and vines for the third time and stopped,

Oh no.

There was one obvious reason that she wouldn't be finding it on the ground.

Abby stepped over to the water and looked in. Sure enough, there it was. She saw the tiny golden wheel glinting under the water. It had to be ruined. The journal had been lying underwater for a full day. Abby shook her head and reached down. She grabbed the journal and lifted it out of the water.

She held it up and let the water run off of it. She shook off the last few drops clinging to the outside of the leather cover. She turned her hand, looking in at the pages from the top and bottom. Surprisingly, the pages inside didn't look bad. Abby untied the leather cord, then she unwound it from the closed cover.

When she opened the journal, her eyes went wide, and her jaw fell nearly to the ground. The pages inside the journal were dry! It wasn't even completely protected by the cover. The top and bottom were open to the air. It should have been one hundred percent completely soaked after all this time, but the pages were bone dry.

Abby flipped through the pages and felt her blood go

cold. It was blank. The journal she had been so worried about, was blank. She turned back to the first page and a chill ran down her spine.

Words magically formed on the page as she stared at it.

She watched in shock, as the first page filled itself in.

In her handwriting...

CAPTAINS LOG

Looking back over the years, I can barely remember finding The Rider in the woods behind my home. She was lost and alone. She was wrecked and broken in both hull and heart. I found her many years after she crashed. I found her in the place she ended up after her last crew was forced to abandon ship. She called to me, in a way. She drew me a map.

The Riptide Rider isn't just an old wooden ship, that's a disguise, a costume. She's an interdimensional research vessel, technically reconnaissance class. She's capable of riding the sideways moving currents of energy that connect all of the fractured worlds and hold the shattered timelines together.

What the builders call, the hyper-dimensional riptide.

When I found her, I found the journal. I didn't know it then, but that meant The Rider had made its choice. It had chosen me, for her captain. As she's obviously chosen you, again.

This journal is self-filling. It's a part of you now, as much as it's a part of the ship. I look back at the early pages and remember seeing them for the first time. I remember how insanely confusing it all was, back then.

In time, you'll understand. I know you will, because I understand. I remember being so confused at the insanity of finding the ship. Now, you're finding it again, after I had to abandon it, tens of thousands of years from

your now.

Before you lose your mind, understand a basic principle. I said that The Riptide Rider is an interdimensional vessel. Well, the fourth dimension is time. Take any singular moment and count slowly to five. You just moved forward five seconds, through the fourth dimension.

There are a thousand things I want to say, but I can't. It's hard to leave you in the dark, but it's necessary. Like I said, one day you'll understand. I do have to tell you one thing. I have to try, even though I know you won't listen. I didn't.

Abby, trust me, you CAN'T save him.

This is my final entry, and the first one I'll someday see.

Welcome aboard The Riptide Rider, Captain Abigail.

Signed, Captain Abigail Watcher.

A True Fixer Upper

Abby blinked and found herself sitting next to the stream, just staring into the water. She didn't remember sitting down. The words in the journal were still dancing through her mind. Her brain was struggling to make sense of the madness she just read. The madness she would one day write, to herself, in the past.

She looked down at her left hand. She was still holding the journal. It was still open to the insanity of the first page. She looked up at the sky. There was still a bright sun, up in the sky above the treetops. She didn't see a giant glowing monkey shedding light on the world.

At this point, she wouldn't have been surprised to see a giant glowing monkey,

Did I injure my head when I fell? Hit a rock? Am I lying in the hospital in a coma?

Some twigs and leaves landed on her head, startling her out of her mental self-diagnosis. Abby looked up and saw a heavyset man that she guessed to be in his thirties maybe. He was looking down at her over the railing of the ship.

He had the dirtiest white shirt on, under the most

heavily stained coveralls she had ever seen. It was almost a crime to call the shirt white. He ran a thick, grimy looking hand through his scraggly black hair and called down to her in a deep, very rough voice,

"The Rider isn't going to repair itself, now, is it?"

She recognized his voice. From up on the deck, the one who carried her up the hill,

THE RIDERS IN NO CONDITION TO SAIL!

He moved away from the railing. She heard him making noise up on the deck. It sounded like he was dragging something across the vine covered wood. Abby just sat and stared. She was still in shock from the journal.

A moment later, he peaked over the edge and called down,

"LOOKOUT BELOW!"

Abby's eyes grew wide as a huge bundle of ropes and boards was heaved over the side. It spun and tumbled and straightened out as it unrolled. The end of the rope ladder slapped against the hull of the ship. The sound dulled by the overgrown vines.

Confused, she just stared at it for a moment. Did he think she was going to climb back up on that ship again? She looked back up and saw him poke his head back over the side. He cocked his head and called down to her,

"What's the problem, Captain? Are you wounded?

Mental? Are you coming up, or what?"

Abby stood up. She looked down at the open journal in her hand,

Is this really happening?

She looked up at the irritated expression on the man up on deck. He looked real. She looked over her shoulder at the hill leading back to the path and back to her home. She could drop this leather wrapped book of insanity right now.

Run home and never leave the house again. Never leave her room again.

She looked at the creek in front of her. She reached out and held the open journal over the water. This was too crazy. She heard the rough voice from above, his tone quite a bit gentler,

"I still remember what you said to me, Captain. Years ago, you told me how hard that first step was for you. Based on what I know about you, I'm sure you'll tell me again, Captain."

Abby looked up. He had a compassionate and patient look, that didn't quite fit his rough face with his scruffy beard. There was something about his expression. She couldn't quite place it. He knew something. He had a secret. Then it dawned on her. He did know something. He knew her.

Abby pulled her hand back and folded the journal closed. She wrapped the leather cord around the cover. Then she tucked the tiny golden wheel through the wrapped cord. She looked at the rope ladder and took a deep breath, letting it out

slowly,

This is insane.

Abby reached down deep and took that first step. The step she knew she would one day tell him about. Tucking the journal into her belt, she climbed the ladder.

Once at the top, Abby saw the big heavy man in his filthy grimy coveralls beyond the forward mast. He was near the very front of the ship clearing away vines and overgrowth with a ragged-looking machete.

It looked like he was trying to gain access to a door that looked like it went into what must be an enclosed stairwell heading down. The raised but slanted area couldn't possibly lead anywhere else but down into the ship.

Abby walked over and looked a little closer. She saw that he had a tool belt on that was overflowing with tools. Some she recognized that were very similar to screwdrivers and wrenches. There were also some tools she had never seen before.

Either way, none of the tools in his belt looked like something you might need on a ship like this,

"Who are you?"

The big man stopped swinging the machete and turned around with a big smile,

"I knew you'd be up."

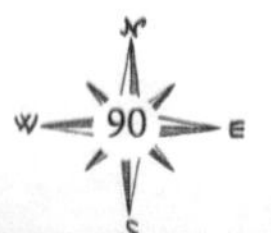

He wiped a grimy hand across his sweaty brow and then wiped it on his filthy coveralls. He held out that same hand, as if he expected her to actually touch it. He introduced himself,

"Technomancer apprentice, class three, Norgren Jorgen Borgen Dorgen."

Abby laughed so hard she had to put a hand on her belly. After a few moments, she stood up straight and wiped a tear from her eye with the end of her sleeve,

"You've got to be kidding!"

The thick man's ample belly jiggled a bit as he chuckled,

"Yeah, I am. My name's Norgren. Those other things are just stuff you've called me over the years."

He gave her a big grin. She hesitated then nodded and considered,

"Things I've called you? Well, I guess I deserved that then. Or I'll deserve it, eventually? Or maybe you'll deserve it later?"

Abby looked up at the sky and seemed to be considering how that worked. Norgren shook his head,

"Captain, if I may, a word of advice you once gave me. May I return the favor?"

Abby nodded. He said,

"Don't get lost on the straight line, just learn to lean into

the curves.”

Abby gave him a confused look,

“What does that mean?”

Norgren laughed,

“I still haven’t figured it out! I was hoping you’d tell me.”

He pointed toward the other end of the ship,

“Perhaps you should start with your cabin, Captain. I already straightened up in there. Once I get the forward hatchway cleared, you can help me down in the engine room. Our first priority is to stop the leak from the water tank.”

Abby cocked her head and looked at him like he was crazy. She thought about the water gushing out of the side of the ship. It had been gushing out as long as she could remember, at least a decade or more. It was the source of the creek,

How is that possibly coming from a single tank of water?

She gave Norgren a very confused look. He laughed and gestured toward her cabin. Then he went back to hacking away at the overgrowth covering the forward hatch.

Abby turned and headed for the cabin, the one she found the journal in. When she saw it last it was dark, gloomy, and dusty, a cobweb infested dungeon. She made a disgusted face as she remembered.

She was careful to avoid the large weak-looking area in the center of the deck between the second and third masts. It looked partially collapsed and full of dead leaves.

Abby pushed open the door and her face lit up with surprise. The difference in the room was mind blowing.

The light brown oak planks of the walls and floor were clean and gleaming. The dark wooden desk looked freshly stained. There were two hurricane lanterns hanging from the ceiling above each end of the large desk.

She saw a narrow bed against the left wall, with several drawers underneath. At the foot of the bed, she saw a silver stand with a long black leather vest and a sword belt hanging on it.

Abby walked over to the bed. Someone left a fancy frilly white dress shirt laid across the bed with a note on it. She lifted the note and read,

Extra boots, socks, foul weather gear, bottom drawer. Breeches, shirts, other sundries, middle drawer. Your sidearm, ammo, wrist bracers, Captain's ring, top drawer. Welcome aboard, Captain Abigail. Signed, Sasha.

Abby grinned.

About ten minutes later, she stepped out of the cabin in black breeches and high leather boots. She put on the white frilly dress shirt, and the long black leather vest over top. She had the sword belt around her waist but left the sword behind.

She didn't even open the top drawer with the sidearm

and bracers and other stuff. She didn't imagine she'd need any of that to help with repairs. She stood there adjusting her belt and tugging at the thick leather vest, when she heard Sasha's voice,

"THERE, is our Captain, Norgren."

Surprised, Abby looked up and saw Sasha and Norgren were standing about ten feet away. They were both smiling, from ear to ear.

That's when Abby noticed that the deck was completely cleared of overgrowth and vines. The wood was polished and clean. The masts stood straight and tall. She turned in a slow circle, her eyes wide and unbelieving,

"How?"

Norgren chuckled, then replied in his rough voice,

"The Rider, Captain. It seems you've brought her back from the dead."

Sasha broke down into tears and wrapped his thin arms around Norgren. He was sobbing, and choked out the words,

"Just look at her. She's just like a young girl, Norgren. I can't take it. This is all so tragically wonderful."

Norgren appeared to be barely tolerating the emotional display and the violation of his personal space. He replied in a deadpan monotone voice,

"Not like, you twit. She is a young girl. She's younger

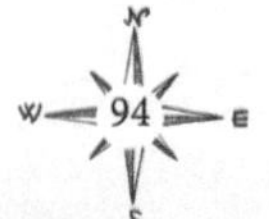

now than the first time we met her in the future. Now get off me."

Sasha pulled himself away and put his face in his hands and sobbed quietly. Abby scrunched up her face and looked at Norgren, she whispered,

"What's his problem?"

Norgren stepped closer, his eyes on the deck, speaking quietly,

"It hasn't been smooth sailing for us, Captain. We have just under a week by my reckoning to get you ready to cast off. And once we do, it's goodbye for good, again, for us at least. Or, until you meet us for the first time, from your perspective."

Norgren looked up and saw Abby's shocked expression. He looked at her with sympathy. He knew she didn't understand,

"The leak Captain, it's imperative we get it fixed as soon as possible. Once we fix the leak, The Rider can begin to repair herself."

He gestured around at the cleared off deck,

"I don't mean this cosmetic stuff. I mean the real repairs that she needs."

Abby's eyes widened,

"It repairs itself?"

Norgren nodded and reached for her arm. Abby held it up. Norgren opened the Velcro retainers on her air cast and pulled it off her arm. Abby was amazed to see that her arm was completely healed. Not even the faintest trace of bruising or pain.

He tossed the cast aside and rebuttoned the end of her sleeve. He looked her in the eye,

"It's the vest, Captain. So long as you wear it, you'll heal. The vest is a part of the ship, this time. My captain, Captain Abby, found the magical leather material. I turned that material into a vest, and I bonded it to the ship."

His expression grew pained with memory and he added,

"Even when the damage is so bad that you don't believe you will, you'll heal. Even when the pain is so crippling that you won't want to, you'll heal."

Something about the specifics in his words made a chill run down her back,

"Am I going to get badly hurt in the future?"

Sasha made a choking noise and looked up suddenly. Norgren held out a hand toward Sasha and shook his head, no. He looked at Abby,

"This is a dangerous time, Captain. We've been your loyal crew for many years, and I'd give my life to defend you. In fact, that's why we're here. But we can't say anything that risks changing the future. I can't explain. There's a lot you have to learn along the journey. Just trust me on this. We're here to

help you cast off. Then it's goodbye, for the last time. Until we meet, for the first time."

Abby felt a tear running down her cheek. She didn't understand it, but she felt them. It was a horrible pain, echoing in her heart. There was a deep sadness coming from both of them. There had to be something she could say or something she could do to make them feel better.

She tried to imagine what the 'Captain Abby' they remembered might do or be like. Something to give them hope that everything was going to be ok.

Abby turned away and looked down at the deck. She looked up toward the back of the ship, to where the raised deck over the top of her cabin was. She looked up where the real wheel of the ship was.

She focused on the pain she felt from them. Suddenly, as if a memory, she saw something. Like she had an idea. She had a flash of who she could be or was. Who she dreamed she might one day be, or who they remembered her to be.

Turning back to the two men, Abby stood as tall and as straight as she could. She didn't wipe away the tears, but she forced her voice to sound strong and normal. She looked into their eyes, one after the other,

"That's how it is then. So, let's get to it. Let's get that leak fixed."

Sasha bawled with happy tears. Even Norgren's eyes got a little wet. He nodded and looked at her proudly,

"Aye Captain."

The Heart of The Rider

Abby stared at the four thick heavy plates covering each of the cube-shaped things, that Norgren called "fuel tanks". Each one was about two feet high by two feet wide. They were arranged in a diamond pattern with a very thick crystal pane over the space in the center of the four tanks.

Behind the crystal pane in the center, was something very small and incredibly bright. It was painful to look at.

The armor-like plates were bolted onto all six sides of the four heavy, safe-like containers, or fuel tanks. Each one had an extremely thick crystal tube coming out of it. Down and away, from the bottom vault. Up and away, from the top vault, etc.

Some weird looking black tar-like substance was filling the bottom crystal tube, which disappeared into the floor. The top vault was pushing out what looked like a continuous tiny tornado. The right tube looked like it was filled with lava.

The left tube had separated from the mounting in the wall. It was shifted slightly down, and that's where all the water was coming from.

Without getting too close, Abby looked up and over

and around and behind the odd 'engine'? She shook her head in confusion. She turned to the right, looked at Norgren next to her, and spoke loudly over the noise of the rushing water,

"Let's start from the beginning! What on Earth am I looking at here? This doesn't make any sense to me! Where is all that water coming from?"

Norgren rolled his eyes. He reached down into the ankle-deep water in the engine room and splashed some on his face. He gestured to the left side tank where the water was coming from,

"Inside each tank is a fixed trans-dimensional anchor! That one feeds a continuous high-pressure flow of water to the rest of the engine!"

Abby pointed at the thick crystal panel in the center,

"And that?"

Norgren spoke loudly,

"The power core is a miniaturized magnetar, Captain! A star harvested by the builders, it's the heart of The Riptide Rider's engine! The engine, is the heart of The Rider!"

A miniaturized magnetar? A star? Three feet in front of me, is a star?

She looked at Norgren like he had lost his mind,

"A STAR?!? How is that possible?"

Norgren cocked his head and blinked at her a few times, before shouting back,

"Just to be clear, Captain! You're asking me, on the day we first meet, how the engine of the interdimensional pirate ship that I've been a member of your crew on, for many years now, is POSSIBLE? Is that your question, Captain?"

Abby stared at him blankly, considering. Finally, she nodded and shouted back,

"You have a point! I think!"

She shook her head. The events of the past couple days had been crazy enough that looking at a miniaturized magnetar wasn't overly shocking at this point. Abby pointed at the bright star at the center of the engine,

"The heat, gravity, radiation?"

Norgren smiled and patted his meaty hand on the central crystal housing,

"Containment fields, Captain! It's very advanced technology!"

Abby looked him in the eyes,

"You said, harvested by the builders! Who are the builders?"

Norgren's eyes narrowed slightly. He shook his head, no.

She remembered what he said earlier up on deck,

This is a dangerous time, Captain...

we can't say anything that risks changing the future...

There's a lot you have to learn along the journey...

Abby nodded, understanding. Well, she had a better understanding of what she was looking at, but she still didn't understand any of it. She shook her head and said loudly,

"Alright then, let's get this done! What is it you need me to do?"

Norgren nodded. He walked over to a tall tool locker on the wall behind them, next to the open hatchway where all the water was flooding out of the room and down to the lower decks. He came back with a thick six-foot long prybar.

He pointed to a large control panel on the wall to their left that had several levers and a bunch of valve wheels,

"I'm going to bypass the engine's fuel regulator and manually open the emergency pressure relief valves! That'll route pressure to the external vents! That will reduce the back pressure that's flooding through the ship!"

Next, he pointed to the dislodged crystal pipe that was spewing water out in every direction from the wall end of the pipe,

"Then we're going to force the feed line back into place over the wall coupling! You're going to have to hold it in place while I seal the connection with a molecular catalyzing adhesive!"

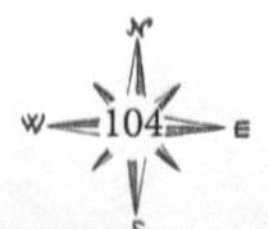

Abby stared at him blankly. After a moment, she asked loudly,

"You want me to hold the prybar?"

Norgren grinned broadly and nodded. He shouted,

"That'll do, yes Captain!"

Norgren handed her the heavy prybar and splashed through the water over to the panel that had sixteen valve wheels on it.

The valve wheels were in a square pattern, four across, four down. The top row of four were all white. The next row down, the valve wheels were all blue. Red below that, and four black wheels along the bottom row.

Norgren pulled down a large lever to the left of the valves, then he turned all four of the blue valve wheels counterclockwise. Abby noticed the flow of water reduced dramatically as he opened each one.

He came back and quickly grabbed the bar. He wedged it under the dislodged crystal pipe, jamming the point of the bar into a gap in the wall behind the engine. He looked at her and shouted,

"Quickly now, Captain! Right now, The Rider is venting water in all directions! Probably looks like a giant antique fountain!"

Together, they got under the prybar and pushed up. The thick crystal feed line shifted slowly, moving in tiny jerks as

they worked it back into place. Once the tube was lined up, Norgren looked over his shoulder and asked loudly,

"You have it, Captain?"

Abby nodded quickly, straining to hold the prybar steady,

"Got it! Go!"

Norgren moved out from under the prybar and over to the connection point where the feed line was spewing water in every direction around the wall. Abby gritted her teeth, straining against the weight and the pressures trying to force the crystal tube back out of place.

She saw him pull a small tube out of his tool belt that looked like a tube of toothpaste. Norgren began squeezing a shiny grey paste around the connection. He smoothed the paste down into the gap with his thumb. Amazingly, it worked!

Abby watched as he worked his way around the end of the pipe. The leak sealed up once his thumb ran across it. The engine room was suddenly much quieter. Filled with the sound of dripping and her heavy breathing. Norgren smiled broadly,

"Molecular adhesive is just a temporary fix. Once The Rider starts repairing herself, she'll do a better job on it."

Norgren tucked the tube of magic paste back into his toolbelt and immediately splashed over to close the four bypass valves and reset the lever. After that, he turned around to grin at her. Abby lowered the tip of the heavy bar to the floor and smiled back at him.

Turning, she looked at the engine and watched in awe as it changed.

The glow from the magnetar core spread out from the center through all four crystal feed lines, causing them all to glow. She heard a faint electromagnetic hum come to life from somewhere behind the back wall. She felt a shudder shake the ship for just a second. The hum settled into a soft gently pulsing background noise.

The water level in the room was slowly dropping. Abby had a huge smile on her face. Norgren was looking around and listening,

"She sounds healthy once again, Captain."

Abby handed him the prybar,

"Well done, Norgren! Very well done."

She cocked her head at him, wondering,

"I'm the captain and Sasha is my steward. What's your title, mechanic?"

He shook his head slightly,

"Ships engineer, Captain."

Abby nodded, and followed up with another question,

"And you said you were a what again? Techno-dancers apprentice?"

Norgren laughed deeply, his belly jiggling,

"'MAN-cer', Captain. Technomancer."

Abby grinned and nodded,

"Sorry, yes, that was it. What exactly is that anyway?"

Norgren rubbed his scruffy chin with his meaty fingers and considered,

"Can't hurt, I guess. Follow me to the galley and I'll explain while we take a breather?"

Abby nodded and stepped aside. She gestured to the door, as if to say, after you. Norgren stowed the prybar back in the tool locker and ducked out of the metal pressure door. Abby followed him out into the passage.

The walls in the passageway and the engine room they just left were metal. The floor was metal grating. Earlier, on the way down, Norgren said the whole engineering section was composed of a combination of metal and carbon fiber.

The Rider was a confusing mix of different types of construction.

Norgren led her to the steel stairway that led up to the deck above them. On the way, Abby saw two short sets of stairs leading down and off to each side into compartments below them,

"Where do those lead to?"

Norgren glanced back,

"Leads down to the maintenance areas for the port and starboard antigravity drives."

Abby nodded calmly, thinking,

Antigravity drives! SWEET!

She followed Norgren back up the stairs and back into the older style wooden ship surroundings. Wood plank decking, walls, and ceiling. Abby shook her head and just smiled. She followed him down the passageway to the galley.

Inside, she saw several tables with long benches. Abby walked around investigating the cabinets and drawers and the strange appliances. She saw wooden cabinets that held a variety of both carved wooden dishes and some that looked more like enameled camping style dishes. The drawers contained silver utensils, towels, dish cloths, things like that.

Surprisingly, she walked over and saw what looked like a very modern cappuccino maker. There was something that resembled a three-chamber ice cream dispenser. There was a small refrigerator, and something that resembled an automated fast-food drink machine.

She laughed as she looked around at the strange mix of technology levels.

Norgren grabbed a bottle of something from the small fridge and twisted off the cap. He settled his large frame onto one of the benches and watched her investigating the galley. He had a sad reminiscent look on his face,

"I'm going to miss this place, Captain."

Abby turned and looked at him with a big smile on her face,

"What was that?"

Norgren smiled back at her. A single tear escaped his eye and ran down his cheek. Abby saw it and stepped closer. Her expression grew concerned,

"Are you ok?"

Norgren looked down and wiped away the tear,

"Just thinking about the past."

He looked back up,

"Your question, Captain. Technomancer. It's a term that comes from my home dimension. A place so rare, it's possibly unique. I know that in all our travels, we never came across another place like it."

Norgren gestured at the bench across the table from him and continued,

"There are many worlds where there's science and technology, and a few worlds where there is magic. Science is by far the most common, magical worlds are rare. But the rarest of all, are worlds where there are both science and magic. Worlds where people have learned how to combine the two."

Norgren took a long drink from his dark glass bottle,

then continued,

"Take pyromancer, for example, that's a fire magician. So, technology combined with magician, equals Technomancer."

He spread his beefy arms,

"That's me."

Abby looked at him with wide eyes. It was a shockingly impressive claim. She thought about something he had said earlier,

"Earlier, up on deck, Sasha was crying. When I asked you why, you said we had just under a week to cast off. You also said The Riptide Rider is interdimensional, which somehow includes time travel. Doesn't make a lot of sense to me, but there it is. Why, if The Rider can travel through time, are we on a deadline?"

Norgren looked down. He fiddled with a tool on his belt. Abby waited patiently. Eventually, he said,

"Imagine a rowboat moving through the water. You see little waves spreading out behind it. That's called a wake. If you were above that water, looked down and saw a wake. You'd know a boat just passed. Little boat, little wake. The bigger or faster the boat, the bigger the wake, and the farther away you can see it from."

He moved his finger across the table as he explained. Now, he put two fingers on the table, moving both across the tabletop. He continued,

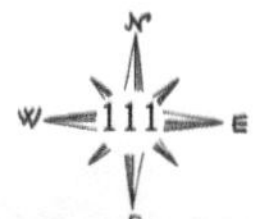

"Now, imagine a really fast boat that can travel in more than one direction at a time. Not just forward, leaving a normal wake, but also riding the riptide across dimensions. That boat is leaving a wake so powerful that it can be seen across multiple dimensions. By the right people of course, with the right equipment."

Norgren held up both hands in fists, touching together,

"Now you add in the dimension of time, and suddenly that fast boat is sailing the riptides while breaking through the dimension of time."

He spread his fingers apart and moved his hands slowly away from each other, demonstrating the growing spreading waves left behind,

"Now, that boat is leaving a wake so powerful that it ripples across other dimensions and also forward and backward in time."

He lowered his hands and looked at Abby. She nodded slowly. She said,

"So, The Rider can sail and remain hidden. She can fly, and risk someone close seeing her. She can ride the riptide across dimensions, and someone is even more likely to see. And if she travels through time, it's almost a certainty she'll draw attention from somewhen."

Norgren chuckled,

"Somewhen, nice. I think you get the gist, Captain. And to answer your question, we're on a deadline because of the

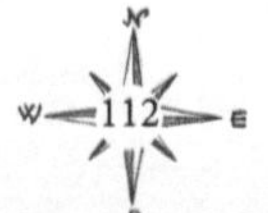

temporal wake that The Rider left behind."

Abby's eyebrows rose,

"She left a wake when she crashed here, however many years ago?"

Norgren shook his head, no,

"Not when she crashed. In fact, that's why she crashed, and why no one found her after. No, she left a wake when you found her and jumped the first time on your own, a couple weeks from today. I can't say anything else about that."

He held up a hand like, don't even ask,

"If the people coming after you follow procedure, they will be here in about five or six days. So, we have to get you out of here, before they show up and kill us all."

Abby looked down at the table. She repeated the words she just heard, in her mind,

Before they show up and kill us all.

Show up and kill us all.

Abby stood up and looked him in the eye,

"Meet me up on deck."

Norgren smiled and nodded,

"Aye Captain."

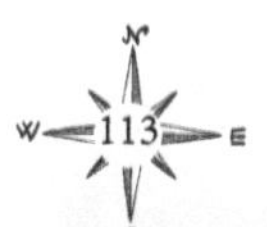

An Order Not a Suggestion

Abby left the galley and headed for her cabin. She climbed the stairs to the upper deck and looked around. Repairing the engine took them a good chunk of time. The Sun was well into late afternoon.

It appeared repairs were complete, up here at least. Everything looked pristine. As she approached what earlier looked like a weak area between the middle and rear masts, she saw what it really was. Two large heavy steel grates over a black material backing, covered a ten-foot by ten-foot opening to the lower decks.

She raised her eyebrows at it as she passed by. Must be doors for lowering down cargo, she guessed. Abby looked up at the raised area above her cabin and saw Sasha standing by the wheel. He grinned broadly and waved at her. Abby nodded politely and walked into her cabin.

Alone, in her cabin, she saw a small plate on her desk with an apple and what looked like a square of cheese. She also saw a cup and a small dark bottle next to it. Abby smiled and shook her head,

Sasha, I'm starting to really like him.

Abby chuckled as she thought about the sweet, weird steward she would one day recruit. As she wolfed down the apple and the cheese, she realized she was famished. She picked up the small bottle and popped the cork.

Sniffing at it, Abby smelled citrus among other things, a hint of strawberry maybe. She shrugged and took a drink. It was good. Sasha knew her pretty well. She smiled, corked the bottle, and set it down.

Next, she changed out of her wet clothes and soaked boots, finding dry replacements for each. She looked around for a dirty clothes hamper. Eventually, she hung the wet stuff on the silver stand by the foot of her bed. She moved around to the side of the bed and opened the top drawer.

She pulled out the arm bracers and slid them on. She looked at the loose leather straps, confused. Removing the bracers, she placed them on the bed. She reached in and pulled out her sidearm. It was unlike any gun she had ever seen in any movie.

Well, that wasn't true. It was like a couple types of guns, jumbled together from things she had seen in a couple of different movies. The problem was that she didn't know how to work a normal gun, let alone whatever this was. She placed the sidearm on the bed and looked at it.

It had an intricately carved and decorated wooden frame with a long thick barrel laid into a carved channel in the wood. It had a long, curved handgrip and for the most part, it looked like an old flintlock pistol from a pirate movie.

The weapon looked like the kind you dumped powder into, then stuffed a ball in. Then you cocked back the big, curved hammer. Then, once you fired it, you tossed it to the side because it took so long to reload.

But this old-fashioned flintlock had a huge black plastic ammunition magazine inserted into the frame just in front of the trigger guard. The magazine looked like it belonged on a big, heavy rifle, it was massive.

Next, she pulled out a ring with an intricate design carved into it, all around the center on the outside edge. Easy enough, she slid the ring onto the middle finger of her left hand.

Then she pulled out what she thought at first was the holster for her sidearm, but it didn't look right. It was a dark rectangular metal plate with a rubber border and two sets of straps on each end.

Shaking her head, she set whatever that was, on the bed. There were two more pistol magazines in the drawer. She picked one up and looked at the ammunition. It looked like a large bullet and a torpedo made a baby, and that baby grew up. She shook her head and set it back down.

There was no way around it. She walked to the door and opened it,

"SASHA!"

Abby walked back over to the bed. A minute later, Sasha stepped just inside the open door,

"Yes Captain?"

Abby picked up one of the black leather bracers,

"How does this work?"

Sasha walked over, took the bracer, and slid it onto her arm. He pulled the leather straps tight from the bottom and looped the end over a tiny dull hook on the forward end near her wrist. He smiled. Abby put on the other bracer and tightened it in the same way.

Next, she held up the rubber wrapped metal plate with straps.

Sasha walked over to a chair and put his right foot up on the chair. He looked at her and waited. Abby walked over and put her right foot on the chair.

Sasha took the plate and centered it on the outside of her right thigh,

"Now, wrap the bottom strap around, and make it as tight as you're comfortable with."

Abby tightened the bottom strap around her thigh. Sasha walked over to the silver stand and brought back her sword. He untied the belt from her waist and passed it through the sword scabbard, then retied it. Next, he lifted the plate into place and passed the top two straps through two small rings just above it that were anchored to the belt and then tightened the straps.

Sasha checked the drawer. He looked around her desk, then looked at her hands. He saw the ring and chuckled. He cocked his head and raised his eyebrows,

"Of course, a ring you can put on all by yourself."

Abby rolled her eyes,

"Get on with it, Steward."

Sasha laughed and slid the ring off of her left hand. He slid it onto the middle finger of her right hand. He carefully lifted her sidearm and handed it to her. Abby wrapped her hand around the grip and noticed that the ring fit snugly into a small indentation on the handle.

Sasha pointed at the metal plate on her thigh,

"Now, just place it against the mag-plate."

Abby lowered the weapon and brought it close to the plate. She heard a "Thunk" sound as the weapon magnetically attached itself to the plate. Or, more accurately, as the plate pulled in the weapon and held it tight. She pulled at it, but the weapon didn't come free.

Sasha touched her wrist,

"Take your hand away, then grab it again."

Abby moved her hand away and then grabbed the weapon again. It immediately came free. She touched it to the plate again and it stayed it place. She looked at Sasha and grinned,

"I like that!"

Sasha stepped over to the desk and picked up the

journal. He walked back to her,

"Never forget your most valuable tool, Captain."

Sasha pulled the sword belt slightly away and tucked the journal under her belt. He pulled his hands away and held them both up, looking her in the eye for emphasis. Then he reached forward and grabbed the journal and tried to pull it out from under the belt. She felt him pulling at it, but it didn't budge.

He let go of the journal and looked up,

"Once it's tucked into your belt, only you can free it. You'll never lose it on accident."

Again, she smiled and nodded.

Abby turned and headed for the door. Norgren was waiting for her when she stepped out of her cabin. Abby looked down, adjusted the thick leather vest, then rested her hands on the thick wide weapon belt and looked up at him,

"Well?"

Norgren had a big smile on his face. He gave her a thumbs up. Abby nodded and looked Norgren in the eye,

"You said, before they show up and kill us all. Before who shows up?"

Norgren shook his head, no. Abby nodded, understanding,

"What's next then?"

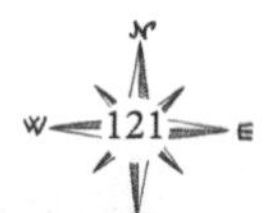

Norgren shrugged,

"The hard part. We have to dig her out."

Abby cocked her head, it looked to her like most of the ship was above ground,

"How much more of the ship do we need to dig out?"

Norgren replied,

"Only about a third of The Rider is sticking out of the ground, I don't think we could force her free with the engines without damaging the antigravity drives and the lower port and starboard masts."

Abby blinked in surprise,

What? The lower masts?

She shook her head. She suddenly had absolutely no idea what this ship actually looked like. Abby suddenly felt the faintest hint of vibration coming from her sternum. She put her hand over the crystal on the silver chain her father had given her. It was vibrating? Humming?

She also felt an echo of the humming. It was strange. It was faint. It was more of a feeling than a sound. She looked straight up, above the ship. It felt like it was coming from up in the sky and echoing against her crystal necklace.

Sasha suddenly called down from above, his voice was higher pitched, and he sounded nervous,

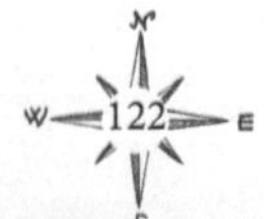

"I don't think we have five days, Captain. Sensors just picked up an approaching temporal wake. It's a very powerful signature, white designation, definitely an Imperial patrol!"

Norgren growled and snapped back,

"Sasha! Hold yer tongue!"

Sasha clapped a hand over his mouth, his eyes went wide, voice muffled,

"Sorry."

Shaking his head, Norgren stormed up the steps. Abby bounded quickly up the other set of steps, taking them three at a time and arriving first. She saw display screens behind and on each side of the large wheel, that she hadn't expected to see. Sasha pointed at one of the screens that looked like a radar display.

There was a small bright white dot moving toward the green dot in the center of the display. There were ripples of energy spreading out behind the white dot. Abby thought to herself,

Wow, it does kind of look like a ship's wake.

Sasha pointed at the screen,

"White, I can't say more than I have. Green is us, reconnaissance class vessel."

Norgren stepped up next to her and grunted in displeasure. He reached forward and pushed the top of the

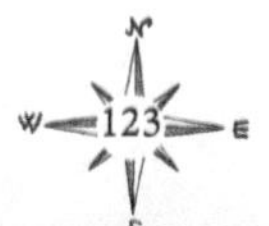

screen backwards until it was laying flat. Then he placed his open palm on the screen and lifted his hand straight up and away. The image stretched up and out of the screen, becoming a three-dimensional holographic display.

Now, Abby could make out that the small approaching white dot wasn't just coming from the right of the screen, but also from behind or farther away. And it was moving directly towards the green dot in the center, The Rider.

Norgren grunted, and gestured at the display,

"This is D-scan view, it isn't showing distance or direction, it's a multi-dimensional representation. They're ahead of us, which means they're coming back toward us from the future. They're also off to the right, which means multiple dimensional shifts away. This is bad, Captain. Signature looks bigger than a frigate, probably a cruiser."

Abby glanced at him. Norgren was shaking his head, he looked defeated,

"We have hours, Captain. Best case, four, maybe five hours. We can't do it. It's not possible to dig The Rider out in less than three or four days, let alone hours. We need to get you as far away from here as possible."

Abby felt a fire begin in her gut. Quit? Run? She hadn't even gotten started yet. She narrowed her eyes and clenched her teeth. She remembered something that her mother had once said to her.

She heard her mom in the middle of a heated argument

with someone on the phone. Abby snuck up and peeked around the door, looking in. Kat saw her watching from the doorway. After she hung up the phone, she looked at Abby's worried expression and spoke coldly,

Someone ever comes to you looking for a fight, you give them every ounce of fight you've got.

Still staring at the white dot in the projected image, Abby asked,

"Norgren, you've known me for many years, yes?"

Norgren looked over at her,

"Aye, Captain, that's right."

Abby turned her hardened gaze on him,

"How many times have you seen me quit, give up, or surrender?"

Norgren's dark scowl slid into a grim looking smile. He shook his head,

"I can't say that I have, Captain."

Abby looked back at the display and nodded,

"Good. Because I'm not going to start this journey by quitting on my first day. How do we communicate on this ship? I'm assuming we don't just run around trying to find each other, every time we need to talk."

Norgren looked at Abby's ears, then turned quickly to Sasha,

"SASHA! SERIOUSLY?"

Sasha's eyes went wide,

"My bad."

Sasha walked in front of Abby, digging into an inner pocket of his suit jacket. He pulled out a small earring and put it on her left ear. Abby noticed that both of the other men had earrings. Norgren had a gold hoop and Sasha a small diamond.

Sasha pointed at his own earring,

"When you want to start a conversation, or reply to one, you just give it a gentle squeeze."

Abby turned to Norgren,

"Can you direct the flow of the hydro-vents down? What are the others? Pyro-vents? Aero-vents? Overpressure vents?"

Norgren looked confused for just a second. He brightened as he realized what she was talking about and asking. He thought about it and shook his head,

"The venting direction can be adjusted, yes. But you'll never be able to use them effectively as weapons. Also, the overpressure regulator uses the same ventilation ports for all of the feed lines, Captain."

She smiled,

"Even better."

Sasha was looking back and forth between them.

Norgren grinned,

"You curious about the ships inner workings Captain, or do I smell one of your crazy plans cooking?"

Abby looked at Sasha,

"Can you teach me the ship's controls?"

Sasha shrugged,

"Sorta."

She nodded,

"That'll have to do. Norgren, get to the engine room. Sasha, you're with me."

Abby stepped up to the wheel and began looking at the various displays, levers, and control panels. She looked at Sasha,

"Start talking."

Norgren shook his head, then just sighed. He knew her well enough to know, there was no stopping her now. He headed to the engine room as fast as he could. Sasha started pointing and explaining. Abby asked leading questions, guiding his instructions to what she needed to know.

A few minutes later, she heard Norgren's voice in her ear,

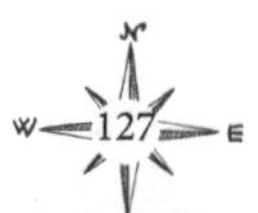

"I'm in position, Captain."

Abby held up one finger to Sasha, stopping him in mid-sentence. She squeezed the earring,

"Direct all overpressure vents straight down toward the ground. Bypass the regulator and open fire valves one and two."

Norgren replied hastily,

"Whoa, Captain! You'll set The Rider on fire!"

Abby jumped up onto the railing at the edge of the deck. Hanging onto a rope line, she leaned out, looking down at the overgrowth piled around the hull. She growled and narrowed her eyes,

Am I the Captain of this ship, or not?

Abby raised her voice,

"How many years under my command did it take for you to start following orders, engineer? OPEN THE VALVES!"

She heard a sigh, followed by,

"Aye Captain."

Fire began shooting toward the ground, from small ports low on the hull, all around the ship. It was scorching the brush, but not enough,

"Open fire valve three!"

The fire intensified, roaring out of the small ports like an

army of flamethrowers. The brush and leaves and vines were all on fire, all around them,

"By the numbers now! Open fire valve four! Quick as you can, open wind valves one and two!"

The flames intensified frighteningly. Then the wind was added to the mix. The raging flamethrowers from the vents became giant welding torches. The ground around the ship was crisping and glowing. Most of the vegetation within fifty feet of the ship was reduced to ash and glowing coals.

Sasha, watching the displays, squeaked,

"Fire alarms popping up all around the hull, Captain!"

Abby glanced at Sasha,

"She'll heal!"

She called out to Norgren,

"Close all fire valves, open all water valves!"

The vents she had turned into torches all sputtered out, but the wind kept flowing, blowing the flames spreading out from the ship higher, like the bellows on a kiln.

Within seconds, mist began blowing from the vents, then sputtering clouds of water, which quickly turned into firehoses pointed at the cleared earth around the ship. When he opened the fourth water valve, the firehose-like water pressure combined with the open wind valves. It turned the vents into high pressure water jets digging into the ground around the ship.

Standing next to her, Sasha laughed. The water jets were beginning to reveal the long, rounded bulges running down each side, along the bottom of The Rider that housed the antigravity generators and the lower masts.

Abby nodded. Her plan was working. In less than thirty minutes, they blasted most of the earth off the tops of both of the antigravity generator housings.

She walked back to the pilot's station and rested one hand on the ship's wheel. She looked at the control panel to the right and pushed the button to activate the anti-gravity drives. She heard a faint low frequency thrumming coming from the drives and felt a gentle vibration through the deck below her feet.

Abby grinned.

She adjusted the dial that controlled antigravity lift power to five percent over the hover/stabilize setting. The Riptide Rider was now very gently pulling up, trying to lift. She squeezed her earring and called down to Norgren,

"Open the remaining two wind valves and raise all overpressure vent orientation ten degrees. Then get up here and see what you think."

Godspeed

Norgren looked over the side of the ship at the growing lake of water and mud. Abby effectively turned the emergency overpressure vents into miniature strip-mining jets all around the ship. The waters around them were churning violently.

He laughed loudly and stepped away from the side, shaking his head. Sasha stood nearby, with his hands crossed behind his back and a big cheesy grin on his face. Norgren looked at Sasha,

"Never doubt our captain, eh?"

Sasha nodded his agreement.

Abby came down the stairs and walked up to them,

"If The Rider crashed here hard enough to get buried in the ground, what are the odds the lower masts are intact and not sheared off from the crash?"

Norgren looked thoughtful and rubbed his scruffy chin with his fingers,

"She should have still had backup power, prior to the crash. It's possible that she went into emergency mode and

retracted the lower masts on her own before impact. If that's the case, they might be mostly intact."

Abby was staring at him with wide eyes. Norgren nodded, and added,

"The masts have solid tritanium cores, wrapped in an ironwood sheathing. We can check the status of the masts in engineering on the damage control display panel in the engine room, Captain."

Abby cocked her head slightly and raised one eyebrow,

"The Rider can do things on her own? Wait... The masts RETRACT?"

Norgren held up a hand,

"Retract is an overstatement, or imperfect terminology rather. They extend slightly, revealing the hinged elbow. That allows the masts to fold back along the outside of the antigravity drives. Otherwise, she would never be able to sail in open water like a normal ship and that would hinder her original purpose. Which was to blend in and operate like a normal ship, in ancient..."

Sasha mumbled,

"Careful."

Norgren looked at Sasha,

"Right, sorry."

Abby looked from Sasha back to Norgren. She looked down at the deck. After a moment, she pointed at Sasha,

"Keep an eye on the radar."

She nodded to Norgren,

"Show me the damage control display."

Norgren nodded and headed for the stairs down to the engineering deck. Abby followed him. She heard Sasha's high-pitched voice call out behind her,

"It's not a radar!"

Abby held out a thumbs up as she walked away,

"Duly noted."

Norgren led her back to the long hatch in the floor, on the crew quarters and galley level. Seeing it closed, she realized it wasn't an obvious entrance to the lower level. It looked more like a storage compartment cover in the floor.

The hatch hid the more advanced section of the ship below them fairly well.

Norgren opened the wooden hatch and headed down the steel stairwell leading down to the metal walls and steel grate floor of the engineering deck. He walked down to the engine room and ducked inside through the submarine-like pressure door.

Abby followed him inside and watched him walk over

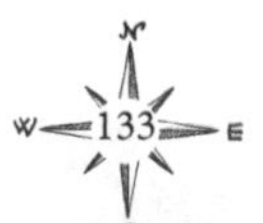

to a blank panel on the wall to the right of the engine. He tapped the center of the panel three times and it flickered to life becoming a display. Abby's eyes went wide.

The display showed the ship in its entirety. A full side view and next to it, a head-on view. It was a black background, with the ship represented in glowing red lines. It looked like an engineer's drawing.

The upper third of the ship was what she had first seen, hidden in the overgrowth of the forest. She had an epiphany and realized that The Rider only looked like a normal sailing ship when the lower two-thirds of the ship was submerged in the ocean.

The Riders head-on profile looked like a pyramid shape that someone had sheared off the top and turned it into the main deck. The bottom two points of the pyramid were swollen out and round, to house the long spinning antigravity drives that ran down each side.

The Rider had nine masts, each row of three in a line from front to back, coming out from the ship, in the same direction as the points of a triangle.

She saw that the lower masts were currently folded back along the outside of the drives, layered one on top of the one behind. The sails were currently rolled up and the crossbeams were folded back toward the rear of the ship along with the masts. When retracted, they would add very little drag to The Rider in the ocean.

Norgren tapped the upper left corner of the screen,

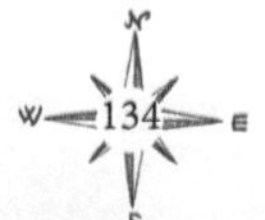

opening a menu. She saw him move his finger down and tap on the damage control option. The screen shifted to a green background. Most of the ship was now black, but the lower masts and small sections of the hull along the bottom of the antigravity drives were highlighted in red.

As she watched, one small square along the drive flickered red to white several times, then shifted to black like the rest of the ship. She pointed to it,

"What was that?"

Norgren looked up from the small device he just picked up and started fiddling with. He looked at the display and touched the bottom. Then he slid his finger to the left, reversing the image, then back to center bringing it forward.

He saw the colors flicker and change in the replay, then tapped the bottom twice sending the display back to real-time,

"The Rider is still repairing the outer hull of the drives, damage from the crash. Red indicates damage, black is fully functioning. She prioritized the drive's inner workings, so she's ready to fly."

He pointed at the red areas along the bottom of the hull,

"Now she's focused on the outer hull. But the masts, crossbeams, and sails are heavily damaged and probably can't be repaired until she's free of the ground."

Abby considered for a moment,

"Would The Rider still be able repair herself, if the lower

masts and sails were submerged in the ocean?"

Norgren went back to the device he was fiddling with, and seemed to be thinking about it for a moment,

"Theoretically, yes. The nanotech repair systems aren't affected by water or weather. But, how would you get her there, Captain? She's designed to fly with all nine sails deployed. With only the upper sails, the wind would constantly be pushing your nose into the dirt."

Abby turned toward him. Norgren stopped and looked up at her. He saw the earliest version of that familiar wild look in her eyes. The look that said she had a crazy idea.

He chuckled nervously,

"Just what did you have in mind, Captain?"

Abby cocked her head and raised her eyebrows,

"Can The Rider hold a continuous steep climb at full speed?"

Norgren began running numbers in his mind. He grinned and stuffed the small device he was fiddling with in his tool belt,

"Steep? Mostly... Full speed, not even close."

He laughed crisply, then held up one finger,

"There's one more thing I need Captain, I'll meet you up on deck."

Abby nodded and ran for the main deck. She ran up the stairs. Crossing the mid deck, she heard Norgren then Sasha, over the earring communication devices,

"Sasha! The captain's hat!"

"OH RIGHT! I'm on it."

Abby laughed and wondered what that was about. She raced up the forward curved stairwell and popped out onto the main deck. She immediately heard the overpressure vents churning and deepening the muddy soup around the ship.

She looked to the west, toward the setting Sun. She saw that they were running out of daylight. Considering what she had in mind, that was a good thing.

Climbing the stairs, Abby saw Sasha staring at the holographic display. He was chewing his nails with a worried expression on his face.

Abby grinned,

"Oh, so that's YOUR job. I was wondering who handled that department."

Abby pretended to look at the displays as Sasha turned a confused expression on her,

"My job? What are you talking about, Captain?"

Abby laughed,

"Being the worrier."

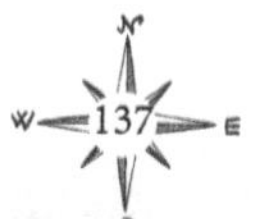

Sasha rolled his eyes and held up a large black hat toward her,

"Take your stupid hat. You'd worry too if you knew that..."

He looked away as Abby turned toward him and took the hat from him,

"Well, never mind."

Abby patted him on the shoulder,

"Worry, never solved a single problem."

Sasha said,

"Yeah? Well, caution has avoided plenty of them."

Abby chuckled and looked at the hat. It looked like a standard black leather, three corner hat that you'd see in just about every pirate movie ever made. She smiled and put it on her head.

Looking across the deck, she saw Norgren come up from below carrying a long, thin wooden crate. He set it down near the rope ladder, then crossed the deck and climbed the stairs. Stepping up next to them he looked closely at the holographic display.

Norgren made an unhappy grunt and shook his head,

"I don't know, Captain. We're running out of time."

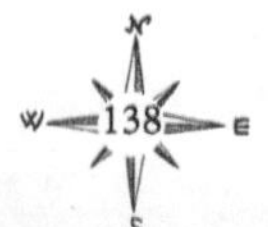

Sasha wrung his hands.

Abby asked,

"How long?"

Norgren shrugged,

"We're down to two, maybe three hours. Based on our location, and The Rider's reduced capabilities. I'm not sure you'll make the coast before they punch into this dimension."

"Punch in? Explain."

Norgren pointed at the two converging dots on the display,

"It's sensors versus concealment. We see them because they have no concealment. They're traveling back in time, crossing multiple dimensions, coming straight toward a fourth dimensional target location, that we're approaching in real time."

He paused for a moment, stumbling a bit over his wording,

"And um... well, they're a military unit. So, their ships... uh, never mind. Point is, what they currently see, is the point of origin. The Rider's wake, when she originally jumped away about two weeks from now."

He turned toward Abby and held up both hands flat. He began slowly sliding one hand under the other, saying,

"Your plan to limp The Rider to the coast and hide her in the ocean is a good one. But only if you can get her there before they enter this time and dimension. Once they arrive, they'll do a broad scan, and they'll spot you if you're still in the air."

He hesitated and looked at Sasha. Sasha nodded for him to go on. Norgren continued,

"There's no travel time, from their perspective. Their ships aren't like The Rider. They leave the point they jump from and instantly they'll be here, from their perspective. We see them moving because the jump isn't truly instantaneous. Not from that far away, temporally."

Norgren gestured at the deck, the wheel, then the sails. He said,

"Their ships aren't designed for stealth and recon like The Rider is."

He looked down and shook his head, groaning. Then he looked back into her eyes and said,

"It would take me way to long to explain it all, and we're out of time. You've got to get her moving, Captain. I recommend slowly dialing up the lift until she pulls herself free."

Abby narrowed her eyes,

"I've got to get moving? Don't you mean, we?"

Norgren gave her a sad look. He shook his head, no,

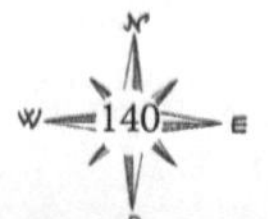

"We're out of options. The best thing I can do to help you now, is to give you the best chance to get away. I'm going to climb down and hang from the bottom of the ladder as you lift away. Just drift clear of the soup and I'll drop down. I'm gonna try to distract em', hopefully disable their ship, or at the very least slow them down."

Still looking at her, he pointed at Sasha,

"You'll come in low and slow and drop Sasha near enough to the coast that he can swim to shore. He'll spend the rest of his time on the way there, trying to help you get up to speed on the controls as much as he can."

Norgren reached into his pocket and pulled out the small device he was fiddling with earlier in the engine room. He held it up for her to see, then tucked it into one of the large pockets in the front of her vest,

"I've done a lot of thinking. We, the engineers, we been passing that along behind the scenes, but we changed a lot of things our last voyage. The Captain I served under was free spirited, very original, and spontaneous. I'm just following her lead here."

He wiped away some tears and sniffed, before continuing,

"I've got to close the valves to divert power and fuel back to the engine. Then I'll climb down and wait until I'm clear to drop. Don't look at that recorder until you're alone and safe in the waters off the west coast."

Norgren started to turn away. Abby saw tears running down his grimy cheeks. On impulse, she reached out and grabbed his thick arm. He stopped. She stepped closer and hugged him. He hugged her back and whispered,

"Godspeed, Captain Abigail."

Abby let go and stepped back. She had tears on her cheeks, but her voice was steady,

"Good luck, my new old friend."

Norgren made a frustrated grunt and turned away, wiping away the tears with the back of his grimy hand. He quickly headed back down to the engine room. Abby watched him go, then wiped the tears from her eyes.

She looked at Sasha. Sasha was silently sobbing into a handkerchief. Abby rolled her eyes and grinned. Playfully, she punched Sasha in the arm,

"Man up, steward."

Sasha lifted his head and gave a brief choked laugh. He smiled under his tears,

"When we get there, just push me overboard. I don't think I can handle telling you goodbye this time."

She thought to herself,

This time. They have both been through this goodbye before.

Abby nodded,

"Will do."

She heard the vents go quiet as Norgren closed all the open valves,

What am I going to do without him?

It was terrifying. She barely had the basics of flying down. Abby put one hand on the wheel and dialed up the lift power another five percent and waited. The Rider was pulling a little harder, but no change.

A few minutes later, Norgren came back up from below deck. He walked over and lifted the lid off of the crate he brought up earlier. Abby saw him take out a very large and dangerous looking thing that roughly resembled a rifle.

He slung the rifle over his shoulder along with a small bag, then walked to the edge. Norgren looked back at her and Sasha for brief moment, then he was gone, over the side and climbing down.

She heard Sasha sobbing again. She slowly dialed up the antigravity drive lift power another ten percent. They both heard bubbles and a sickening sucking sound from below the ship. They felt The Rider begin to lift.

Abby glanced at Sasha,

"Give me eyes over the side. Make sure he's ok."

Sasha ran to the side and leaned over,

"I see him, Captain. He's at the bottom and hanging from

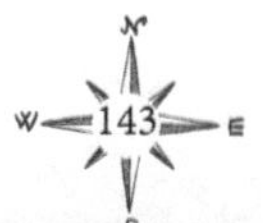

the ladder. You're almost clear."

Abby put her free hand on the drift control. Tweaking it, would set The Rider sliding gently sideways. Sasha called out from the railing,

"He's giving us a thumbs up. You can drift clear of the mud, Captain."

Abby gently shifted the drift control knob to the left. The Rider slid sideways in the air. In a moment, she heard the faintest grunt from over the side.

Sasha looked back at her,

"That's it. He's down, Captain."

Abby pushed the antigravity lift control dial in, setting it to automatic. She pulled the wheel back as far as it would go, setting The Rider to maximum climb. She grabbed both power levers and slid them slowly forward. A light wind hit them from behind, billowing the sails.

The Rider's nose lifted gently as she started sliding forward toward the trees, thick slimy mud dripping from the bottom.

Fly By Night

Abby did her best to keep The Riptide Rider low and close to the trees. It was a delicate balance. She was trying to push the ship as fast as possible, but too much speed pushed her down toward the ground because of the damaged and retracted lower masts.

~ ~

Her first flight caused dozens of calls to local radio stations. They described a drunken looking ghost pirate ship, skipping and bouncing along the treetops through the night sky.

~ ~

Abby looked over at Sasha, gripping the railing in front of him for dear life, his eyes wide and terrified. She asked loudly over the wind,

"So, you said this is the quarterdeck?"

Sasha nodded,

"Yes, Captain! WATCH THAT BRIDGE!"

Abby eased back on the power levers and The Rider

lifted, clearing the bridge. As surreptitiously as she could, she let out a deep breath at the close call. She called over,

"Yeah, no worries. I got this!"

Sasha closed his eyes and took a deep breath, trying to calm himself. The Rider swooped across the sky. Abby tried to avoid brightly lit areas where the population was denser. She caused quite a stir in some medium and small sized towns.

Sasha yelled over to her,

"The more people that see us, the more likely we are to set off an anomaly alert!"

Abby eased the wheel to the right, gently turning away from the approaching city lights. She yelled back,

"What's an anomaly alert?"

Sasha looked down, shaking his head slowly. He mumbled,

"We're going to die."

Abby asked,

"So port, is left? Why not say left?"

Sasha quickly raised his head. His wide eyes stared straight ahead, he shouted,

"PLEASE JUST FLY THE SHIP!"

Abby leaned her head back and laughed loudly. The wind

whipped across the deck, pushing them forward powerfully. The ground directly beneath them was a blur of motion. The rapidly pulsing thrum of the antigravity drives gently vibrated the deck beneath her feet.

She felt more alive than she had ever felt in her entire life. She shouted loudly,

"THIS IS AMAZING!"

Sasha looked at the D-scan holographic display and called out,

"They're almost here, Captain!"

Abby yelled back,

"I can see the ocean, Sasha! I've never seen the ocean before!"

"That's where they'll bury us."

"What was that?"

"I said, where is my hairbrush?"

Abby gave him a scowl. She shouted,

"YOU'RE ABOUT TO JUMP INTO THE OCEAN!"

Sasha rolled his eyes. He heard Abby call out,

"I'm going to bring us down over there! I'm slowing her down!"

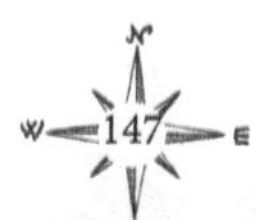

Abby eased the power levers back. She pushed the wheel forward, gently lowering the nose and letting The Rider brush the tops of the thin low trees. As they cleared the last trees and approached the beach, she backed the power way down.

She eased The Rider down almost to the sand, as they reached the water. She pulled the power levers slowly back to full stop and set the lift dial to hover.

Sasha was looking back over the aft railing. They came to a stop about four football fields from the beach. He nodded,

"Easy enough. I'm a good swimmer."

From behind, jokingly, Abby pushed him toward the rail. Sasha squeaked and turned around,

"I was kidding!"

Abby laughed and wrapped her arms around him,

"This has been the greatest and second saddest day of my life, Sasha."

Sasha's eyes watered up and he embraced her,

"Same here, Captain."

Abby let him go and stepped back. Sasha looked at the holographic display and furrowed his brow,

"We don't have time for a long goodbye. Get to deeper water, Captain. With luck, we'll meet again."

Abby nodded and smiled,

"Sasha. I hate eggs."

Sasha laughed,

"I KNEW IT!"

He gave her a deep bow before turning around and jumping into the ocean. She heard him splash into the sea. Abby turned back and grabbed the wheel. She felt a tear running down her cheek. She was alone now, again.

It was terrifying, but she had been trained for this. She grew up spending most of her time alone. It hurt, but she was strong, like her mother and her father. It also helped to know that Norgren and Sasha would become two of her best friends, eventually.

She sniffed and shook her head. Abby couldn't imagine how hard it had been in the future, telling them goodbye and abandoning The Rider. She eased the power levers forward, pulling back on the wheel to keep The Rider in the air.

She looked at the display. The bright white dot was nearly on top of her. She felt her heart race and reminded herself that they were going to punch in hundreds of miles behind her. Back where The Rider laid hidden in the forest for so many years.

Over the next couple minutes, she had to ease up on the power levers as the ship dipped too low. She could feel the gentle pull of the ocean as the lower masts dragged in the water. She looked at the scanner. They were almost on her.

She had to get the antigravity drives below the waves. Sasha told her that was the key to staying off their sensors. Whoever they were, they would be scanning for technology more advanced than it should be for this time period.

She looked back toward the beach. It was out of sight except for some distant lights. She hoped she was over deep enough water. Abby pulled the power levers back to full stop and the wind died. The sails drooped then pushed back on the crossbeams, catching air and slowing her. She shifted the sail controls to hoist.

She looked up and saw the sails being drawn in and rolled up. She pulled the lift dial out of automatic and twisted it to five percent below hover. The Rider was silently sliding forward through the air. Gently sinking closer and closer to the water below.

She felt inertia pull her gently forward and The Rider quickly slowed as she touched the ocean. Abby pulled gently back on the wheel, keeping The Rider level as she dragged against the water.

The ship began pushing up a gentle wake in the water as she slowed more rapidly. In a moment, she was floating in the ocean. The ship gently rocking as it came to rest.

Abby looked at the display. The bright white dot suddenly flashed an ominous red, giving off a pulse that spread out from it in every direction. Like a single ripple in a pond from something breaking the surface.

Again, she felt the echo from her crystal necklace, but

much stronger this time. She put her hand over the crystal under her shirt. She felt the direction the echo came from. The crystal her father had given her, had somehow sensed the temporal disruption.

She thought back to that day. Had he known what he was giving her? They were walking the creek in the woods, when he suddenly stopped and crouched down. He looked her in the eyes. She didn't see it at the time, but looking back on the memory, he had something else on his mind. He was smiling, but his eyes were serious.

She remembered the sound of his voice as he held up the crystal and then put it over her head. He said it was a very special kind of crystal. He said she must try to never lose it or give it away. The more she focused on it, the more she remembered.

Whoever they were, they were here. Abby looked at the display. The interdimensional wake left by their travel was beginning to fade.

She reached deep water at the last possible moment. Following Sasha's instructions, she pushed all of the display screens down flat. She put her hand over the holographic display and pushed her hand down, shutting it off.

Reaching behind the arm that the wheel was mounted on, she flipped a hidden toggle switch and set The Rider into camouflage mode.

Wooden panels rose up from behind each display and each set of controls. The panels then folded forward and locked

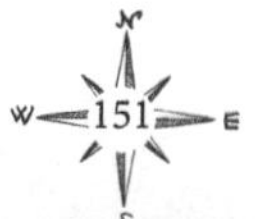

into place, hiding everything that looked out of place on an old wooden sailing ship.

Abby took a long slow look all the way around the ship. She didn't see any other boats, or people, or lights in the area. She walked down the stairs from the quarterdeck and entered her cabin.

She closed the door behind her and hung up her hat on a hook next to the door. She sat down at her desk and pulled the recorder out of her vest pocket that Norgren gave her. It had a small display screen and three buttons. Abby pushed the first button.

She saw Norgren's sad expression as his face appeared on the screen. He forced a smile for her,

"Captain Abigail, my dearest friend. I'm sure you're scared and confused and probably pissed off that Sasha and I couldn't come with you. Our job was just to get you off the ground and get you out of there. Our secondary consideration was to minimize the affect our interaction would have on your future. Those were your orders, Captain."

He looked down and wiped away some tears,

"I wish we could have stayed with you. Even now, I'm tempted to tell you to come back and get us. You have no idea how hard it is, knowing we can't stay with you. Meeting you changed..."

He stopped and looked off to the side for a second, then he looked back and started over,

"No, no personal history. You'll live it yourself. I knew we'd be tight on time, so I prepared this as a backup. I need to teach you how to use the jump drive. Your first jump is the most important. But it's been a long day. The first thing you need to do, is get some sleep. Yes, I know, you're the captain. But, for the first time, you're going to follow my orders."

He sat up straighter and gave her a goofy grin. Abby laughed. He continued,

"First, go over to the door and open the plaque mounted to the left. Just push the first button on the recorder again to pause. Also, you can hold the button down to back up if you need to hear something again. You can pause, I'll wait."

Abby laughed again and paused the recording. She found the plaque next to the door. It had the skull and crossbones of the Jolly Roger and underneath it said,

TIME 2 CAPTAIN UP!

Abby grinned and grabbed the top of the plaque. It swung open revealing a small, recessed control box with several switches. She pushed the button on the recorder again, Norgren continued,

"Now, just flip all three switches, to the down position. That locks down the forward stairwell, the cargo hold doors, and the quarterdeck control panels. Next..."

Abby hit pause and flipped all three switches down. She pushed the button,

"...on the other side of your door, you'll see a crossbar on

a swivel mount. You grab the handle, and you lift the crossbar about a foot straight up, then you can swing it down and across your door. That'll secure you inside, so you can rest. Do that now. Get some rest. Tomorrow, we'll go over the jump drive."

Abby paused the recording and locked the crossbar over her door. She walked over and tossed the recorder onto her bed. She was smiling and crying at the same time. She barely knew Norgren, but she already loved him like some crazy older brother.

She hung her belt and weapons on the silver stand, then sat down on the bed and pulled off her boots. After shrugging off the thick leather vest and hanging it up, she got comfortable on the bed.

Abby laid her head back on the pillow and picked up the recorder. She hit the first button again. Norgren continued,

"Now, since you ignored my orders to get some rest, let's continue. The jump drive..."

Abby paused the recording and laughed loudly. After a moment, she pushed play,

"...is activated by the drive key that hangs from the leather cord that binds your journal closed. A great deal of its automatic operation is subconscious. Mastery of the manual controls can take a lifetime."

He held up a computer tablet, turning the screen to face her so she could see. On the screen she saw a larger-than-life expanded drawing of the tiny golden wheel hanging from the

cord on her journal.

He touched the screen and moved the tiny disc on the face of the wheel, showing that it was actually three small rings that moved independently. She saw the inner gears turning and spinning in response.

He switched the picture on the screen. She saw a picture of the strange brass device on her desk that had a small eyepiece, tiny mirrors, and other moving parts. Norgren raised his eyebrows at that picture and gave her a look. He set down the tablet and continued,

"Manual control is VERY complicated, but you're in luck. The Rider was built to travel back in time and research the past. She was designed specifically to hide and remain invisible to others. The builders didn't want to risk causing changes that could destroy their time in the future."

Norgren held up the tablet again. This time showing an image of a harbor with several dozen old ships anchored in the bay of some port city in the past. He pointed at one of the ships amongst the others,

"That's The Rider, in the 16th century, or 17th? I don't exactly remember when I took this."

He set the tablet down and looked back at the camera,

"The ships jump drive was designed to accommodate the research teams. Book toting science nerds, who didn't have time to spend mastering complex controls. The researchers would complete their observations and then return the ship to

be used by another research team."

Norgren held up his tablet like it was a book in his hand,

"To put the automatic function of the jump drive simply. You hold the journal in one hand and the key in the other. You focus your mind on your destination, one hundred percent total concentration. Then you squeeze the key and activate the drive. The ship will jump you where you want to go."

Norgren set the tablet back down and sipped on what looked like a cup of coffee, then continued,

"That's putting it very simply. There are later ship designs, much more advanced, like the Imperial warships."

He gave her a very stern look,

"Never go toe to toe with one of those! They'll eat The Rider for breakfast with their shields and energy weapons. Also, there are other mechanisms for time traveling. Far more advanced than anything else ever created. Like these, for example."

Norgren reached down and picked something up. He held up what looked a lot like the crystal her father gave her the day before he died, with a silver chain running through the inside of it. He held it close to the screen for her to see. It looked almost identical to hers.

Abby sat up straight in bed with her eyes fixed on the small recorder screen. She reached up and put her hand on the crystal under her shirt. She thought about the strange vibration like echo feelings she felt from it. Norgren continued,

"This is a personal time portal generator. It can move a single person through time and across dimensions. Or, a very small group, standing very close together. The transportation range is about ten feet in every direction from the crystal."

He looked at the crystal for a moment and smiled. He looked back at the recorders camera,

"Captain Abby, my captain, got her hands on this one and came up with her backup plan to send us back to help you. This generator is how me and Sasha got to you."

Norgren set the crystal to the side and continued,

"The small more advanced portal generators were built much later in time than The Rider. Much harder to detect than a ship, almost no wake. Designed for more clandestine single operative missions back in time. Think spies and assassins..."

He stared off to the side for a moment, then shrugged,

"What can I say? The original builders were long gone. The Empire that replaced them was declining into decadence and corruption, infighting and treachery. Long story short, many of those secret operatives were corrupted by evil agendas and ended up causing the Empire a lot of problems. They retired all of those operatives."

Norgren drew a finger across his throat, meaning the builders killed all their clandestine operatives,

"They gave the confiscated personal generators to battleship captains as escape devices. So that, at the very least, they would be able to find out what happened to the ship.

Which brings me to my last warning."

Norgren leaned forward and looked at the camera very intensely,

"I said they retired all the solo operatives. Well, they retired all but three. Three very specialized, very powerful individuals."

Norgren held up three fingers in sequence as he counted them off,

"A telepath, a cyborg, and a mage. The Empire calls them The Renegades. They are the most powerful and most dangerous human beings of all time."

Norgren sat back. He looked at the screen for a moment, thinking,

"I've probably screwed up everything, telling you all this. But I realized once I started talking, that the odds of you starting over and meeting all of our old crew again are probably nil. I wanted to give you the best chance to start over, and that means knowing what's going on."

Norgren had tears in his eyes again. He blinked and shook his head. After a moment, he wiped away the tears and continued,

"The second button is a long boring explanation of the ships systems and controls and my thoughts on things. Including a couple of upgrades I never got around to finishing. Please don't push the third button, Captain. Save that, in case you do run into the younger me again. Do me that one favor, let

him, or me, push that button. Godspeed."

The recording ended. Abby got up and went to her desk. She set the recorder down and picked up the strange brass object he had shown her on the tablet. She couldn't even imagine what it's function and purpose was.

She set it back down and looked at the journal. She put her finger on the cover and traced the pattern of the compass rose etched into the leather.

Her eyes went wide as she suddenly heard Norgren's voice over the earring communicator. It was faint and cutting in and out. It sounded like he was in a war zone.

The Renegade

Hundreds of feet above the forest where The Riptide Rider rested for so long, an atmospheric anomaly occurred.

Norgren looked up and saw what appeared to be ball lightning forming in the sky high above him, a small sizzling, crackling sphere of pure electricity. It suddenly expanded into a massive open ring of electricity and fire, giving off a cascade of sparks and thunderous noise.

The instant the temporal rift opened and ripped a hole in the sky, a dark craft shot out from within it. The ring of lightning and fire snapped closed immediately after the ship passed through. Norgren lifted his weapon and took aim at the cruiser. He had to hit them fast, before they got their bearings.

The Imperial Cruiser, The Cronos, was an arrowhead shaped craft with a visually camouflaged hull, a blended and mottled mix of black and dark grey colors. The ship slowed to a stop after the portal snapped closed behind it.

The whole process lasted only seconds.

On the bridge of The Cronos, High Seeker Yano Vain stood up from his command chair and looked over at his junior officer in charge of sensors and weapons, Punisher Travin

Lore. The High Seeker's voice was lofty, entitled, cruel, and demeaning,

"Punisher Lore, sweep the area and ensure we are undetected. Fry anything with a matching signature echo. Then do a thorough scan and report back. The Emperor's Hand must have sent us early for a reason."

Punisher Lore tapped at his control screen and scanned the area for any signals of active resonance. The initial sweep was tuned to detect any sensors, scans, and even low-tech electronic recording devices, that might be directed at them. He saw none.

Next, he activated a longer range, much broader sweep with their sensors. The more thorough scan would detect anything that the onboard A.I. deemed inconsistent with current technology.

He activated the sweep, at the exact same time that Norgren pulled the trigger on the long, square barreled Strakaker rifle.

Lore saw the glowing signature of the high-tech weapon directly below them. His eyes widened in shock, and he called out loudly,

"TL-14 weapons fire! Directly below!"

The Strakaker fired a Rubik's Cube sized block of synthadiamond shards compressed around a small, powerful sonic disruptor at hypersonic speed. Just before hitting the target, the sonic disruptor sent out an ear shattering pulse of

vibration and energy.

The systems operator sitting next to Punisher Lore didn't wait for the High Seeker's order to raise the shield. He slapped his hand down on the emergency activation pad shunting power directly to the shield emitters. He did that, just a half second too late.

The sonic disruptor pulsed through the block, expanding it into a five-foot-wide cloud of razor-sharp synthadiamond shards. The pulse also weakened the hull of The Cronos just before impact.

The glistening shards, moving five times faster than sound, shredded the lower hull of the ship in the rear starboard section. They flashed through the ship, damaging the drive systems, life support, killing half a dozen imperial soldiers, and then shredded the upper hull on its way out. All of it happened in 0.1 seconds.

The shield surged to life as The Cronos began to tilt and drift. The pilot moved his hands on the control screen trying to keep the ship stable. Fire and smoke were rising from inside the damaged hull.

High Seeker Vain narrowed his eyes, furious. He stepped to the sensor display and gripped Punisher Lore's shoulder painfully, speaking harshly,

"Give me a visual."

Lore gritted his teeth against the pain. He entered the commands and brought up the display, showing a man on the

ground below. The pudgy, scruffy bastard was standing next to a small pond of soupy mud in grimy coveralls, giving them the middle finger. He began reloading the single shot Strakaker rifle.

The insolent wretch had a wide grin on his face. High Seeker Vain shouted,

"DEPLOY LEGIONARIES! I WANT HIM ALIVE!"

The bridge sub-commander spoke to the computer in front of him,

"Deploy Legionaries, non-lethal only, capture the hostile."

The computer's sweet and gentle feminine voice replied,

"Deployment commencing."

Norgren saw a hatch open near the rear of the ship. He inserted another block of ammo in the Strakaker, but the replacement firing charge jammed and wouldn't go in. Stupid black-market vender must have sold him replica tech, which wasn't always perfect.

Half a dozen humanoid robots dropped to the ground from the damaged cruiser. They looked like men in black armor, but Norgren knew they were combat robots. They carried nets and shock sticks. They immediately spread out to minimize Norgren's ability to hit more than one of them at a time.

That's when Nero arrived.

There was a bright flash on the top of the nearby hill, from the same spot where Sheriff Baker found Abby lying half conscious.

Norgren looked up toward the flash. In the moonlight, he saw a man dressed in ornately designed black clothing with long blonde hair tied back in a ponytail. He stood with his hands clasped casually before him, smiling pleasantly.

To Norgren he looked like a long-haired priest about to perform a wedding. But Norgren knew better, he would never forget that angular face and those slightly pointed ears. Not after what he saw...

The former engineer of The Riptide Rider knew he was looking at one of the Renegades.

Years back, the crew of The Rider searched the aftermath of a battle between the empire and the renegades. In the wreckage, Galahad found an intact server bank and Norgren hacked it, replaying recorded scenes of the battle.

Norgren remembered seeing Nero in the holographic replay. The cruiser above him was just a gnat, compared to the unimaginably powerful mage. Nero could call down lightning at will, raise magma from the mantle, or casually wave his hand and churn the ocean.

As a Technomancer, Norgren knew that Nero could harness the power contained inside the elements of earth and sky, and he could bend them to his will.

Nero looked at Norgren, then he calmly looked around at the robots and the ship overhead. He looked back at Norgren and nodded cordially.

On the bridge of The Cronos, Punisher Lore saw the temporal field activation on his screen and shifted the sensor display to the man in black. The A.I. computer operating system immediately recognized Nero. Red lights pulsed on the bridge.

The sweet feminine voice of the ship's computer announced over the PA,

"Emergency Alert. Renegade Watcher detected. Launching emergency disaster beacon."

High Seeker Vain saw the display and recognized the Renegade. His heart raced and he very nearly soiled his uniform from panic. Shaking, he spoke to the men around him,

"Emperor's light, protect us. Sub-Commander, re-task the Legionaries, try to buy us time. Activate damage control teams, alert all weapons divisions. Prepare for emergency landing sequence."

A missile carrying the emergency beacon launched from the top of the cruiser. It streaked up into the sky. The missile was programmed to leave the atmosphere and maintain a stable orbit, looking like random space junk. The beacon would then begin broadcasting a multi-dimensional alert.

Nero looked up at the missile and put one hand over the crystal hanging around his neck. He reached up with his other hand and pointed at the rapidly climbing emergency beacon. A small portal opened in front of the missile, sending it across the dimensions.

Nero watched the missile vanish and winked at the cruiser,

We'll keep this gathering private, thank you.

Crossing his hands behind his back comfortably, Nero began walking casually toward Norgren, his expression calm

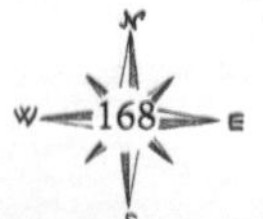

and friendly.

The legionaries changed direction and ran around the soupy pond of mud toward the Renegade. Nero's ice blue eyes shifted over to the robots. He stopped walking and held out one hand in their direction.

One after another, in rapid blinding succession, lightning began striking the robots and the ground all around them. Norgren shielded his eyes from the cataclysmic display of power. In seconds, dozens of lightning strikes fried the robots, leaving them sparking, twitching, and partially melted on the ground.

Nero looked up toward the cruiser with a frown and shook his head, as if to say knock it off. He gestured at the cruiser dismissively, silently saying go away. Then he turned toward Norgren and began walking again.

Norgren finally got the propellent charge to lock into place. He pointed the rifle at Nero. The man in black just grinned and continued walking toward him.

High Seeker Vain watched Nero look up at him and shake his head, then dismiss him like a beggar before continuing toward the infidel that damaged his ship. He put his hand back on Punisher Lore's shoulder,

"By the Emperor's light, we have been given a chance. Target the Renegade and fire every single weapon on this ship at him. Do it now!"

Lore tapped his screen, targeting Nero with the weapon

systems. He toggled 'fire all' on the weapons control panel and pushed the button to fire on the target.

From where he stood, Norgren saw a dozen bright green lasers fire down at the man in black. The lasers hit a round invisible shield around Nero and were deflected away in a dozen different directions.

Norgren dropped onto his back and held the rifle up in front of himself like a shield that was far too thin. The scattered lasers cut through dirt and trees and rocks all around the area. Glancing past the rifle, Norgren saw the man in black narrow his eyes, irritated.

Nero held out one hand toward Norgren. The Strakaker rifle was jerked away and flew into the mage's outstretched hand. Nero tossed the rifle into the soupy pond of mud, then turned his attention to the cruiser.

With the bright lasers still being reflected from, glancing off, and dancing across his invisible projected shield, Nero held out both hands toward the cruiser. He held his hands as if gripping an invisible ball, then began moving his hands like he was spinning it.

The air began spinning around the ship.

Norgren shielded his eyes from the wind and flying debris of the sudden tornado that was gripping the cruiser, causing it to begin spinning in mid-air. The engines whined loudly in protest.

Norgren rolled onto his left side and shielded his head

with his right arm. He reached up with his left hand and
squeezed his earring, speaking quickly.

Nero moved his hands faster and faster. The tornado,
centered on the ship, stretched down to the surface. Trees were
ripped from the ground and thrown into the distance.

The Renegade thrust both hands toward the ship and
made grasping gestures, then he ripped his hands down to each
side. Two thick powerful arcs of electricity stretched down
to the Earth, draining all of the ships electrical power into the
ground.

On the bridge of the cruiser, the lights dimmed, the non-
critical systems all went dark. The emergency backup lights
came on, bathing the bridge in faint red light.

Everyone on board was pinned to a wall or holding
on to railings and control panels for dear life. The ship was
spinning in a tumbling circle at ridiculous speed, with suddenly
powerless inertial dampening systems. The Sub-Commander,
gripping his restraint harness, shouted,

"CORE POWER CRITICAL! ENGINES FAILING!
SHIELDS FAILING!"

Nero looked back at Norgren and smiled. The tornado
immediately dissipated. The Imperial Cruiser, behind him, was
spinning so fast it looked like a blur. Most of the crew were
already dead, smeared across various interior surfaces. Smoke
and fire poured out of the cruiser in every direction.

Norgren watched as the spinning two-hundred-foot-long

ship fell from the sky and crashed to the Earth, exploding into a gigantic fireball. The shockwave from the explosion blasted branches and small trees away from the impact area.

The force of the explosion, the wave of fire, and all the burning debris parted around Nero and Norgren like they were rocks in a stream, protected by the mage's shield.

Norgren knew he was a dead man. He rolled onto his back, reaching behind himself to prop himself up. He raised up slightly and looked at the man in black. Nero took several steps closer. He spoke in a soft, calm voice,

"Where did she go?"

Norgren shook his head, no.

Nero's face took on a look of displeasure. He raised his hands out to each side, palms down. He slowly rose from the ground. Hovering in the air, he lifted his left hand toward the sky and spread his fingers. Lightning began pounding into the ground repeatedly, about fifty feet away. It was slowly coming closer.

Nero shouted down at him,

"WHERE IS THE DAUGHTER OF JUSTINIUS THE WATCHER?"

Norgren huddled into a ball, mentally and emotionally crippled by the furious effects of the continuous lightning strikes. The cracking and deafening sound of air being vaporized, the shockwaves from the ground being blasted, the blinding light, even the ozone smell assaulting his nose.

Nero suddenly felt an echo from his time portal generator. He looked to the west as he felt The Riptide Rider jumping away from this world and time. After a moment he looked back down at Norgren, his eyes were filled with rage.

Atoll

Abby's eyes went wide as she suddenly heard Norgren's voice over the earring communicator. The transmission was faint at this distance, cutting in and out. It sounded like he was in a war zone. She heard what sounded like extremely high winds in the background. She heard Norgren shouting,

"...have to run! Do it..."

The deafening sound of arcing electricity drowned out Norgren's voice. The electromagnetic interference caused loud static over the connection for about ten seconds, then she heard,

"...UMP! JUMP! JUMP! ABIGAIL, JU..."

The roaring winds were replaced with the sound of a massive engine of some kind. It was whining in the background. It sounded like it was struggling to keep some massive machine moving. The sound of the engine was changing, fading. She heard,

"Capta... ...ou have to jump th... ...ore he finds it and kills you."

The sound of the whining engine ended with a loud

explosion, followed by the roaring wind and the shockwave, and screaming from Norgren. Then the transmission went silent for several moments.

Abby picked up the journal with one hand and grabbed the key between the fingers of her other hand. She hesitated, suddenly unsure about departing immediately,

Do I need to be moving forward? Does The Rider need to be in the Air? Can I jump the ship while it's sitting in the water? Is it still damaged?

Abby heard an unfamiliar man's voice. He sounded like he was standing close to Norgren,

"Where did she go?"

The question was followed by silence. Then she heard the sounds of lightning pounding on the ground very close by. Then she heard the stranger shouting, demanding,

"WHERE IS THE DAUGHTER OF JUSTINIUS THE WATCHER?"

Abby's blood froze in her veins. Her mind raced with a furious flood of thoughts,

Justinius the Watcher? Justin Watcher?! MY DAD?!?

Oh my god, I can't leave my mom!

Norgren just said,

Capta… …ou have to jump th… …ore he finds it and kills you.

Her mind automatically filled in the blanks. Captain, you have to jump the ship before he finds it and kills you.

Norgren said HE, not THEY. He! One of the Renegades! Norgren was in danger! Oh my god... NORGREN!

Abby was thinking of her ship's engineer, as she squeezed the jump drive key and felt it 'click'.

In less than a second, several things happened. To Abby, they played out slowly. She heard the spinning pulsing build up of electromagnetic energy. The room around her and everything in it were suddenly doubled in her vision. It felt like gravity increased and she stumbled. She heard the painfully loud, warbling, low frequency pulse.

Abby felt weightless for a split second, then The Rider dropped three feet and slammed down onto a body of water. Abby landed painfully on her butt, crying out. Her stomach heaved and she gritted her teeth to avoid throwing up.

She scrambled to her feet and threw open the door, running for the rail. Then, she emptied her stomach over the side of the ship.

After the heaving stopped, Abby stood up and wiped the tears from her eyes with her sleeve. Her eyes were so blurry with tears she was seeing green and blue shimmering lights on the wooden deck by her feet. She blinked her eyes several times and wiped her mouth as she looked up.

Her eyes went wide, and her mouth dropped open in shock at the awesome vision above her.

The aurora borealis filled the entire sky above her. Shifting rippling waves of green and blue fire covered the sky from horizon to horizon. Abby turned in a circle, unable to believe her own eyes. She staggered unsteadily and leaned hard against the railing next to her, staring up at the sky.

The ship suddenly leaning toward starboard, jerked her out of her reverie. She looked around quickly, thinking maybe she drifted onto a beach she hadn't seen or rocks or some other ocean hazard.

There was no land in sight. Not in any direction. The ship was definitely leaning. Abby moved closer to her cabin door, fear running its cold wet fingertips down her spine. She either hit something, or something grabbed hold of the ship.

A long, thick, glistening, black tentacle shot up over the starboard railing and wrapped around the forward mast. It was black and blotchy purple, and slimy. Abby screamed as a second tentacle lashed out of the water and wrapped around the center mast.

Abby ran into her cabin and slammed the door. She raised the crossbar and slammed it down across the door. She was breathing fast and shallow. She felt the ship being pulled further to starboard. The ship was leaning at a precarious angle. She was starting to panic,

What if it capsizes the ship?

She heard her mother's voice echo in her mind,

Someone ever comes to you looking for a fight, you give them every

Fight...

Abby looked over her shoulder at the silver stand. She turned and rushed across the room. She threw the leather vest around her shoulders, then quickly buttoned it up,

Don't panic. Keep moving. Fight.

She put on her sword and sidearm and tightened the belt. Out on the deck, she heard an ungodly, high pitched, screaming, squealing noise. Goosebumps covered her arms and she shivered involuntarily.

Abby took a deep breath and narrowed her eyes,

It's time to fight. The time for fear is over.

Prioritizing, she decided this would have to be a barefoot fight, no time for boots. She lifted the crossbar and pulled open the door. The ship tilted even further, getting close to forty-five degrees of tilt toward starboard.

She grabbed the pistol off her thigh and looked at it. It had two controls, a hammer, and a trigger.

She looked over the rail in the direction the tentacles had come from. There was a mass of dark flesh rising out of the water with sickly purple splotches on it. She needed to be higher. She ran awkwardly across the angled deck to the rear mast.

Leaping off the deck behind her, she took two running

steps up the mast and caught a support rope in her free hand. She saw more of the dark mass coming out of the water. Abby cocked back the hammer and aimed at the creature.

She heard a voice in her mind,

Please! Help me!

Her face contorted in confusion. What had she just heard? Was someone caught in the monster's jaws? She couldn't see any jaws. She was in the middle of the ocean. Where had that person come from?

The Rider tilted even further, as the creature pulled itself higher from the water and Abby saw what was attacking it. She heard the voice in her mind again,

PLEASE!!!

From here, she could see the bulk of the dark creature was butted up against her ship. It's front end against the hull. Down by its tail end, there was a long thick eel-like creature with a flat wide head and nasty jaws.

The eel was biting down on the blotchy purple flesh between the narrower part of its body and its tail. The eel was thrashing its thick body, trying to tear the dark flesh.

She hesitated only a second. Then she raised the pistol and aimed toward the eel, just slightly away from the dark creature screaming for help. She pulled the trigger, and surprisingly there was no recoil.

The bullet fired out of the pistol in one cough-like pop.

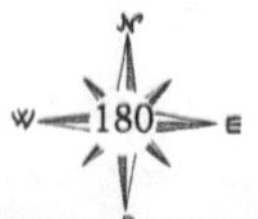

Then it immediately shrieked with a tiny fiery propellent like a huge bottle rocket and streaked forward like a missile, leaving a trail of smoke in its wake. It screamed into the water next to the eel and detonated like a bomb.

The concussive shockwave from the surprisingly large explosion blew her off the mast and she landed painfully on her back, grunting from the force. The ship rocked hard to port as the tentacles released and retracted. The Rider rocked back and forth several times before settling.

Abby lay on her back on the deck for several moments, groaning. That hurt. She slapped the pistol against the mag-plate. THUNK. She sat up and shook the fog from her brain as she scrambled to her feet.

Walking slowly over to the side, she looked out and saw most of the eel's body was slowly disappearing below the water. A smaller piece was drifting away on the tide. The large dark creature with tentacles was nowhere to be seen.

Her head was throbbing and her back ached something fierce. She leaned close to the edge and shouted incredulously,

"YOU'RE WELCOME!"

Abby shook her head and went back into her cabin. Everything felt like a dream, or a nightmare rather. She sat down and pulled on her boots. A yawn escaped her lips as the adrenaline faded.

She still needed rest. But she wasn't going to ignorantly fall asleep on some alien world, in the middle of a pack of dark

fleshed, chubby, tentacled whales and thick, wide mouthed eels.

She grabbed the journal and tucked it in her belt. Then she stepped over to the door and grabbed her hat. She stopped and considered for a moment. Abby walked back over and grabbed the spare magazines out of her top drawer and dropped them into one of the large lower pockets on her vest.

Opening the door slowly, she half expected to see the deck crawling with eels and giant crabs carrying torches and pitchforks. Outside her cabin, everything was quiet. She made her way across the deck, watching the railings carefully. She grabbed the handle on the door to the stairwell leading below deck. It was still locked.

Abby leaned her head back and groaned at the sky. She stalked back across the deck, grumbling in irritation. She went into her cabin, and toggled the locks hidden behind the plaque next to the door.

After unlocking the ship, she made her way down to the engine room and triple tapped the engineering display panel. She shifted it to damage control and was happy to see that most of the red was now gone. The lower masts still had some minor damage, but she didn't think that would keep her from flying.

Abby stopped in the galley on her way back up and found another small brown bottle that looked like the one Sasha left for her on her desk. She grabbed it and headed back up. She carefully stepped back out onto the main deck. Looking around, she saw that everything was still quiet.

About halfway to the quarterdeck, she stopped. She suddenly remembered hearing a voice in her mind. In the heat of the moment, she totally forgot about that. Did she hear that fat little whale thing talking to her? Had she imagined that?

She shook her head and walked up the stairs to the quarterdeck. She flipped the camouflage switch off and watched the wooden concealment panels open up and then retract out of sight. The display screens all tilted up toward her at an angle and flickered to life.

She found the section of the control panel for the masts and sails and switched the lower mast setting to deploy. She heard the muted sounds of the lower port and starboard masts deploying underwater. They were working and almost fully repaired.

She was about to be mobile.

Next, she needed eyes. Abby looked at the D-scan. Sasha told her it had other functions, but he never got a chance to show her. It was still on the original multi-dimensional view setting. She didn't see any dedicated buttons or external controls for it.

She thought about what Norgren did to the display down in engineering. Abby tapped the upper left corner of the screen and saw a menu open. She grinned and scrolled through the various options.

She found a setting labeled tactical, with the options of short, medium and long. She selected medium range tactical. The screen now displayed the area all around the ship, out to

about a hundred miles,

WOW! That's medium?

There was activity happening on the scanner, near the edge of the sensors medium range. She saw one large green signature, and a dozen much smaller red signatures all around it,

Kinda looks like it might be a gathering place? With some ships nearby?

Pulling the cork on the small brown bottle, she took a big swig. Her face contorted into a grimace,

UGH! THAT'S RANCID!

It was disgusting. There was a sickly-sweet aspect that she absolutely hated. She pushed the cork back in and dropped it into a pocket as she looked at the display one more time,

Maybe if I come in low and slow, I can get a look without drawing attention.

Abby adjusted her hat, tightened her belt, and narrowed her eyes. She thought about the plaque next to her door inside her cabin. It was Time 2 Captain Up.

With a quick flip of the protective cover and toggling the switch, she activated the antigravity drives. She heard the slow rise of the low frequency thrumming and felt the gentle vibration through the deck. Abby smiled and dialed up the lift power to ten percent.

The Rider lifted slowly out of the ocean. Abby let her rise about fifty feet into the air, then she deployed the sails and set the drives to hover.

She went to each side, looking over the rail at the lower masts and sails sticking out from the ship at an angle. She smiled broadly. The Riptide Rider was the craziest thing she had ever seen,

She's a beautifully weird ship. She's perfect.

Abby stepped behind the wheel and pushed the lift dial in, setting it to automatic. She grabbed the wheel with one hand and on impulse, pushed the power levers to full throttle.

An instant hurricane blasted into the ship from behind, stretching the sails to their limit and throwing Abby forward into the wheel. The Rider dipped forward and almost slammed into the ocean, but the burst of speed pulled Abby back and the wheel with her.

Clinging desperately to the wheel of the slowly climbing ship, Abby got her feet under her just as she heard a sputtering engine coughing noise from behind. Before she could turn around the rear afterburners engaged, again pulling her back.

Abby grabbed the wheel tightly with both hands and braced her feet, pushing the wheel forward and leveling out. She was accelerating at an incredible speed! Abby laughed loudly,

This crazy thing has freaking AFTERBURNERS!

Looking back, she saw three bluish white jets of flame

that shifted to red, shooting out of the back! The Rider was roaring across the sky!

Abby glanced at the scanner display and made a squeak. She was already well over halfway to the group of unknown signatures on the display. She quickly pulled the power levers back to half thrust and pulled back on the wheel. The afterburners flickered out and The Rider lifted silently higher into the sky.

So much for low and slow.

Abby pushed the display screen flat. She placed her palm flat on it, and then lifted it away as she had seen Norgren do. The image lifted up into a three-dimensional display. Abby leveled out at about a hundred feet and continued forward. She switched the display to close range.

Now she recognized the larger signature as some kind of structure in the ocean, with about a dozen small craft moving around it. As she got closer, she backed the power levers down even further. She rolled the wheel gently to port, leaning The Rider toward the scene below for a better look.

She saw that the smaller craft were boats, one larger and slower, most of the others were very small and very fast. She also saw that the structure had what looked like a large water cannon in the very center. Mounted in an opening in the roof, it was firing at the boats that got too close.

Abby kept The Rider in a gentle bank, circling around the Atoll.

She needed a friend. She needed someone to keep watch while she slept. She was in an alien world, and down there was at least one local who desperately needed help. She decided that the defender in this conflict was the safest overall bet.

Pushing the wheel forward, she lowered The Rider closer to the ocean. She turned into her circling path, and straightened out, heading almost directly toward the structure, just slightly off to one side. Hopefully she could get close enough before she was noticed and then slow down at the last moment.

She was close enough now to see the different types of small watercraft around the structure. She saw them throwing flaming objects onto the huge tarp-like roof. The water cannon blasted the little boats and washed the flaming objects off the tarp that stretched out all around it.

Some of the boats were very small and tried to get close enough to get inside under the low outer edge of the tarp roof.

Abby reduced thrust to about ten percent, letting the generated wind die down to a breeze. The Rider was now gliding silently and gently forward. She banked slightly to the right, so she could see down toward them over the starboard rail.

The scene had a dream-like quality, bathed in the green and blue lights of the aurora filled sky. With her left hand on the top of the wheel, she controlled the gliding turn closer to the structure. She reached down with her right hand and pulled her weapon off the mag-plate on her thigh.

She saw small prickly looking creatures on most of the boats. They looked like half-sized men made out of black chunky cactus bodies. There were a handful on the larger square boat, but there was also something else.

On a high-mounted seat, near the back, she saw a tall gangly-looking fish-man. In the green and blue aurora light, he was glistening with the colors of the sky. He had fins and spiny things around his head and shoulders and arms.

The instant the fish-man saw her, they all turned to look at her. The cactus men were unreadable, but she saw the expression on the fish-man. He narrowed his eyes. He was not happy to see her.

The structure under attack looked like a giant circus tent with no walls sitting in the ocean. The only apparent way in was under the side of the low outer edge of the massive tarp roof.

Abby looked up as her slow banking turn started to pull her away from the structure. The man sitting in the turret-like water cannon turned to look at her. His normally well combed black hair was messy and chaotic.

It was Sasha!

She immediately pulled the power levers to full stop and kept The Rider in a gentle turn so that the atoll was directly to starboard. Abby slowed to a stop, just a couple hundred yards away.

She was too far to make out fine detail, but she saw the

fish-man pointing at her. Good, she was pulling some of their attention off of Sasha. Several of the smaller boats turned away from the atoll and came straight at her.

Abby stepped up to the starboard rail. She cocked back the hammer and aimed at the nearest boat. As it got closer, she saw the little cactus man in the front aiming some kind of rifle at her! She panicked and started to duck on instinct as she pulled the trigger. Her aim was way off.

The bullet-missile thing, whatever it was, shot out off to the side. It wasn't pointed anywhere close to them. But then it ignited and roared forward like a missile, leaving a tiny trail of smoke in its wake.

It banked in an arc toward the boat, dropped just underneath the water as it hit and detonated. The boat exploded into a thousand flaming bits and dripping chunks of little cactus men flew in every direction.

Abby stood up straight with a big smile on her face,

The torpedo bullets are guided missiles!

She took aim at the next boat in line. She reached over with her left hand and cocked back the hammer. The boat quickly turned and headed away from her, angled off to the left. Two more boats turned in the same direction and sped away.

The rest of the boats harassing the atoll headed off that way as well. The fish-man in the big chair on the back of the larger boat stared at her as he followed the rest. She felt a cold shiver run down her spine as she heard a faint whisper in her

mind,

We'll see you again. Real soon.

Abby put her weapon on the mag-plate. THUNK. First the splotchy fat whale thing, now the fish man,

Can everything on this weird world send thoughts into people's minds?

She waited and watched the boats get smaller as they sped away. Once she couldn't see them anymore, she turned The Rider toward the atoll and eased the power levers forward.

As she approached, she saw the edges of the tarp rising. Submerged poles were coming up from underwater, lifting the edges of the massive tarp in four places and opening the structure into four main areas.

She saw a tall round central building surrounded by a wide tiered platform, separated by a series of railings. She was closing in on a section that had a number of small boats tied up at several small docks.

Abby let The Rider glide slowly past the docks and banked around to the next area, where she saw that the tiered platform had a wider floor of floating connected panels filling the space between the section dividers.

The raised platform nearest the main building looked like an oceanside dive bar combined with a deli or a buffet. The outer main floor was covered in round tables with about a dozen people standing among them.

Grinning and waiting, as Abby came into view, everyone erupted into a standing ovation. She smiled at the cheering and clapping. She saw a lot of smiles and a lot of appreciation.

Sasha walked out from the structure toward the tables, carrying a tray. Abby never would have guessed she'd see him barefoot in tattered brown pants, and a darker brown homemade looking shirt. He smiled broadly at her as she came into view.

Abby pulled the power levers to full stop, then dialed down the lift to five percent below hover. She set the sails to hoist and let The Rider slowly settle into the water. Soon, The Rider was floating gently next to the atoll.

Abby pulled the big lever at the rear of the quarterdeck and heard the clanking of the chain as the anchor dropped away. That's when a much younger Norgren came running out from the central structure, looking at some device in his hand. He looked panicked, shouting,

"NO! NO, NO, NO! RAISE THAT ANCHOR!"

Abby raised her eyebrows in surprise but did as he said. She reversed the long heavy lever and heard the slow clanking of the chain being hoisted back in. She looked at him and waited. He looked at the thing in his hand for several moments until the anchor was all the way retracted,

What was the problem with lowering the anchor?

Abby just stared at him as The Rider bobbed gently on the low waves. Norgren and Sasha both looked much younger

now,

These two won't know me, gotta remember that.

Norgren turned in a slow circle, holding the thing in his hand lower toward the water. Finally, he nodded and looked up. He gave her a thumbs up, then held up one finger, wait. He ran off around the inner platform.

Sasha caught her eye. He waved and grinned. He put his hands together like praying and bowed. Meaning, thank you, she thought. Abby smiled and waved back.

A few minutes later, Norgren came around the outside of the atoll in a small heavy-looking boat. He pulled up next to The Rider and stopped.

Abby leaned on the rail and looked down. Norgren had on a clean white T-shirt under some surprisingly clean coveralls. He looked up at her,

"I'm guessing you're not from around here, eh?"

Abby shook her head, no,

"You're not wrong. Going to tell me why I can't drop anchor here?"

Norgren nodded,

"These waters are leviathan territory. Not some shallow five or six miles like most of the planet. If you grab enough weight and jump overboard, you're looking at almost forty miles of black below you. The really big ones don't like coming

near the surface, but the younger ones have been known to explore the twilight zone. So, we don't dangle bait to draw them up."

Abby felt a queasiness in her gut and took a step back from the railing. Norgren laughed and asked,

"More of a flyer than a sailor, yes?"

Abby smiled and nodded,

"How'd you know?"

Norgren pointed towards the rear of the ship,

"You tried to drop anchor in deep ocean. Even if it weren't as deep as it is, anchors are for shallows, not deep ocean. No ship carries a deep-water anchor with a chain five miles long."

Abby chuckled,

"Guilty."

Norgren gestured over his shoulder, toward the inside,

"You're welcome to come in. Have a bite, a drink, whatever you want, on the house."

Abby shook her head and held up a hand,

"That's not necessary."

Norgren cocked his head and grinned,

"Those thugs were about to make an example out of us. We turned away one of their slave barges yesterday. Refused them food and supplies. If you hadn't come along, every single one of us would have been tossed off a Syndicate ship screaming, chained to sinkers."

Abby gave him a puzzled look,

"Sinkers?"

Norgren chuckled,

"Just like it sounds, heavy metal rings that'll pull you down as far as down goes."

He chuckled again at her sudden grimace, adding,

"The Twilight Syndicate will be back, and not just to kill us. They'll also be looking for you and that sky ship of yours."

Abby cocked her head at him questioningly,

"Shouldn't you be leaving then?"

Norgren nodded,

"We've got some time. I need to pack some tools and other things that are hard to replace. Syndicate is based out of a massive atoll about a day's sail from here. So, we've got at least two days to be gone. By my reconning."

Abby thought about the older Norgren saying they had at least five days and the enemy showed up in five hours. She grinned and mumbled,

"Your last timing was a bit off."

He looked up at her,

"What was that?"

Abby quickly said,

"It's past time I get off this ship."

Norgren nodded his head and gestured to his boat,

"Come aboard then, I'll have the lads get your ship tied off to the atoll."

Getting The Band Back Together

Abby locked down the deck and the quarterdeck control panels after setting The Rider to camouflage mode. She checked her weapons and tucked the journal in her belt before climbing down the rope ladder to Norgren's small boat.

As he turned the sturdy little craft back toward the docking area, Abby looked back and saw two men attaching long poles to the side of her ship, fore and aft. Then they attached the other ends of the poles to the atoll, securing her ship to the structure. The poles would prevent her ship from drifting away or drifting into the structure.

Norgren took her to the inner docks and led her around the wide tiered platform that wrapped around the entire building. She followed him around to the restaurant-like gathering place where all the others were.

Abby walked in, to the sound of more applause. She grinned at the odd-looking assortment of dark but smiling faces and held both fists up in victory. The men around the tables cheered and applauded. Abby smiled broadly and put her hands on her hips, looking back at them.

Sasha walked up to her and offered her a cup that looked like it was carved from wood. Abby picked it up and sniffed it,

OH MY GOD! What is that? Jet fuel?

She raised her eyebrows expressively,

"Thanks, you are?"

Bowing slightly,

"Sasha San'Strobien. At your service, Captain...?"

Abby looked him in the eye,

"Captain Abigail, of The Riptide Rider."

Sasha turned around to the men in the room and spoke loudly,

"FRIENDS! Three cheers for our savior! Captain Abigail!"

Abby looked around at the small crowd as she watched them all raise a fist and shout in unison,

"HUZZAH! HUZZAH! HUZZAH!"

Saving the day and being cheered for, put the biggest cheesiest grin on her face. Most of the men went back to talking, a few were still watching her and clapping softly. Surprisingly, she heard one dissenting voice,

Can we wrap this up and get the hell out of here please?

Abby looked around but couldn't tell who said it. The sentiment didn't match any of the smiling faces she saw.

Sasha turned back to her,

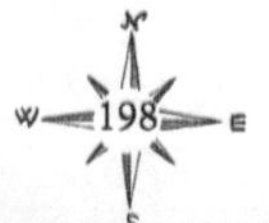

"Captain, what can I get for you? Absolutely anything you want. Just name it."

Abby looked around at the tables, wondering what her choices were. She saw a few small cups, made of tarnished and battered metal, but most of them were on the floor.

She saw a few empty plates still on tables, but most were also scattered around the floor from the battle she interrupted. She saw some stuff she thought might be food, but nothing she recognized.

Abby looked back at Sasha and shrugged,

"I could use a bite. What do you recommend?"

Sasha looked at her thoughtfully for a moment, then he nodded,

"You strike me as a chowder kind of girl."

Abby smiled cautiously and gave him a thumbs up. Sasha grinned happily and headed off through the door into the main building, the same door that Norgren had come out of when she first saw him.

Grabbing an empty chair, Abby sat down and looked around. She started to take a sip from her cup, then sniffed at it again. She blinked her eyes a few times from the fumes and changed her mind. She set the cup down and waited.

A few moments later, Sasha walked up to her table with a big steaming bowl. Norgren followed him out of the kitchen, carrying a plate and utensils. Sasha set the bowl down in front

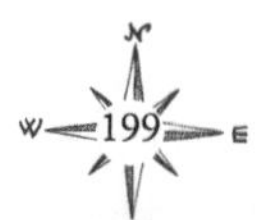

of her, smiled briefly, then quickly headed off to check on everyone else.

Abby noted that many of the men were saying their goodbyes and heading for their boats.

Norgren set the plate down next to the bowl of chowder. It had what looked like four sausage patties and a crusty piece of bread. He set down a nice-looking set of silver utensils, then moved around to the far side of her table and took a seat. He sat and stared at her, just smiling.

Abby picked up her spoon, then looked at him curiously,

"You about to judge my table manners?"

Norgren chuckled and shook his head, no,

"I'd like to have a word with you, Captain. But I don't want to intrude. I can come back if you'd rather eat alone in peace?"

She pointed her spoon at him,

"If you don't mind me eating, I won't mind your talking."

She dipped out a spoonful of the white soup and saw a couple of small purple cubes of something next to some kind of meat, and what she thought might be pepper. Abby glanced up at Norgren,

"What is this?"

Norgren's smile slipped. He looked at her spoon, slightly

alarmed. After a moment, he looked back up at her,

"It's just chum chowder."

"And those little purple chunks?"

He raised an eyebrow,

"Where on Earth are you from? Those are potatoes."

"Oh, ok. I'm used to white potatoes."

Abby blew across the steaming spoon and watched his eyes grow wider,

"You're used to land-grown potatoes? Now I'm really curious about where you're from."

He laughed softly and smiled. Abby cocked her head,

"What do you mean land-grown? Where else would you... You know what, never mind, I'm hungry."

Abby tried the chowder as Norgren nodded in reply. The chowder was fantastic. It was perfectly creamy, peppery, the potatoes were slightly salty when she bit into them. She made some loud 'this is the yum' groans,

"That is absolutely delicious."

Norgren grinned happily,

"Sasha is a pretty good cook."

A group of men called over to Norgren. He turned and

waved and called back to them, saying goodbye and good luck to the group. He reminded them to head away from the Syndicate's territory.

Abby made a mental note that now, all of the customers were quickly heading for their boats. She had a feeling that they didn't agree with Norgren's assessment of how much time they had before the Twilight Syndicate came looking for payback.

While all of that was going on, Abby tried the sausage. It was amazing. Whatever kind of meat she was eating, which she figured was probably fish. It was better than any sausage back on her world. That thought made her wonder,

Or back in my time? Is this Earth?

The men here were all humans, and Norgren said, 'where on Earth'. But what about that fish man, and those little cactus men? She shook her head and just focused on enjoying the food.

Abby looked up and noticed Norgren was watching her again, grinning,

"I'm glad you like Sasha's cooking. That's actually part of what I wanted to ask you about. My first question I guess, is why are you alone? The rest of your crew holding up below deck, waiting to see if this is some kind of trap or what?"

Abby laughed and shook her head, no. She finished chewing,

"It's funny you ask that. I'm actually in the market for a new crew at the moment."

Norgren's face was suddenly beaming,

"Well, you're in luck, Captain! I know two chaps who are looking for an immediate career change. Their rundown combination boat repair and restaurant just went out of business, due to some disagreements with the local crime boss and all."

Abby grinned at him and finished the last piece of sausage. As she was chewing, she mumbled,

"Gotta warn you... the pay sucks... that's if you actually... get paid at some point."

Norgren waved a hand dismissively,

"We're not trying to get rich."

She chuckled,

"Ship like The Rider, could be dangerous work at times."

Norgren nodded,

"Probably beats prolonged torture and certain death at the cruel hands of the Syndicate."

Abby picked up the bowl and drank the last of the chowder. She wiped her mouth with the back of her sleeve,

"That was one of the best meals I've had in a long time."

She burped loudly and gave Norgren a serious look,

"Where I'm going, there's a very good chance you can

never come back..."

She leaned forward and emphasized,

"...to this world."

Norgren's eyebrows went up and his mouth dropped slightly open in shock. He looked over at The Rider, then back at her. At first, he looked confused, then he started to smile. In her mind, she heard his voice,

She's got to be joking. That's not possible.

Abby continued staring at him. It took some quick thinking and serious effort to avoid freaking out from hearing his thoughts. This was a weird world. She was starting to think that maybe it had something to do with everything here being bathed in the green and blue aurora lights.

Like maybe all of their thoughts were just a little looser than they should be and tended to slip out from time to time. She kept the serious look on her face. After a minute, Norgren leaned toward her,

"You're serious?"

She nodded. Norgren furrowed his brow and looked down at the table. After a moment, he looked back up at her,

"No matter how I turn it around, it still beats torture and death."

Sasha approached so quietly that neither of them knew he was there, from off to the side he surprised them,

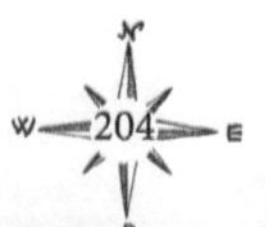

"Sign us up, Captain."

Abby looked over at him then put her foot on the chair between her and Norgren. She shoved the chair away from the table and nodded towards it. Sasha came closer and sat down. He sat up very straight and put his hands in his lap, a pleasant smile on his face.

She narrowed her eyes and looked at Sasha a bit skeptically. She looked back toward Norgren,

"Let's not be overly hasty here gents. We've established that you're looking for thankless and underpaid work that's just barely better than slave labor. We've also established that I'm looking for exactly that kind of help."

Abby spread her hands, asking,

"But what's in this for me and The Rider? What skills do you bring to the table?"

She tapped the bowl with her spoon, glanced at Sasha,

"Other than making an exquisite chowder."

Norgren sat up a little straighter and squared his shoulders. Abby was laughing in her head. He hadn't expected an interview. Norgren made a fist and pointed at his chest with his thumb,

"If you don't already have one, you're going to need an engineer. I'm your man, Captain. Not a thing exists that I can't repair, reverse engineer, or repurpose into something useful."

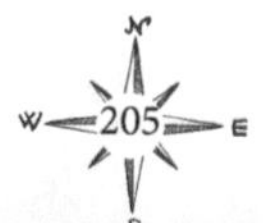

Sasha grinned and set his clasped hands on the table,

"And obviously, every captain needs a good steward."

Abby nodded in reply to Norgren, then looked over at Sasha and gave him her best quizzical look. She looked down at his ragged handmade clothes,

"Are you trying to insinuate you're a good steward?"

Sasha sat up straighter, clearly offended,

"Don't judge by the issued uniform of this paltry failing establishment, Captain."

Abby chuckled and nodded,

"That's fair, what exactly is a steward?"

Sasha and Norgren both started laughing, but quickly stopped when she just raised an eyebrow and continued to stare at Sasha. Sasha held up his hands, like 'whoa',

"Oh, uh apologies, I thought you were kidding."

He touched his chin with one hand, gesturing nervously with his other hand,

"Well, a steward uh cleans, and cooks, and obviously sees to the captain's daily needs and is basically..."

Sasha gestured at her, and smiled,

"...HER assistant, and closest confidante, and advisor, if needed."

Abby started shaking her head,

This is amazing. I don't even have to ask them to be part of my crew. They're begging to sign up just to avoid dying.

She realized that the captain of The Rider before her, must have been exactly where she was now, at some point in her journey. Otherwise, these two might not have been here since the Syndicate was about to kill them.

Norgren poked at the table with one stubby finger,

"Now, look here. We're both hard working, Captain. You'll not find better on this ball of salt and water. I promise you that!"

Abby looked at him confused for a second, then realized what was going on. He must have misunderstood her shaking her head. He thought she was declining their application to join her crew.

She waved his comment away,

"You're hired. Both of you. But I don't believe we have as much time as you think. I want to get underway, as soon as possible. I don't want the Syndicate to catch The Rider lounging in the waves with her sails down."

Sasha had a huge smile on his face. Norgren smiled also and nodded,

"You won't regret it, Captain. If you'll maneuver The Rider around to the cargo dock on the far side, I'll meet you over there and get her secured. Then just swing her boom

over the dock and we'll get our sundries and tools and other valuables loaded up."

Abby gave Norgren a serious look. She glanced at Sasha, then back to Norgren,

"That's it though, right? You two are onboard, so to speak? You'll not back out on me, or quit, or give up, or throw in the towel when things get rough? Not even if you run into something terrifying that you never would have expected?"

Norgren and Sasha looked at each other. Sasha shrugged and nodded. Norgren nodded back at him then looked at Abby and stood up. He held out his hand. Sasha stood up and did the same.

Abby stood up and shook Sasha's hand, then she shook Norgren's hand. Norgren thumped the table with one meaty fist,

"Done deal, Captain. We're your crew now."

Abby nodded,

"Good. Now, what's a boom?"

Norgren gave her a confused look,

"A wha... A boom, Captain. The boom."

He pointed towards The Rider. Abby glanced at the ship when he pointed, then she looked back toward him. She cocked her head and thought about it for a second.

Abby narrowed her eyes at him slightly,

"I've just decided I don't like repeating myself, engineer."

Norgren's eyes opened wider,

"Oh, you're serious! The boom is a long swinging arm rigged with ropes for loading cargo, Captain."

The two men looked at each other alarmed, then back at her. Norgren cocked his head curiously,

"How long have you been The Rider's captain, Captain?"

Abby tilted her head and looked up towards the ceiling, like she was thinking about it. She looked back at him,

"Four or five hours, I guess. Maybe years, technically? I'm not positive how that works, it's been a crazy day."

Norgren and Sasha both looked at her with wide eyes and open mouths, unbelieving. She shrugged and smiled broadly,

"Either way, once I get The Rider in place and you get her secured, you can come aboard and show me how to work the boom. Sasha, get packed. Norgren, get those poles off my ship. Hop to it men!"

Abby took off her hat and stuffed it into her vest. She ran to the edge of the floating floor and leapt off the atoll and into the sea.

She was having the time of her life. She swam

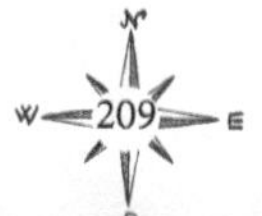

underwater toward The Rider. It was easy to see her ship with the lights of the Aurora in the sky. The Rider looked odd from this viewpoint.

Abby looked down and almost freaked out. She was not alone in the water.

She calmed quickly and continued swimming, looking down. The ocean was full of life. Most of it, what she could see, was either highlighted by the light of the auroras or farther down giving off its own light.

Far below her was a massive whale-looking creature that had stripes of red glowing light running down its sides and back. There were huge schools of glowing fish moving and shifting like tiny parts of one large fluid shape.

She got to The Rider and put her hand up on the bottom of the rope ladder. She couldn't take her eyes off the amazing and wonderous scene below.

~~

Norgren and Sasha watched their new captain run off and leap into the sea. Both of them were shocked, stunned, and slightly alarmed by the insanity of that interview. Norgren asked absently,

"Did she just say hours, maybe years?"

Sasha looked at Norgren and sounded optimistic,

"I think we got lucky. If she's only been a captain for a few hours, then she's clearly a natural. If it's actually been years,

then she's just a little forgetful."

Norgren nodded,

"I hope you're right and she isn't just crazy."

Both men moved quickly to follow her orders.

Run Like Smoke and Oakum

Abby climbed the rope ladder and hopped over the railing. Looking around the deck with a grin on her face, she shook off the excess seawater. She stepped into her cabin and unlocked the controls and deck access points.

She felt her socks squishing around in her boots as she walked up the stairs to the quarterdeck. She laughed and shook her wet hair out, then took a moment to tie it back out of the way,

Taking a quick swim probably wasn't the best idea.

Norgren untied the stabilizing poles and just dropped them into the ocean. No point in stowing anything since they were abandoning the atoll.

Abby nodded at him and eased the power levers forward just slightly. The wind whispered up behind her and eased the ship forward. The Rider moved with a gentle rocking motion from the extended lower masts dragging through the water below.

Looking up, around, and behind her, Abby suddenly wondered how that worked. When she slammed the power levers to max, a hurricane of wind hit her sails. Now, just the

slightest touch of power caused a faint breeze,

Does The Rider somehow manipulate the air around the ship?

Abby chuckled at herself,

The Rider can time travel, but controlling the wind is far-fetched?

Abby laughed loudly at her own silly thoughts and shook her head. She maneuvered The Rider to the far side of the atoll and found a much larger raised dock, compared to the smaller ones she saw on her way in. This one was built for a ship more her size.

She eased The Rider up next to the dock, then she pulled the power levers to full stop and gently shifted the drift control. The Rider slid slightly sideways and bumped up against the rubber cushions on the dock.

Norgren was waiting. He secured The Rider with mooring lines, attaching them to the forward and aft cleats on the side of the ship. Cleats that Abby hadn't even realized were there. She watched over the side of the railing and raised her eyebrows,

Good to know!

Norgren walked to the edge of the dock and opened the gate in the railing. He took on a serious expression and saluted her,

"Permission to come aboard, Captain?"

Abby grinned and nodded. Norgren stared at her a

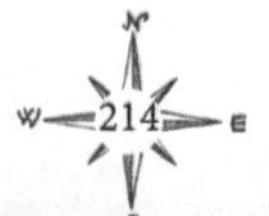

moment, then lowered his hand slightly and spoke in a low voice,

"You're supposed to say, permission granted."

He straightened up and raised his hand back up to salute. Abby sobered up and looked serious. She saluted him back,

"Permission granted."

Norgren nodded and stepped aboard. Abby held up a hand, stopping him,

"You're not going to do that every time are you?"

Norgren laughed loudly and shook his head, no,

"It's just an old custom. For new crew, the first time aboard. But visitors and passengers better ask every time, or risk being confused for pirates."

Abby nodded,

"Good to know."

Norgren pointed up, drawing her attention to what looked like a thinner, shorter square mast attached to the main mast,

"That's the boom, Captain."

The boom sat on a hinge attached to a swivel at the bottom, mounted on the main mast. She saw ropes and pulleys attached to the end and secured along it's length. Abby nodded

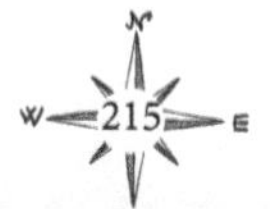

and smiled. She had been wondering what all that mess was about.

Norgren moved quickly and efficiently. He untied the bindings, lowered the boom, and swung it out over the dock. He showed Abby which ropes were involved and how to work everything.

By the time Norgren was done, Abby noticed that Sasha had already spread a thick cargo net out on the dock. He was currently carrying out a crate. She saw several large canvas bags and what looked like luggage already on the net.

Abby went into her cabin and changed out of her wet clothes. She now had a small pile of wet stuff. She put on her last set of dry clothes. She chuckled at the thought that now she had a steward to take care of stuff like that.

Toweling off the inside of her leather vest, she put it back on and tossed the towel on the pile. Once she had her weapons on and the journal tucked in her belt, she headed back out.

Abby walked over to the railing and watched the two men going back and forth into the building. There was a growing stack of crates and bags and luggage on the net. Abby looked around a bit. Her eyes went up to the open top of the canvas roof.

There was someone sitting in the water cannon turret! It looked like a young girl. Abby called out to Norgren and Sasha,

"OY! Who's that?"

They stopped and looked at her. Abby was pointing

toward the top of the atoll. From where they were, they couldn't see above the canvas. Norgren looked at Sasha and jerked his head toward the building,

"Check it out."

Sasha nodded and ran inside. Norgren went back to loading. Abby looked up at the girl. It was hard to make out fine detail, but it looked like she was scanning the horizon with a small handheld telescope.

The dark-haired girl lowered the telescope and turned her head toward Abby. She pointed at something in the distance, to the rear of The Rider. Abby felt a knot in her stomach, the girl saw something in her telescope.

Abby ran up the stairs to the quarterdeck and looked at the scanner. She felt that knot in her stomach twist with panic. There was an entire armada bearing down on them. A hundred ships, at the least. One of the enemy ships was massive. It was easily twenty or thirty times the size of the atoll, if not larger.

Looking over the rail, she saw Norgren tying the wrapped netting to a rope that was attached to the boom. She yelled over at him,

"PICK UP THE PACE! WE'VE GOT COMPANY!"

Norgren looked up at her confused,

"But the Syndicate won't be here for days, by my…"

Abby shouted,

"THEY'RE ALMOST ON US! MOVE IT NOW!"

Norgren finished tying up the net and ran onboard to work the boom. Abby went back to the controls and found the cargo hatch toggle. She flipped it up and saw the cargo doors opening. The two doors were lifted by small hydraulic arms that pushed the doors up and out to each side of the opening to the hold.

She looked up and saw Sasha's and Norgren's big net full of stuff was moving through the air, with Norgren working the ropes of the boom.

Sasha came running out of the building, pulling the young girl along behind him. She looked like she was maybe eleven or twelve. Abby wasn't sure, but the girl was pretty small.

She had long messy wavy black hair that looked like it wouldn't recognize a brush if it saw one. She was wearing what looked like a repurposed potato sack with a string tied around the middle.

Abby called out as Sasha came running up,

"Who is she?"

Sasha shrugged, his voice high-pitched and excited,

"I HAVE NO IDEA! She must have been a stow-away on a boat and got left behind!"

Abby growled and narrowed her eyes,

"Nothing to be done about it now. We can't leave her here for the Syndicate."

She glanced at the scanner. The armada was making a move. A couple dozen smaller craft were accelerating and getting closer much faster. Maybe they had somehow detected her scanning and knew that she saw them.

Abby looked up at Norgren,

"You got everything you need?"

Norgren nodded without stopping. Abby looked at Sasha,

"Get those ropes off my ship!"

Abby looked down at the small girl and faintly heard Norgren mumble,

"Mooring lines, Captain."

The small girl looked up at Abby. Abby swallowed nervously. The girl had extremely unnerving solid black eyes. The feeling passed quickly. Abby shook it off and called down to her, while pointing at the quarterdeck next to her, over near the railing,

"You, park it, right there where I can see you."

The girl walked up the stairs and sat down near the railing, never taking her eyes off Abby. Sasha ran back on board,

"We're free!"

Abby slid the drift control to the side and The Rider moved away from the dock. She dialed up the lift to about thirty percent. Everyone felt the deck heave upwards as a deep vibrating wood groaning sound came from below. The Rider jerked violently as she lifted from the water.

Norgren, obviously concerned, looked up at Abby,

"She didn't like you pulling out of the water that fast, Captain! You put a lot of strain on the lower masts!"

The Rider was free of the water. Abby unfurled the sails and yelled back,

"She might not like it, but she did it!"

Checking the sails, Abby set the lift controls to automatic. She took Norgren's warning to heart and pushed the power levers forward gently.

Abby looked behind them and saw that the lead vessels were airborne. She didn't see any sails. They weren't like The Rider. They were low tech, with wings and propellers. They were smaller than The Rider, but they made up the difference in numbers. There were a lot of them.

The wind filled the sails, and The Rider began gliding forward away from the atoll. Abby flipped the switch to secure the cargo hold doors. Norgren ran to the bow and disappeared into the forward stairwell.

Abby looked down and noticed Sasha standing there wringing his hands. She laughed quietly and slowly pushed the power levers up to fifty percent. Looking back, Abby saw that

the flyers were falling behind. They weren't quite airplanes. They looked more like hang gliders with two-man seats and large fan propellers.

Norgren said she strained the lower masts, so she left the power setting at fifty percent. The last thing she wanted was to snap a mast or something. She glanced over at the small girl. She was still staring at Abby with her disturbing black eyes.

Sasha climbed the stairs and moved to the aft railing, watching the ships behind them falling further back. Abby watched the scanner occasionally. They were still falling back. The lead ships were about to fall out of the short-range scanner. She switched to medium range.

Now she could see the long line of the armada stretching out behind her. They were spread out in a long line, going all the way back to the hundred-mile outer limit of the medium range scan.

Abby looked closer at the display. She saw a handful of other ships of various sizes in range of the scanner, but they were scattered randomly, not part of the enemy armada. What caught her attention was the far end of the enemy armada near the limit of the scanners medium range setting.

She leaned down toward the display. They were spread out in a line at the back. The line looked like the beginning of a circle that went off the edges of the scan. Abby felt a knot in her gut again. She shifted the scanner to long range,

Oh no...

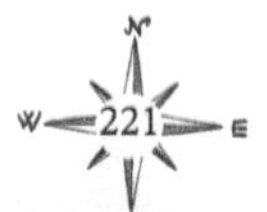

They were fewer and farther between, but the circle of enemy ships went all the way around them. They were in the middle of a giant circle that spread out over hundreds of miles,

How is that reaction speed even possible? They had to have already been there.

Abby switched the scanner back to medium range. She saw a small grimy finger point at one of the ships ahead of them. She looked to her right at the small girl standing next to her. Her black eyes were boring into Abby's soul. Abby heard a tiny voice in her mind,

Brother.

Abby stood up straight and looked down at her with wide eyes, thinking,

Your brother is on that ship?

The small girl's eyes went wide with surprise. She nodded, once. Abby frowned and pointed back to the spot by the rail,

"I told you to park it, over there."

The younger girl seemed to shrink just slightly. She moved back to the railing and sat down. Abby shook her head,

This is no place for a child.

Abby looked back at the scanner. The boat the small girl pointed at was in front of them, just slightly off to the side. Frowning, Abby turned the wheel slightly to the right, veering

her course toward the boat on the scanner that the girl pointed out,

Maybe we can take a minute to drop her off with her brother.

Norgren came up out of the stairwell and ran his bulky frame across the deck. He came up the stairs and walked over to stand next to her,

"I got the cargo secured in the hold temporarily. I didn't unpack the net, just secured the whole thing to the bulkhead. Captain, what are those turrets on the mid-deck level, tucked off to the port and starboard sides of the cargo shaft?"

Abby's eyebrows went up,

Turrets?

She looked at Norgren,

"I have no idea!"

Norgren walked around her to the other side. He looked down at the control boards,

"Permission to investigate, Captain?"

Abby grinned and nodded. She turned her attention back to the long low-riding boat that they were approaching. She angled off to the left, and called out to the others,

"HOLD FAST! We're going to bank right to investigate this boat."

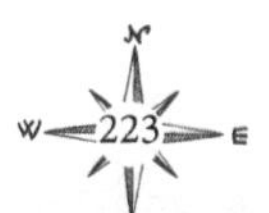

Sasha came up on her left side and grabbed the railing at the front of the quarterdeck. The small dark-haired girl turned to the side and put one arm through the railing next to her. Norgren looked up and grunted, then went back to investigating the controls.

Abby noticed he was putting his hands on things and closing his eyes as if concentrating. She turned her head slightly his way,

"What are you doing?"

Norgren glanced at her, then went back to what he was doing. He sounded distracted,

"You could say... um... reading the manual... Captain."

On her other side, Sasha said,

"He's a Technomancer, Captain."

Abby shook her head. She already knew he was a Technomancer. But he was doing what, reading the ships mind? She'd have to follow up on that later. She banked The Rider to the right and pulled back the power levers to ten percent thrust.

They passed over the ship in a low right hand banking turn. It was a long narrow skiff with six cages on it. Abby saw about a half dozen of those little black cactus men and one angry looking fish-man.

Next to her, looking down at the boat, Sasha pointed at the fish-man,

"Twilight Syndicate, Captain. Slave barge, the same one we turned away and refused to give supplies to."

Abby leveled out The Rider as they pulled away. They were being hunted and chased by hundreds of ships. Her thoughts bounced back and forth like two parts of her were playing ping pong,

We don't have time to mess with this.

But it's a slave barge.

We need to escape the ARMADA of Syndicate ships chasing us!

But it's a SLAVE barge!

Abby thought about it for a few more seconds, then made an angry growling noise and went back into a right-hand turn. She angled the turn gently, aiming to make one big circle as she built up speed. She wanted to be pointed away from the Syndicate ships behind them, after they rescued the slaves.

Abby continued banking around to the right. She pushed the power levers forward opening her circle up as she pushed The Rider to higher and higher speed. Abby looked over at Norgren,

"You got it figured out yet?"

Norgren nodded,

"Almost there, Captain."

Abby was getting close to the angle she wanted, she

shouted,

"HOLD FAST!"

She banked a hard right, lining them up with the slave ship, and then slid the power levers up to eighty percent power. The wind furiously hurled them forward. Abby had The Rider low, the lower masts just barely clearing the water.

Norgren opened his eyes and looked at Abby. His eyes were wide, his voice excited,

"VERY interesting ship, Captain!"

Abby nodded crisply, her eyes on the slave ship ahead.

Still staring at her, Norgren jerked his head toward the barge,

"You saw that they all had rifles, Captain?"

Abby nodded again,

"You can fly her?"

Norgren scrunched up his nose and bobbed his head from side to side,

"Uh... sort of, yeah."

Abby flashed him a quick thumbs up,

"That'll have to do. You have something I can cut those cages with?"

Norgren dug around in the big pockets of his overalls then dropped a small tool into one of the large lower pockets of her vest.

Something suddenly came over Abby as they flew toward the enemy and certain danger. Adrenaline, excitement, maybe the spirits of her ancestors, she wasn't sure what it was. She just felt different. She had no fear.

Narrowing her eyes, the grey-haired personality of Captain Watcher stared straight ahead. Abby's voice sounded different to Norgren and Sasha, colder, harder,

"Up ahead are evil men, lads. We're about to bring em more fight than they can handle."

Captain Watcher looked to her left at Sasha,

"You have one job, steward! Don't take yer eyes off that kid you dragged aboard me ship!"

Sasha nodded quickly, his knuckles white from gripping the rail in front of him,

"AYE CAPTAIN!"

The Riptide Rider was rapidly bearing down on the slave ship. Norgren nervously cleared his throat,

"Again, forgive me captain, but they all have rifles!"

Captain Watcher nodded crisply, her demeanor and her voice were harder than steel,

"Won't be a single shot fired. Throw me a ladder, then take the wheel. HOLD FAST!"

At the last possible moment, Captain Watcher pushed the 'hoist all' button on the sail controls. She watched the sails furl up, then retracted the lower masts and pulled the power levers to full stop. She spun the wheel to the right, turning the ship ninety degrees.

The Rider was now moving through the air at high speed on inertia alone, headed toward the slave ship directly to port. She was flying just above the waves, held up by the loudly thrumming antigravity drives.

Captain Watcher turned her gaze to port. Beyond the railing, she saw the eyes of the fish-man growing larger as The Rider rapidly slid sideways through the air toward his slow little boat.

With an evil grin, she dialed down the lift and banked The Rider into a right lean while sliding the drift control nob full to port.

The Rider dipped into the water, pushing up a huge wave ahead of her as the water tried to slow her down. The antigravity powered drift control kept the ship moving. The leading wave kept growing.

A split-second before impact, Captain Watcher released the drift control and killed power to the antigravity drives.

The Rider dropped fully into the water and slammed into the slave ship with a bone jarring impact. Norgren cringed at

the sound of wood groaning and cracking. The massive wave that The Rider pushed up in front of her washed the slave barge clean of everyone not in a cage.

Captain Watcher ran to the port side of the ship and leapt over the railing. She grunted in pain as she came down hard on one ankle that twisted on the wet bars of the cages. The fall was a little farther than she calculated.

Dropping from the top of the cage to the deck of the skiff, she pulled out the tool Norgren gave her. It looked like a battery-operated angle grinder. She pushed the button and put the spinning blade to the first lock. It sliced through the metal lock like cheese.

Captain Watcher moved forward, calling out to the slaves as she moved and cut,

"Get to The Rider! Get up the ladder! We're getting out of here!"

There were only three slaves in the cages, all of them on this side of the barge. The three cages on the far side were empty. Good, that saved time. She knew she was still standing on her twisted ankle only because of adrenaline.

She cut the last lock and opened the cage. The lone slave inside, a young man with dark hair and black eyes, ran out and ran toward The Rider. He immediately climbed up the rope ladder when he got there.

Captain Watcher dropped the cutter back into her pocket and ran back toward the ship.

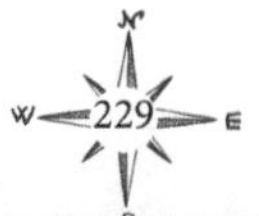

She grabbed the ladder as a small black dart hit her from behind and lodged in her left forearm. It was needle-thin and about two inches long. She stared at the tiny black spine for a second in shock and confusion,

What is the point of such a tiny dart?

Without thinking, she drew her weapon as she spun around. She immediately cocked and fired at the fish-man pulling himself up and over the front of the skiff. The torpedo bullet rocketed forward into his chest and detonated.

The shockwave from the explosion slammed her back into the hull of The Rider hard. Her head exploded with pain from the impact. She cried out and fell forward onto the deck of the skiff.

Captain Watcher slapped her weapon onto the mag-plate. THUNK. She climbed to her knees growling at the pain. She looked up and saw that the barge was quickly sinking bow first. Her torpedo bullet blew the entire front of the ship off.

She pulled herself up with the bars of the cage next to her and turned toward The Rider. The barge was sinking fast, falling away from her ship. Captain Watcher clenched her jaw and ignored the pain,

Always time to whine about stuff later.

She took two running steps and leapt off the edge toward the ladder. She just barely managed to catch hold, shouting,

"NORGREN! GET US IN THE AIR!"

The Rider slowly rose out of the water as the lower masts extended back out into place.

Captain Watcher climbed the ladder toward the deck. She suddenly felt dizzy and shook her head. When she did, she saw the side of the ship moving like a blur...

Abby suddenly shook her head and looked around, confused. She heard someone calling her name. It didn't sound right. The words had an odd smell to them as they moved slowly through the air in front of her. She looked up and saw one of the slaves reaching for her hand.

It took her a second to focus. She saw a young man with long dark gangly hair and solid black eyes. Her vision was blurring badly. She reached out for his hand as her world started to darken.

Sasha and the dark-haired young man pulled Abby up and over the railing. She tried to stand and cried out in pain, going down on one knee. She could hear her heartbeat pounding in her ears. Sasha called out next to her, his voice smelled strange too,

"She's been poisoned! Toxopnustus dart!"

Abby grabbed ahold of Sasha for stability. She leaned her head back and yelled out in a scratchy voice,

"BORGEN! GET US STOUT OF BEER!"

She heard Norgren shout back something that sounded like, shut the truck. Sasha pushed Abby over gently, lying her down on the deck. He rolled her onto her side. His voice

burbled like he was underwater,

"Don't worry, Captain. I've served enough drinks to speak intoxicantese."

Sasha shouted up to Norgren,

"SHE SAID GET US OUT OF HERE!"

Norgren nodded and eased The Rider forward, away from the nearest Syndicate ships. He pushed the ship higher and faster. Abby smiled as she felt the wind sweeping the deck. She looked up and saw Sasha wringing his hands and looking worried.

Abby looked at her arm, where the dart had hit her. There was a black spot about the size of a nickel around the tiny hole in her skin. The dart seemed to have fallen out.

The small dark-haired girl ran up to the young man and began moving her hands in a rapid series of gestures. The young man said something to Sasha that Abby didn't understand.

It was more than just the poison distortion. It was a language she didn't understand. It sounded beautiful, but that didn't really help.

Sasha was shaking his head,

"I don't speak whatever the hell that is!"

The young man repeated the words louder and harsher. In her mind, Abby heard,

I need herbs, spices, roots, tinctures, extracts. Medicines!

Abby reached out and grabbed Sasha's leg. She choked out a string of babbling nonsense,

"Mitigable tuff! He aunt's burbs, pieces, boots, stinksters!"

Sasha's eyes went wide and excited,

"Medical stuff! He wants herbs, spices, roots, tinctures! Got it, Captain! NORGREN!"

Abby tried to hold on, but she was done. Her strength left her. She went limp and rolled onto her back. She thought about the slaves she just saved from the syndicate,

It probably cost me my life, and it was worth it.

She knew she was dying. She felt it. She sensed it from the others. Abby relaxed and stared distantly up at the green and blue lights in the sky above, wondering,

Is that where I'm going now? Up there?

She fought to the last second as her eyes forced themselves closed. She slid off the deck of the ship into the blackness around her. Her mind drifted off, the poison spinning her imagination up, to mercifully distract her from the end.

She saw fish-men swimming through the air, being chased by fat little whales with tentacles. She saw little, black, cactus-looking men marching around in little formations. Their short stumpy limbs all moving in unison.

Far away in the distance, there was instantly a bright light. The light was looking at her. It strangely reminded her of extreme mom-judgement.

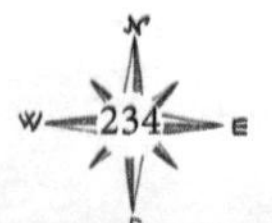

Radiation, Turrets, And A Mad Scientist

It felt like her brain exploded into wakefulness. Abby's eyes went wide open, then squeezed closed again as she fought the urge to vomit. She instinctively pushed away the bowl of noxious stink that Sasha was holding under her nose. She shook her head, then looked around.

She was sitting on the side of the deck, leaning back against the rail. Sasha sat back and lowered the bowl. He smiled over at the young man squatting on her other side. The dark-haired young man smiled back at Sasha, nodding. The young dark-haired girl by her feet began packing things back up into jars and envelopes.

Abby saw a gritty-looking paste smeared on her forearm where the dark spot had been. She looked back toward the girl and saw an assortment of crushed leaves, little bowls of pastes, powders, and other odd-looking stuff arrayed out in front of her feet.

Whatever that black-eyed young girl just mixed up, it really did the trick. Abby started to get to her feet, but Sasha put a restraining hand on her shoulder,

"Easy Captain. You were just poisoned, and you have a broken ankle."

Abby turned a stern gaze in his direction. There were hundreds of Syndicate ships closing in on them from every direction. She narrowed her eyes just slightly,

"Sasha. I don't know what the three of you just did, but sincerely and with all my heart. Thank you."

She looked to her left, meeting the black eyes of the young man then the girl,

"Thank you."

Abby looked back at Sasha,

"Now get out of my way."

Sasha shook his head but moved out of the way as ordered. Abby got her good foot under her and hooked an arm over the railing behind her. Carefully, she got up. She gently put some weight on her injured ankle. She didn't feel any pain. She remembered what the older Norgren told her,

It's the vest, Captain. So long as you wear it, you'll heal.

Abby grinned. She took a couple of careful steps. It wasn't even tender. Sasha had a grimace on his face, as if he expected her to fall. The young man and the girl were staring at her with equally confused and concerned expressions.

Abby checked her weapons, made sure the journal was safely tucked in and jerked her belt a bit tighter. She looked at Sasha and patted him on the shoulder,

"Excellent work, steward. Now, see to our guests, food

and drink if you can find it."

Abby walked to the quarterdeck, away from their shocked expressions. Testing her ankle, she bounded up the stairs. It felt completely back to normal. She put her hand on Norgren's shoulder, where he stood behind the wheel,

"I'll take it from here. Good work getting us out of there. What's our status?"

Norgren looked at her with raised eyebrows and stepped to his right. He looked down toward her boots then back up at her and shrugged, turning his attention to the control panels. He spoke with an exaggerated casualness,

"Running from a shrinking circle of hundreds of enemy ships is our status. How's the broken ankle, Captain?"

Abby grabbed the wheel with one hand and checked the scanner, she replied just as casually,

"It itches a little."

Norgren chuckled. Abby saw on the display that there were still about a dozen of the Syndicate fliers behind them, about thirty miles back. Widening the display, she could see the rest were tightening the noose around them. Abby looked over at Norgren curiously,

"Why so much trouble over The Rider, Norgren?"

Norgren glanced over at her, then went back to the control panel he was fiddling with,

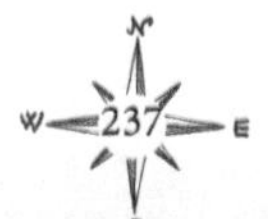

"There's nothing like The Rider anywhere in the world, Captain. They must want her bad."

Abby nodded. She looked back behind them, then her eyes went up to the glowing auroras in the skies overhead,

"We could climb to a thousand feet or more. Just stay out of their reach."

Norgren gave her a concerned look,

"We'd never survive a climb that high! The radiation density zones would fry us long before we got to half that height!"

Abby cocked her head and raised an eyebrow,

"The WHAT?"

Norgren held up one finger and then fiddled with the menu on the scanner. He pulled up a programming screen and typed in some parameters. Nodding, he pushed another button.

Suddenly, there was a layer of light red air that started at about a hundred feet above the water. At two hundred feet up, the red became darker like blood. At three hundred feet and above, the air was almost black.

Norgren pointed at the light red area,

"It's just a rough simulation, but close enough to cook with. Pun intended. At a hundred feet and up, continuous exposure to the radiation will kill you in about a day."

He pointed at the layer where the red turned darker,

"Starting at about two hundred up to three, you might have about an hour or two and maybe survive if you drop back down fast."

He moved his finger to the black,

"Hit three hundred feet and above, you're dead. Your body just won't realize it for a little while."

Norgren gestured up toward the blue and green auroras covering the sky,

"The whole world is continuously bombarded by high energy protons and radiation from the Sun. That's why most life on the surface stays within about ten degrees of the equator, north and south. That's where the magnetic fields of the planet are strongest, offering the most protection."

Abby made a queasy looking face and changed the subject,

"What did you learn about those turrets you mentioned?"

Norgren grinned,

"One is insanely cool, but not really helpful. It's a rotating reclining chair-like turret that can be very finely adjusted for precision movement. It has a powerful telescope mounted on it for studying the stars and their precise positions."

Abby nodded,

Charting star locations makes sense for teams researching the past.

"And the other?"

His grin shifted to a big cheesy smile,

"The other is a heavily modified forty-millimeter quad-barrel anti-aircraft cannon."

Abby laughed loudly, then turned a wide smile his direction,

"Excellent. Let's get it unpacked. But first, I want you to study the scanner and find me the thinnest part of their perimeter. Pick out where you'd punch through."

Norgren nodded and began studying the scanner. Abby went down the stairs and saw Sasha herding the passengers into the forward stairwell,

Good man. He's taking them down to the galley.

Abby turned toward her cabin and stopped in her tracks. She saw something weird under the starboard stairs to the quarterdeck. She moved a few steps closer and squatted down, looking closely into the dark shadowed corner.

There was something black and just a bit shiny, about the size of a small loaf of bread under the stairs. Abby drew her sword and leaned in, looking closer. It was a chunk of one of the cactus men,

Must be from the boat I blew up when I first arrived at Sasha and Norgren's atoll. Eww, gross...

Abby called Norgren down to join her and pointed it out to him,

"I'll keep an eye on the scanner. You get something and chuck that thing off the side of the ship."

Norgren looked shocked,

"Captain! That's a Toxopnustus drone, like the dart you got hit with. One of the Twilight Syndicates servant races. They are almost impossible to get your hands on. It could come in very handy."

Abby leaned in and stabbed the chunk of black cactus-looking whatever he just said. She pulled it out from under the stairs and lifted her sword, looking at it. It looked like a funky shaped sea anemone. Best she could tell, it was about half of one of the cactus men's legs.

She gave Norgren a skeptical look,

"THIS, is useful to us? How so?"

Norgren chuckled,

"I'll be back, Captain. Give me five minutes."

Abby shook her head and set down the sword, leaving the chunk attached. She went back up to the quarterdeck and watched the scanner. She adjusted their course slightly, adjusted speed, trying to keep them out of range of any of the Syndicate's boats and fliers.

She watched Norgren come running up from below deck

with one of the crates he brought onboard. He ran into her cabin with it!

What the...

She yelled down,

"Hey! What are you doing?"

Norgren ran out and back to the forward hatch, calling over his shoulder,

"Two minutes, Captain! Almost done!"

He came back up with two small barrels and ran those into her cabin also. After another minute, he came out and tossed some scrap wood from the crates over the side. He grabbed the sword with the cactus man chunk on it and went into her cabin,

What the heck is he doing?

Another minute went by. Norgren came out and called up to her,

"Come look Captain!"

Abby checked the scanner one more time,

Still nothing close to us.

She ran down the stairs and walked into her cabin. Inside, Norgren was in the middle of pouring water from a pitcher into a fish tank that he secured to the wall with leather

straps. It was on the opposite side of her cabin from her bed.

Abby saw some kind of dark sandy dirt in the bottom of the fish tank. The chunk of Toxic-poop was sitting on top of the dirt and her insane engineer was pouring water on it.

Abby held out both hands, and said very matter-of-factly,

"Ok. You have lost your mind, if you think, you are leaving that, in MY cabin!"

Norgren chuckled. He stood up and looked over at her,

"It's harmless right now, Captain. Its spines aren't even producing poison in this state. It has to be somewhere that you can keep an eye on it. If you want to regrow it."

She looked at him like he just confirmed that he had in fact, lost his mind,

"I'm sorry, but... REGROW IT?"

Norgren nodded, smiling reassuringly,

"They're living drones Captain. They can come in pretty handy, if you're creative. Also, they are one hundred percent loyal to whoever is nearest to them when they are grown."

He pointed at her, then gestured around at the room,

"Which is another reason it needs to be here in your cabin. I can think of a hundred uses for one. It's a bio-engineered lifeform. It'll regrow into a full-sized drone. Heck, cut that fully developed drone into five pieces, and you'll

eventually have five full sized drones!"

Abby looked down and shook her head,

I brought a mad scientist onboard.

"I'm not agreeing to this. I just don't have time to have you flogged right this minute. Get back to your duties, engineer. Unpack that cannon turret and watch the scanner while I check on our guests. I still need you to find me the thinnest part of the enemy perimeter."

Norgren looked at the aquarium and smiled, pleased with himself,

"Aye Captain."

Natives Amongst Us

Abby walked into the galley, removing her hat as she entered. She saw that Sasha had the four former slaves seated at one of the tables and he was standing nearby while they were eating.

Everyone stopped eating when she stepped through the door. There was an older man and woman, the young man, and the girl they brought from the atoll. Abby saw the facial similarities, the same long black hair. They all had solid black eyes,

We just saved a family!

Abby remembered Sasha saying the girl was likely a stow-away, on a boat that stopped at the atoll. The pieces fell together in her mind,

Stow away? Close! She escaped from the slave barge that they refused to resupply! She pointed at the slave barge on the scanner and said, brother! Holy sneaking freaking potato chips! We DID just save a family!

Abby had the biggest smile on her face. As she watched them, the mother and the daughter both put their hands in their laps and lowered their heads. The young man lowered his head slightly, but he kept glancing between her and his father,

to see what was going to happen.

The father of the group stood up and bowed his head, he began mumbling in that beautifully odd language. Abby held out a hand toward him, open palm, in a 'stop' gesture. He stopped talking and just stood with his head bowed, glancing up at her carefully.

Sasha started to say something, but Abby held out one finger toward him and he stopped talking too. She walked around the table and put one hand on the father's shoulder. Abby gestured toward his seat with her other hand.

He looked at her nervously, but slowly and hesitantly sat back down. Abby slowly reached down and pushed his plate closer to him. She looked him in the eyes with a smile, nodding, thinking,

You're welcome here. You're safe here. Relax and eat.

Tentatively, he smiled back at her. Abby walked around to the other side and stood next to the young girl. The father's smile faded, and he watched Abby closely. The young man was watching her closely as well. Even the mother had raised her head just enough to see what Abby was going to do.

Abby put her fingers under the girl's chin and very gently lifted her head upright. The poor girl looked terrified and confused. Abby was thinking,

You're not prisoners anymore! You're safe here!

All four of them were staring at her now. Abby stood up straight and lifted her head high, then she pointed at the father

and nodded at him. He sat up straighter, still looking a little confused.

Abby smiled and nodded at him. She pointed at the mother, son, and daughter and again stood straight and tall, again nodding at them.

The father's eyes brightened with revelation and expressed his sudden understanding. He spoke to his family in their odd language. In a few moments all of them were sitting up straighter, smiling, looking relieved and extremely grateful.

The mother started crying tears of relief. Her family was safe. Abby smiled and gestured toward their plates. She touched the young girl's hair and smiled at her when she looked up.

Abby turned her attention to Sasha as the family began talking quietly amongst themselves. Sasha shook his head in amazement,

"You're a surprisingly good communicator, Captain."

She walked closer and put a hand on his shoulder,

"I grew up with trees, rabbits, and squirrels."

Sasha looked extremely confused, but Abby let it go as if her response made perfect sense,

"We're heading for a fight. Norgren and I can handle it. I need you to stay here. Keep them here. Be calm but be firm. I don't want these kids or their parents anywhere near the main deck when bullets start flying. You understand?"

Sasha bowed with a flourish,

"Understood, Captain."

Abby looked him squarely in the eye,

"One more thing. When you feel The Rider starting to maneuver, you take a seat next to that girl and hold on for dear life. Try to get them to do the same."

Sasha nodded crisply,

"Aye Captain."

Abby walked back up the forward stairwell and stepped out onto the deck. The cargo bay doors were open, and she saw a hideously beautiful monstrosity of a gun turret rising from below. She heard a chain drive mechanized cranking sound coming up from the shaft.

Her eyes were wide as she stared at the deadly looking contraption.

A wide round turret base supported the central gunner seat, and the two double barreled cannons mounted on each side. She saw armor plating across the front, and the rest of it absolutely bristled with tubes, vents, pumps, gears, and a ton of pieces and parts she couldn't even identify.

Abby bounded up the stairs laughing. She relieved Norgren from the wheel. He stepped to the right and checked the scanner. Together, they discussed some tactics. After a few minutes, they had a rough plan.

They pointed The Rider toward a fairly thin part of the Syndicate's ship perimeter. They deliberately avoided the obviously thin area farthest away from the large main vessel. Abby agreed with Norgren, that was most likely a trap.

If the main ship of the armada was six o'clock on the perimeter, the assumed trap sat at high noon. Abby flew The Rider toward ten o'clock, but her real target was a gap around nine.

She knew the Syndicate were communicating, since they reacted immediately to her scanning them earlier. She wanted them to think she was going to try to breach their ten o'clock location. She pushed toward it at fifty percent power.

When the time was right, she planned to veer to port, push The Rider to maximum thrust, and hopefully punch through their line without a fight.

The gun turret stopped rising and Abby heard a series of automatic bolts lock it into place. The swivels mounted on each side of the gunner's seat automatically shifted and unlocked. The four barrels, currently raised for storage, lowered themselves into place.

Abby heard ammo belts begin moving, tiny clanking chain-like noises. She heard charging handles shifting and locking. She suddenly realized that the older Norgren must have modified the original cannon.

It was basic, old, World War Two technology. But she was pretty sure they didn't have that kind of automation back then. Abby looked over at Norgren,

"Get down there and get in the seat. Put your hands on her and get familiar with your new girlfriend."

Norgren made a face like a kid on Christmas,

"ME? Really? You serious, Captain?"

Abby laughed,

"Still don't like repeating myself, Engineer."

Norgren laughed loudly and headed down,

"Roger that, Captain!"

Abby watched him run down and jump into the gunner's seat. He was grinning from ear to ear. She saw the turret rotate left and right, the barrels raising and lowering. Norgren placed both hands on the controls and closed his eyes in concentration.

She turned her attention back to the scanner. It looked like they would be in visual range soon...

The scanner, the consoles, everything around her became blurry. Abby saw a dark hazy room appear around her, several fish-men standing around the table in front of her. She saw one of them pointing at a map and moving his lips, she heard,

The sky ship has changed course...

Her thoughts became a flurry of images and sounds. She saw flashes of maps. She heard snippets of plans. The sounds became a rapid jumble of communications between dozens of

ship captains. It stopped as quickly as it started. She had just enough time to think,

What the hell was that?!?

She suddenly had the impulse to do something. It might have been her subconscious or instincts, she wasn't sure which or why, but she changed her plans. Abby heard what sounded like her own voice, but different, in her mind,

Shock and Awe! Punch a hole! DO IT NOW!

The visage of the grey-haired Captain Watcher grimaced and gripped the wheel of The Rider firmly. She shouted down to Norgren,

"GUN BARRELS TO PORT! PREPARE TO FIRE!"

Norgren swung the 40mm cannons to port, hands on the grips, fingers on the triggers. Captain Watcher brought The Rider down as low as she could. The tips of the lower masts tracing two thin lines through the water below.

She saw the enemy ships getting closer. They were a mixed match. Some looked like fishing ships, others like ships designed for war. She assumed that all of them had been repurposed for fighting by the Syndicate.

As she approached, she saw a few arrows beginning to arc into the air from the nearest enemy ships. They wouldn't get anywhere near The Rider. Captain Watcher knew they were using them for range markers.

She saw a single deck-mounted harpoon launcher fling

a massive bolt toward her ship. It got much closer, but still fell short.

She grinned evilly,

Thanks for setting my range.

Captain Watcher banked The Rider hard to starboard. She kept the ship outside the range of the enemy's weapons and faced her port broadside at the enemy line. She leveled out, cut thrust, and yelled to Norgren as she walked toward the port side of the ship,

"Warship! Red striped sails!"

Captain Watcher stepped up to the port railing and put one foot up on the rail. She leaned forward and shouted as loud as she could, hoping the enemy would hear her calling for their end,

"OPEN FIRE!!!"

Norgren squeezed the triggers and all four of the forty-millimeter cannon barrels roared to life. Massive flames were spitting out the front of the barrels as the four cannons churned out a combined fire rate of nearly one thousand rounds per minute. Roughly sixteen shots per second.

The cannons fired a combination of three explosive rounds for every magnesium tipped tracer round. Norgren's first shots were slightly high and off to the left. He dialed in his aim using the laser-like tracer rounds, bringing the explosive rounds dancing across the bow of the target.

The terrifying, panic-inducing, hells fury roar of the cannons carried far across the water. It chewed fifty feet into the bow of the warship's hull in less than ten seconds.

Norgren stopped firing.

Every living creature in visual range looked at the burning and sinking remains of the big warship as it began its final journey beneath the waves. They watched the cloud of burning wood shrapnel blown off the rapidly sinking ship, raining down into the water all around it.

Captain Watcher heard alarm bells ringing from all the nearby ships. They had no hope of victory and zero chance of survival against The Riders cannons. The alarm sounds were spreading to other ships farther away.

The enemy heard the roar of the cannon and saw the laser-like effects of the tracer rounds. They saw the devastation caused by the explosive shells. They watched the massive warship tipping under the waves after just the first ten seconds

of the engagement.

None of them were willing to fight anymore.

Orders or not, every ship in range of the captain's vision was veering away and putting distance between themselves and The Rider.

Captain Watcher tipped her hat in salute to the fallen enemies. She looked at Norgren and nodded farewell for now.

Norgren raised his fists and shouted. Abby laughed and smiled down at him.

The battle was over before it started. She dialed out the scanner and double checked the area. She could see the break in the line of enemy ships growing wider by the minute. She turned The Rider into the growing gap and pushed the power levers to fifty percent.

Norgren started to stand up and climb out of the turret. Catching his eye, Abby shook her head no. He nodded and lowered himself back into the chair. Once they were set on course, Abby pushed the power levers slowly up to eighty percent. They rapidly left the Syndicate armada behind.

Once they had a good fifty-mile lead, Abby whistled down at Norgren. He climbed out and made his way to the quarterdeck, still grinning. She pointed at the scanner,

"You know this area. Where do our guests live? Or at least, where can we drop them off that's safe?"

Norgren pointed up in the sky,

"See the grog ladle? Follow the handle east, Captain, the Levash Tu'an Islands are that way. Dangerous waters though. If The Rider weren't in the air, I wouldn't even suggest it. But it's the most likely place for them to be from."

Abby looked up and chuckled. She turned the wheel slightly to adjust and followed the handle of the Big Dipper, to the east. Looking around, it was hard to see with the auroras, but she saw other constellations that she recognized. So, this was Earth after all. Or at least some version of it,

"Norgren, make sure the cannons are ready to stow. Then see if you can wrangle our guests up to the deck. If they see home, we want them to point it out to us."

Norgren nodded, heading down,

"Aye Captain."

He stopped by the cannons and hesitated, then he turned back toward her,

"You sure you don't want to just throw a tarp over it? Keep it handy?"

Abby looked at him. He had a huge grin on his face. She shook her head and smiled, before checking the scanner display and keeping the ship on course. She saw Norgren put on a pouty face, then prep the cannon for storage. He headed below deck.

She flipped the turret controls to stow and waited for it to clear the doors, then flipped the switch to close the cargo doors. There were just a few small ships randomly scattered

around in range of her scanner.

Abby watched them until she was sure that none were on a course to intercept. She thought about that a moment. Why had she thought to consider that?

In the relative peace of the moment, she reflected on a few other things. Her maneuver with The Rider that swamped the slave barge by sliding in like she did and clearing its deck of crew, had been perfectly executed. Everything she had tried to do so far had been nearly as perfectly executed.

She also suddenly remembered that right before coming in range of the enemy line, her thoughts had churned like crazy. What were those images in her mind? Why had she decided to change her plans at the last second?

There was a variable at work that she couldn't quite understand, somewhere in this whole strange equation.

Abby settled The Rider about thirty feet above the waves and running at fifty percent forward power. No reason to run blindly into an ambush.

It was beautiful here. The green and blue auroras bathed everything in fairy fire. The ocean glistened and sparkled under the phantom fires in the sky.

Before long, she saw Sasha come up from below deck. He stood up straight and stretched his back. He was just the slightest bit too tall for the confined spaces below deck.

As Sasha walked toward her, she saw the family following behind him. The father was carrying the young girl,

asleep on his shoulder. The mother and son were following behind him. Norgren brought up the rear.

Abby caught Norgrens eye and gestured for him to join her.

Sasha led the family to the base of the stairs and waited, watching her. Abby nodded to him and gave him a thumbs up. When Norgren climbed the stairs to the quarterdeck, Abby gestured to the wheel,

"Keep us on course."

He nodded,

"Aye Captain."

Abby walked down the steps, then to her cabin door. She gestured for the father to come closer. He did so, bowing his head almost continuously at her. Abby opened her cabin door wide, letting him see inside. She pointed to herself, then laid her head to the side and closed her eyes, then gestured to her bed.

Next, she gestured to the girl and spread both hands wide, looking from side to side into the distance. She stopped and looked straight into the father's eyes. Thinking to herself,

Please understand! Where the hell do I take you? Where does she sleep at night?

Surprisingly, he quickly nodded several times and turned away. He looked at the stars and walked across the deck, staring at different parts of the sky. Abby followed behind him.

The father called to his son, softly. When the young man joined him near the bow, they spoke softly back and forth for a few moments.

The young man turned to Abby and said a word she didn't understand. He turned back toward the bow and raised his hand, looking and pointing into the distance. Abby moved up behind him, just off to the side. She looked along the length of his arm to where he was pointing. Almost directly ahead, just slightly to port.

Abby patted him on the shoulder and walked back to the quarterdeck. The family gathered at the bow, speaking quietly but very excitedly amongst themselves.

Abby relieved Norgren at the wheel, and adjusted course about five degrees to port.

Sasha lead the family down to a guest room with extra bunks. Norgren found it earlier while searching the ship. The mother and the father took turns standing watch near the bow. Keeping an eye out for signs of their home.

Abby eventually ordered Sasha to go and get some rest, just to keep him from doting on her excessively.

The stars shifted as The Rider glided silently over the ocean. A dull lonely hour passed. The blue and green auroras danced overhead. The vibration of the antigravity drives lulled her to sleep.

She started to slip, but her head jerked up. Abby shook it off and then yawned. She was already exhausted when she first

arrived in this world. She almost jumped out of her skin when Norgren suddenly spoke from behind her,

"Going to try to tell me you're not falling asleep on your feet, Captain?"

Abby looked back at him and scowled, then she turned back to watch the horizon in front of them. She heard Norgren chuckle,

"Would be better you get an hour or two of rest, rather than collapse due to lack of it. We need you, Captain."

Abby lowered her head and sighed. He was right, and she knew it,

"Alright, engineer. You wake me in..."

"HYLO, SHTO! SHTO!"

The father, standing at the bow, franticly waved his hands at her. Abby cut thrust and let The Rider slowly drift to a stop. The father ran below deck. Norgren shook his head, then he stepped up next to her,

"You still need rest, Captain."

Abby nodded,

"I agree, fetch my steward, if you would please."

Norgren's eyes went wide. He gave her a strange look as he walked away,

"If I would? Please? You must be exhausted beyond reason, Captain."

Abby growled and Norgren laughed as he headed off. She looked up toward the brightening horizon and saw what she thought were islands far ahead in the distance. Why had the father stopped them? Very soon, the whole family came up from below.

They were followed up from below by Norgren and Sasha. They were talking quietly as they approached her. She heard Norgren saying something about rest and Sasha nodded his head quickly.

She knew they were going to try to get her to sleep and she didn't have time for that right now. Abby called down to them before they reached the stairs,

"Bring me some coffee, steward!"

The two men looked at each other in confusion. Sasha looked back up at her,

"Medicine for a cough, Captain?"

Abby rolled her eyes,

"Bring me something that will wake me up, until I have time to get some rest."

Sasha and Norgren both opened their mouths to speak, but Abby shouted then quickly lowered her voice,

"NOW! Please."

They both turned to run back below decks. Norgren stopped after only a few steps, realizing she hadn't told him to go anywhere. He turned back toward the quarterdeck, shaking his head. Then he changed his mind and headed toward the bow anyway.

Abby was watching the family by the bow. They were behaving strangely. The father, mother, and son were all down on their knees, facing the rising sun. The young girl was on her feet, both hands held out to her sides, fingers spread, palms towards the sky. She leaned her head back just slightly and began singing.

Sasha was already below deck, but Norgren stopped in his tracks and stared at her. The young girl was singing without words. Her voice was powerful and rich despite her youth and size. The sounds coming from the young child were captivating and magical.

After a few minutes, it grew more intense. The tempo of her wordless song changed, the sounds coming faster and becoming almost violent in nature.

That's when the leviathan rose out of the water directly in front of the ship. Abby watched as it's blotchy purple bulk slowly emerged. It was long and whale-like in overall shape. She realized the one she saved from the eel must have been a tiny little baby.

The water was shedding off of its massive body like it was a submarine surfacing. But this creature was no submarine. It was the size of an aircraft carrier. It had massive shoulder-like muscle bulges that had long thick tentacles coming out of

them.

Abby was frozen in shock. She had never even imagined that something so large was even possible. It towered above The Rider. Its front end was so large that she could no longer see the rest of the unbelievable creature. Then she realized it was staring at them.

Her mind had automatically associated it with the closest thing she knew, a whale. She realized this was no whale. Its eyes were widely separated, yes, but definitely oriented forward on the front of its body. Unlike a whale that had eyes on the sides of its head.

This creature was a predator, a hunter. She realized the small girl was still singing. The family still on their knees, bowing forward.

Abby couldn't believe her eyes. She saw the thin tip of one of the leviathan's tentacles lift out of the water and very gently touch the young girl on the side of her head. It was slow and gentle. It stroked her hair.

The young girl's wordless song shifted to slow drawn-out sounds that were softer and went from low to high and then slowly faded to silence.

Abby took a sudden breath. She hadn't even realized that in her shock she had been holding her breath, frozen where she stood. She heard a deep groaning tone from in front and underneath the ship. The sound vibrated the entire ship. The leviathan was making a sound like whale song. Then it lowered slowly into the water.

Abby and Norgren were still staring at where the massive creature had been, when the father shouted at her,

"VERO VEY!"

He was pointing at the largest of the islands in the distance and waving his hand forward, saying go. Abby swallowed and took a deep breath. Adrenaline coursing through her veins. She breathed out slowly. Her hand was shaking as she reached for the power levers. She pushed the ship forward, very slowly, very carefully.

Reception

The family was still at the bow of the ship. The father and the mother were taking turns going from laughing with joy to crying with relief. They must have believed they were lost to the slavers. Now they were in sight of home and their little family was safe.

That's what Abby thought anyway.

She was starting to relax as Norgren and Sasha came walking toward her. She took a deep breath and quickly shook off the last of the adrenaline from seeing the massive leviathan. She adjusted her hat and put on her best 'Unshakable Captain' look.

She heard Sasha saying to Norgren,

"And I missed it? A REAL LEVIATHAN?"

Sasha was carrying a large black ceramic coffee mug. It looked like a normal coffee mug you might see for sale in any retail store. Abby smiled. They came up the stairs and Sasha turned the cup and offered her the handle.

She laughed when she saw the white skull and crossbones on the black cup. She stepped back from the

wheel gratefully, letting Norgren take over. Abby accepted the steaming cup from Sasha.

Sasha was grinning at her. Obviously anticipating praise for what he brought her. Abby raised an eyebrow at him with a small grin and looked into the cup. She saw the lightly browned edges around the white foam,

NO FREAKIN WAY!

Abby raised the cup and sipped carefully. Then she moaned in appreciation. It was a cappuccino. Delicious and perfect. When she lowered the cup, she smiled softly at Sasha. She turned her head to Norgren,

"An extra ration of rum for the steward."

Sasha beamed, smiling proudly. Norgren chuckled. She walked to the rear and leaned back against the rail, enjoying the bittersweet steaming cup of warm liquid. She heard Sasha talking to Norgren,

"I can't believe I missed it."

Norgren waved his hand dismissively,

"You're better off. I nearly soiled myself."

Sasha laughed. The two men started chatting, but Abby stopped paying attention. She took her time and enjoyed her fancy sweet coffee. She watched the islands slowly getting larger. She saw boats in the water as they approached.

The islander boats appeared to be made from two long

wooden canoes with a wooden platform built across the top. The canoes were spread out wide beneath the platform. From a thin central mast, the islander boats had tall thin diamond shaped sails.

Each of the boats she saw had three to four men and one woman. The men were fishing with nets. The women she saw were either singing, sitting like they were meditating, or sprinkling flower petals into the water around the boat.

Abby noticed Sasha and Norgren were looking around wide-eyed. Norgren glanced back at her,

"This is amazing, Captain! No one gets this close to the Levash Tu'an Isles, except the natives of course. Too many strange accidents happen to boats that try to get this close. I can't believe who we rescued off that slave barge."

Abby raised an eyebrow, questioningly,

"If it's that dangerous, why would people keep trying to get close?"

Norgren spread his hands, gesturing at the water around them,

"Simple, it's the absolute best, most profitable fishing location in the whole ocean. Well, more accurately, the best location is as close to the Levash Tu'an Isles as you can get without sinking."

She raised her eyebrows and nodded,

That makes sense.

They were close enough now, that the people on the boats saw the family leaning out over the railing of The Rider. All of them were waving excitedly. At one point, the father helped the young girl step up onto the railing and the fishermen they passed erupted into cheering,

Did we bring back their lost princess or something?

They were getting close to the main island. Abby relieved Norgren from the wheel and reduced forward power to ten percent. The Rider began slowing, she handed her empty cup to Sasha and leaned close to him, speaking softly,

"Check the crew quarters below and find something nice that fits you. We brought back someone special, and I want us to look competent not lucky. Might even score a payday out of this deal."

Sasha nodded and ran off for the lower decks. Abby pulled off her earring and handed it to Norgren,

"On your application, you said you could reverse engineer stuff? I want two more of those, on the same channel, quick as you can."

Norgren laughed,

"There are so many things wrong with what you just said, Captain. But I get the idea."

Abby furrowed her brow in confusion,

"What did I say that was wrong?"

Norgren held up the tiny earring,

"One, I don't have to reverse engineer magitech that I already invented. Two, you can't add new devices to an existing set of whisper-comms. And three, I have several pre-made sets in my gear, down in storage."

Norgren grinned at her, and added,

"Bigger ships with large crews, fishing fleets, they all love these. Use to sell a couple sets a month before the Syndicate moved into the area and put us out of business."

Lightbulb. Abby said,

"That's how the Syndicate captains were communicating!"

Norgren nodded and tossed the whisper-comm into the ocean. Abby watched it fly over the rail, then made a shocked face at him. He waved it off,

"Worthless without the rest of the set. I'll go grab another set from storage, Captain."

Shaking her head,

"Alright then."

She thought about it a second, then said,

"Like I told Sasha, check the crew quarters below for something nice to wear. I'm pretty sure you'll find that one of the rooms has plenty of stuff just your size."

Norgren gave her a very puzzled look as he headed off below,

"Ok... that's not completely weird at all..."

Abby reduced forward power to full stop. The water around the large island was getting shallow. She checked the scanner, switching it briefly to a close-range depth finder view.

This was as close as The Rider could get to the main island. She hit the button to hoist the sails, then she retracted the lower masts.

Islanders all around were staring at the ship with wide disbelieving eyes. Like they were watching magic happen right in front of them. Abby thought about old Norgren and his Technomancer modifications. She chuckled,

Technically speaking, they are watching magic happen.

Abby dialed down the antigravity drives and let The Rider sink gently into the water. In moments, the ship was floating in the slow-moving shallow water. Abby dropped anchor, then looked toward the front of the ship and the family standing at the bow.

The older three of the family unit were waving and shouting to the rapidly growing throng of islanders. Every boat in the area was paddling or sailing closer. The fishermen and the praying women on the boats, all of them, were clapping, laughing, waving, cheering.

They reminded Abby of raving fans at a concert she saw on television.

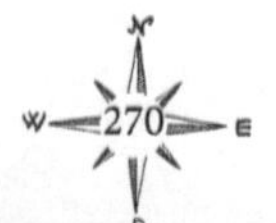

Months ago, she sat down to watch her favorite band. The band Abby refused to admit was her favorite because the lead singer had the same name as her mom. Abby looked around and laughed.

The islanders on the boats around them looked like raving screaming teenage fans at a 'Kat, Bunny, and The Sisters of War' rock concert.

She remembered her mom walking into the living room and sitting down to watch. She had the fakest innocent look on her face and said,

Oh look, it's that bunny-cat group you like, sweetheart.

Abby laughed at the memory. Looking back, she knew her mom was messing with her. She tried so many times to get Abby to admit that she liked the group because of the lead singer's name.

~ ~

The idea that she could just jump The Rider back anytime she wanted, crossed her mind. The idea that she could just jump home and pickup her mom, comforted Abby. It made leaving her world, her home, and her mother behind, a little easier.

She could just jump back, to her mom...

The thought passed quickly, but it planted the seeds of a future disaster.

~ ~

Abby whistled loudly at the family up at the bow of her ship. They turned to look, and she gestured for them to come closer. Abby walked down the stairs and over to the starboard railing.

She opened the boarding gate and signaled for one of the larger nearby boats to pull up alongside. The men on that boat pointed toward the island. Abby looked that way and saw a much larger boat headed toward them.

The family joined her by the gate. The mother gave Abby a hug, she had tears of joy in her eyes. Abby smiled at her. The father shook her hand. The young man and the small girl didn't approach her, but both smiled at her when she looked at them.

Abby turned back to the rail and looked at the larger approaching boat. She saw a half dozen men wearing something like shaman outfits. They wore colorful bead and seashell covered garments, feathered headdresses, and lots of face paint.

She also saw a very old looking man standing in front of the shamans. He had a bald head and no face paint, but he was wearing shimmering colorful robes with lots of gold and silver trim.

Sasha stepped up next to Abby. She looked over at him. He had on black dress pants, and an untucked fancy looking white shirt. Then she noticed that his hair was slicked back, caked with a heavy coating of some kind of hair product. She smiled and resisted laughing.

He smiled happily and gestured at his outfit,

"Yeah?"

Not laughing, was not easy. Abby nodded and kept her cool,

"Close enough for now. We'll uh... Well, we'll work on it."

She saw Norgren headed toward them as well. This time, she did laugh. He traded his clean white T-shirt for a smudged and ratty black T-shirt. He had on the same coveralls.

Surprisingly, he was also wearing the toolbelt that 'old Norgren' wore. He was pulling things out of the pouches on the belt and looking at them. His expression was a mixture of confusion and excitement.

Abby thought back to the last time she saw old Norgren. She remembered seeing him pull the rifle out of the crate and slinging it over his shoulder before climbing down the ladder. He didn't have the toolbelt on then.

He must have left it behind, for his younger self to find. Sadly, Abby realized he went over the side knowing that it would most likely cost him his life to buy her time. Her expression serious, her eyes slightly haunted, she nodded respectfully at Norgren as he approached.

The large boat pulling up alongside them had four canoes under its wide platform, two on each side. There were two small structures, like square beach tents you changed clothes in. The tents stood side by side in the center of the platform.

This boat didn't have sails. It was propelled by six very

large and muscular men with long poles, three on each side of the platform. They all had matching facial tattoos. They were the closest thing Abby had seen to a 'military' looking unit.

They pulled up close enough to grab the rail and pull both boats together. Leaving no gap between them. The big islander boat was very close to The Rider's height, just a short step down to the islander platform.

The older bald man in shiny robes stepped to the edge and Abby noticed his eyes were different from the others. They looked normal like hers and Norgrens. He opened his mouth to speak, but immediately closed it again.

Confused, Abby looked behind her. The small young girl had one hand up. She turned and made a series of complex hand gestures to the young man with her. The young man said several things to the old man in robes.

The old man bowed deeply and stepped aside. The young girl casually walked past Abby, hopped off The Rider, and walked into one of the small structures on the islander boat. Everyone on their boat was bowing and deferring to her.

Abby stared at the tent in stunned silence for several minutes. When she finally looked around, she saw that every single islander was waiting patiently with smiles on their faces,

Who the heck did I rescue? A princess? Her family isn't being treated like royalty.

Abby looked around again. While a lot of people were looking at her and her crew, no one was talking. All of them

were just standing there waiting patiently. Abby looked at Sasha. When he looked back, she raised an eyebrow and subtly spread her hands like, what do we do now?

Sasha stood where he was and held out one hand from near his waist, indicating be patient. Abby shrugged and nodded. She looked back at the islanders. Abby realized, she didn't see any weapons, anywhere.

She thought about the leviathan they saw. Maybe these people never needed weapons. After about ten very long minutes, the small girl came back out. The difference was mind blowing.

The filthy haired dirty kid wearing a potato sack came out in the most sparkling, jewelry encrusted, princess style dress that Abby had ever seen.

Her hair was clean and tied back into a single braid. She had a thin shimmering crystal tiara on her head. The tiara had a large round dark purple gemstone dangling from the front and hanging in the center of her forehead. The rising sun cutting through the green and blue auroras made the crystal tiara look like it was glowing with dancing colors.

Her dress looked like it was made of black silk and covered in glittering purple diamond dust. The dress also had thick shoulder pads, with two leviathan-like tentacles that curled out and hung directly off to each side.

Abby looked down. The strange princess girl was barefoot. Abby raised an eyebrow at the girl's bare feet, then she looked around. Everyone was barefoot. She looked up, saw

the islands, and thought,

Well, ok, that makes sense.

The change in the young girl's demeanor was equally as shocking. She came out of the small structure with her head held high. Her eyes were wide open and looking around. Her hands were together in front of her, her fingers curled together and interlocked.

Every single person in sight bowed. After a second, Sasha bowed as well. Norgren grunted, then followed suit. Abby looked at them, then looked back to the girl. The young girl was staring at her expectantly.

Abby shrugged and gave a brief bow as well. Almost imperceptibly, the small girl gave Abby a brief nod, as if saying, good enough. The overall message was pretty clear. She was in charge here.

The small girl walked back toward them. She stepped up in front of the old man, who was still bowing. She made a gesture to the young man that Abby thought was her brother. The young man said something loudly, and everyone stood up.

The purple princess made a series of hand gestures. The young man translated to the old bald man that Abby thought was like the king or the chief maybe. Abby saw shocked expressions on the faces around her, as the young man continued speaking.

The islanders were looking at Abby in amazement, while he continued talking,

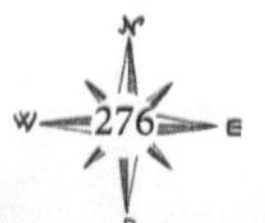

He must be telling everyone what an amazing rescue I pulled off.

When the young man stopped talking, he stepped in front of Abby. He bowed deeply to her, then left The Rider and walked over to stand behind the princess. The mother and father did the same thing but did not stand behind the princess. They jumped off the large boat and swam to a smaller boat that immediately paddled away to the main island.

Abby stepped in front of the gate, once they were all off her ship. The old bald man in shiny robes stepped up in front of her. He bowed briefly, then said,

"Our high priestess has requested that you allow her to honor you. She asks that you join us for a feast this night. A feast to celebrate your bravery and your grace. She asks that you allow us to reward you for your incredible service to the Levash Tu'an people."

He bowed again deeply, stood up, and stared at Abby expectantly. Everyone was staring at her. Abby had wide eyes and her mouth was partly open with shock over the old man speaking her language.

Abby snapped out of it and nodded,

"We would be honored to join you. Thank you, I accept."

"We will send a boat out for you, when the great fire gives way to the night."

Abby nodded politely. She stood and watched as they untied from The Rider and headed back toward their island. She waited until the islanders were all well out of hearing

distance. Then she spun around and glared at her grinning crew,

"The Syndicate wanted The Rider sure, as a bonus! That armada had us surrounded impossibly fast! When we left the atoll, there were already hundreds of boats spread out over hundreds of miles..."

Abby pointed at the big boat carrying the high priestess,

"...LOOKING FOR HER! The high priestess of the richest fishing grounds on the planet, that just escaped from their slave barge! Escaped their barge, onto YOUR ATOLL!"

Sasha's mouth dropped open with realization. Norgren nodded,

"That makes sense."

Abby slammed the gate closed and growled. She shook her head and looked at Norgren,

"You saw that maneuver I pulled, when we swamped the slave barge?"

Norgren grinned,

"Most impressive piloting I've ever seen, Captain."

Abby raised her eyebrows,

"I never flew a boat, or piloted, or whatever you call it, before yesterday!"

Norgren looked confused,

"How is that possible?"

Abby pointed a finger at his chest,

"THAT, is exactly what I want you to figure out."

She looked at Sasha and jerked her head toward her cabin,

"I have laundry I need done, steward."

Sasha laughed and headed toward her cabin,

"I told you every captain needed a steward, Captain."

Abby started to follow Sasha, but Norgren stopped her with a hand on her arm. She turned back around. He held up one finger as he looked closely at her vest. He shook his head slightly then lifted her hand and looked closely at the ring that unlocked her sidearm, again he shook his head.

He checked her wrists under her sleeves, frowning. Finally, Norgren looked up at her hat. He stared at it for a moment and his eyes lit up,

"I think I found the answer. Can I take a closer look at your hat, Captain?"

Abby pulled it off and handed it over, then stalked off toward her cabin,

"Take turns with Sasha keeping watch. I'm exhausted to

the point of cranky, I need a nap.”

Abby walked into her cabin and saw Sasha gathering the wet clothes from her fixing The Rider's engine. He also gathered up the other wet stuff from her impulsive swim. Sasha smiled at her and headed out,

“Sweet dreams, Captain.”

Abby growled at him jokingly and fell back onto her bed.

She was too tired to even take her sword belt off. Abby laid her head back and closed her eyes. It seemed like two seconds later she woke up to someone knocking on her cabin door.

Abby squinted at the door and pretended not to have heard it, laying her head back and closing her eyes again. Ten seconds later, she heard knocking again.

Groaning, she sat up on the edge of the bed,

“Go away! I quit! You fly the stupid ship!”

She heard Sasha's gentle voice through the door,

“I have cough medicine.”

Abby rubbed the back of her neck, fighting to open her eyes,

“In my cool black pirate mug?”

She heard Sasha's voice more quietly, off to the side,

"Is that a pirate symbol? It looks like a poison warning label."

Norgren grunted loudly, and pounded his fist on the door,

"There's a boat of islanders bearing down on us, Captain."

Abby groaned again loudly,

"Just come in already."

Norgren opened the door and Sasha walked in carrying a big tray. Sasha walked over and set the tray on her desk. Then he offered his hand to help her up. Abby scrunched up her face and took his hand, letting him pull her to her feet.

She tugged at her vest and belt, then squinted at Sasha,

"I like having a steward. You can stay."

Sasha chuckled and gestured toward the large tray on her desk. Abby walked over to the desk and smiled happily, looking at her big steaming pirate mug. She picked it up and smelled the sweet aroma of cappuccino.

From just outside her door, Norgren grumbled and mumbled,

"You'll spoil her rotten."

Sasha stuck his tongue out at Norgren as the big man closed the door and walked away. Abby chuckled at her crew

and looked back at the tray. Sitting in the center of the tray, she saw a large porcelain bowl of clean water with a folded washcloth on the edge.

Abby sipped her coffee and looked over at Sasha. He was putting her cleaned and folded clothes and spare boots back in the drawers. Abby sipped more coffee, then smiled happily,

"Did I mention you can stay?"

Sasha laughed,

"You did, as a matter of fact."

Abby looked back at the bowl,

"What exactly am I supposed to do with this?"

Sasha turned and saw Abby looking at the bowl, he stood up and faced her with a smile. When Abby looked over at him, he pretended to be splashing water on his face and made a big exaggerated dramatically refreshed smile.

Then he pretended to be dipping a cloth into an invisible bowl and wiping the back of his neck, then under his arms. He spread his hands and made a 'duh' face,

"Combat shower, Captain!"

Abby made a disgusted face as Sasha walked out laughing and closed the door behind himself. Abby took him up on the first part, she put her face down to the bowl and splashed the freezing water on her face.

She stood up and took a couple of deep breaths. That water was ice cold. She looked at the washcloth. She thought about it a minute. She looked at the bowl again. Finally, she laughed and shook her head,

"Nah."

Abby stepped out of her cabin and looked over toward the rail. Norgren dropped the ladder down to a smaller boat. Sasha stood nearby watching.

She walked up the stairs to the quarterdeck and switched The Rider to camouflage mode, sealing all the displays and consoles. She went back to her cabin and flipped the switches, locking down the hatches and consoles. She pulled her door closed and looked at it. She cocked her head, confused. She turned toward Norgren,

"I need your brain over here!"

Norgren trotted over,

"Captain?"

Abby pointed at her door,

"How do I lock this?"

Norgren grabbed the latch and tried to open the door. It didn't budge,

"Is this a trick question?"

Abby shook her head, reached out, opened her door then

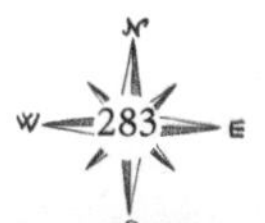

closed it again. She looked at Norgren,

"Well?"

Norgren tried the door again. It still wouldn't open for him,

"I don't know, Captain."

Norgren pulled out her hat and handed it over. He scratched his chin,

"The hat mystery, I solved. Save the door mystery for after dinner?"

Abby put on her hat and nodded,

"Sounds good. Let's eat."

The three of them climbed down into a long wide outrigger canoe. There were two islanders in the canoe that rowed them to shore. The rowers were dressed in fancy shell decorated vests, with headcovers that had a few feathers sticking up from the back.

Approaching the beach, Abby saw a small delegation waiting to greet them. The rowers beached the canoe, then got out and pulled it forward onto the sand. Abby got out and walked toward the waiting delegation with Norgren and Sasha close behind.

She walked up toward the old bald man. He had on a similar fancy outfit to what he was wearing earlier. He was holding his arms open in welcome. Abby stopped far enough

away that he couldn't do something weird like reach out and hug her. Norgren and Sasha stepped up and stood on each side of her.

The old man gestured to his left and right. From his left, a fancy dressed young man with a tray walked in between Abby and the old man. There were about a half dozen very small wooden cups on the tray.

The old man grabbed a cup and gestured to Abby and her companions. They each grabbed one. The old man held up his cup,

"We welcome these honored guests, with a toast to the gods of the deep."

Abby glanced at Sasha and gave him a questioning look. Sasha nodded vehemently. The three of them raised their cups and drank when the old man did. It tasted like spoiled coconut water! Abby coughed gently and set her cup back down. The others did the same. Norgren had a grin on his face.

From the old man's other side, a young girl came forward with a necklace of pearls and shells and wildly cut and polished gemstones. The young girl smiled and lifted the necklace over Abby's head, settling it onto her neck. Abby smiled at her,

"Thank you."

The old man clapped his hands and the islanders around them moved away. All except for two that were carrying torches. He gestured for Abby and her crew to follow him. He turned away and led them toward a dark path into the forest.

The torch bearers split up. One followed close behind the old man. The other fell in behind Abby and her companions. Both of them held their torches high, so that everyone could see.

Following the old man down the dark and winding path, Abby pulled Norgren and Sasha close on each side of her. She handed the pearl and gemstone necklace to Sasha,

"Put that in the ship's treasury. Which you are now in charge of."

Sasha smiled and inspected the necklace. Abby turned to Norgren,

"Earlier, you said you solved the mystery."

Norgren nodded and spoke softly,

"Autonomic Motor Neurogenesis."

Abby scrunched up her face for a moment, then said,

"Uh... what?"

Norgren chuckled, he looked over and gave her an odd look,

"You ready for this?"

"Lay it on me."

He nodded,

"My hypothesis is that you acquired that hat from the

original captain of The Riptide Rider, an older version of yourself. She was captain of The Rider for at least ten years. Which explains why that hat works for you. The older you, is an exact deoxyribonucleic acid match."

Norgren pointed up toward her head for emphasis, and continued,

"That hat was designed for the older you, by an older version of myself. He designed it to record and transfer all of her stored neural patterns and muscle memories to a younger her. All of which implies that they both knew that all of this was going to happen. Care to ask me how I know all of this?"

Abby's eyes were wide, her heart beating fast. She guessed,

"You recognize your own work?"

Norgren nodded.

Abby took a deep breath and let it out slowly,

"I was going to tell you. We just haven't had a calm moment until this one we're having right now."

"I figured that was the case."

Abby put a hand on Norgren's shoulder,

"Remind me when we get back to the ship. I have a recorded message for you... from you."

Norgren nodded. They walked in silence for a few

minutes. They looked around at the strange vegetation and the odd bugs that jumped from tree to tree like frogs but looked more like grotesque fairies.

Sasha asked,

"Was my older self, your older self's steward?"

Abby nodded,

"He wasn't the ships master at arms, that's for sure."

They all laughed, as they followed the old bald man in the shiny dress through the strange dark forest.

The First Dawn

They emerged from the path through the forest into an enclosed and secluded area. Abby smiled in wonder at the picturesque beauty before her. Her eyes were immediately drawn to a small crystal-clear lake in the center that sparkled with green and blue diamonds reflecting the auroras above.

The forest wrapped around this side of the lake, giving way to a sandy beach around its edge. The other side of the lake was overshadowed by a dark and looming mountain. Abby looked up at the small waterfall coming from a wide crack in the side of the mountain, pouring into the rippling waters below.

Her eyes followed the water down, then she looked beyond the lake, under the overhanging rock. She saw a carved ledge that appeared to lead to a cave opening that disappeared into the mountain.

The half dozen shamans from the boat were on their knees along the edge of the beach. They faced the shallow lake and the stone ledge. Their bodies swayed, arms held high, as they chanted and sang in deep throaty voices.

The old man bowed deeply to Abby. When he stood, he turned and pointed toward the cave with a solemn expression.

He immediately turned away and walked back toward the path, leaving the way he had come.

The torchbearers handed their torches to Norgren and Sasha. Then, they also, turned back and left along the dark path through the forest.

Abby watched them go. Then she looked first at Sasha, then Norgren,

"This isn't creepy at all."

Sasha swallowed and looked nervous. Norgren chuckled. Abby grabbed the torch from Sasha and led the way toward the lake and the cave beyond. Sasha followed closely on her heels. Norgren brought up the rear. They crossed the shallow lake.

On the other side, Abby saw carved steps and followed them up to the stone ledge at the mouth of the cave. She stepped toward the cave with her torch in her right hand. She heard her own voice in her mind, as if from a memory, some advice, or maybe training,

Always carry things with your left hand, your right hand is for your weapons.

Abby grinned and thought,

Autonomic Motor Neurogenesis, for the win.

She shifted the torch to her left hand and held it before her as she climbed the steps and entered the cave. Thankfully, it was a short walk through a narrow cave until it opened up into a large dome-shaped room that had the look of an old magma

chamber.

Immediately upon entering, Abby saw three thick square rugs in front of them. A fourth rug, in the center of the room, was occupied by the young high priestess. Against the far wall, facing them, Abby saw a smaller than normal, throne-like wooden chair.

The high priestess didn't move when they came in. She continued to kneel on the single square rug in the center of the chamber. Abby assumed the three squares were meant for her, Sasha, and Norgren. She looked at the priestess and cocked her head curiously,

Why is the "High Priestess", on her knees? Why is she facing an empty throne? Why isn't she on the throne?

The young girl, still in her crystal tiara and her sparkling purple gem encrusted dress, turned around and pointed at the carpet squares behind her. Abby took her place on the center square, nodding to the others to join her. All three of them knelt down and rested on the carpets, waiting.

After a few moments, Abby realized she could still faintly hear the shamans chanting and singing on the beach outside. A cool soft breeze blew through the chamber. The flames of their torches flickered and danced toward the entrance behind them. The wind was coming from deeper in the mountain.

The torches flickered out and the chamber was plunged into pitch darkness. Abby heard Norgren set his torch on the floor next to him. She set hers directly behind her.

The young priestess in front of them took a deep breath, then sang softly in her sweet and wonderful wordless way. Her voice was raw musical sound that melted away anger and fears and put the monsters of one's soul to sleep.

Abby felt herself relaxing deeply. She felt a powerful sense of calm settle onto her like silk chains. She heard Norgren and Sasha shifting around. They laid down on their carpets and fell asleep. It didn't upset Abby that her crew fell asleep. Everything was ok.

She suddenly noticed that there was another passage leading into the chamber. Abby saw a faint blue light coming from an opening behind the small wooden throne. The young priestess bowed forward, her hands outstretched, her forehead near the floor.

The blue light grew brighter and brighter, until the source of the light floated into the room. At first, it appeared to be a thin hovering disc-shaped thing. Its outer surface seemed like a liquid, translucent, its surface layer flowing around itself.

As it got closer, Abby saw that it wasn't actually a disc. It had short, tapered wings on each side. Not like flapping wings, more like it was swimming through the air. The blue light emanated from a hollow crystal lattice ring that floated inside the liquid disc.

The softly glowing light source turned in a gentle bank, swimming into the room and around the wooden throne. It was the shape of a small manta ray! Abby's eyes went wide in awe of the beautiful thing. It swam up near the ceiling and circled around, back toward the passageway it came from.

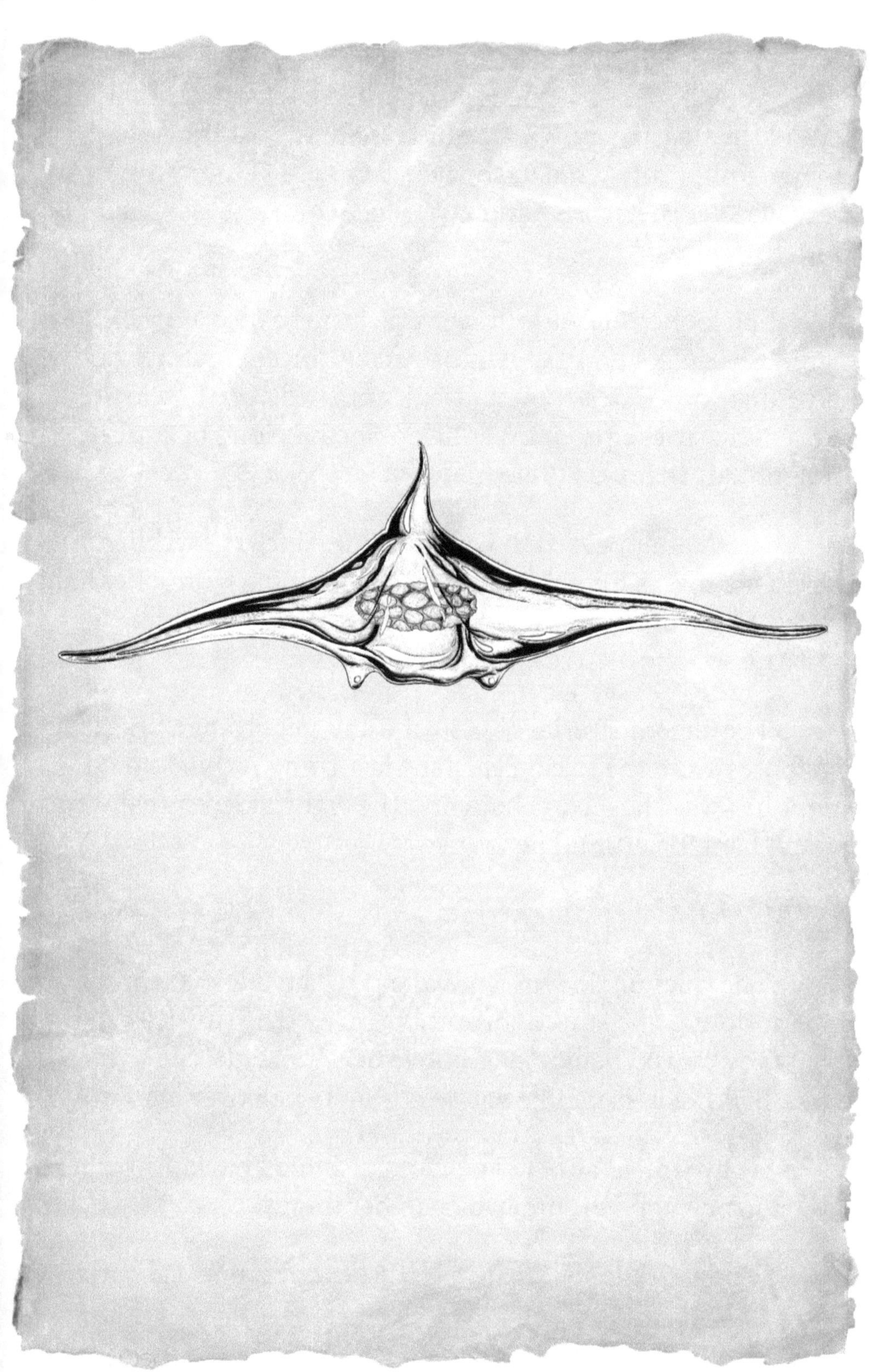

Abby heard movement and looked back down. Following behind the floating glowing liquid manta ray, Abby saw a woman unlike any woman she had ever seen before. Abby's eyes grew wide with surprise and awe. The woman was amazingly unique.

She looked about four feet tall, but she also appeared incredibly thick and heavily muscled all throughout her body. She didn't look like a stereotypical fantasy dwarf. She looked like a miniature female power lifter. She had long beautiful straight hair that was braided down her back.

Her hair appeared to be light blue, since everything in the chamber was highlighted by the swimming manta ray light source. She wore a simple robe, so sheer that it would have embarrassed the men to witness it.

The sheer material of her robe and her strange physical attributes were the reason that the last thing Abby noticed about her was the silver chain and the eight-sided translucent crystal hanging around her neck,

She has a time portal generator!

The thick little woman walked to the wooden throne and sat down. She stared into Abby's eyes. The tiny floating manta ray moved behind and above her. It backlit the sheer dress, making it seem like she was glowing all over her body.

Abby smiled at her. The woman smiled back. Abby heard a very strong and feminine voice in her mind,

Welcome, child of Justinius and traveler across time and worlds.

The strange woman's thoughts were so powerful, it felt like they vibrated through her. Abby made a soft almost laughing noise. It was an incredible sensation, and she was giddy with joy at being recognized for her actions.

The fact that the woman was speaking directly into her mind didn't upset her in the least. Nothing could upset her right now, in this induced lethargy and calmness. Abby thought back to her,

Who are you? And forgive me, but what are you?

The short thick woman cocked her head slightly to the side, as if considering. Abby heard her sweet powerfully resonating voice again,

I am the first Dawn. A creation of the builders, much like but infinitely different from the ship that brought you here. I was one of the first watchers. Sent back to study the past, and never heard from again. I was custom built and engineered to infiltrate a race of creatures that looked similar to the builders but were in fact very different.

She gestured at her body, emphasizing the physical differences between her and Abby. She continued,

My mission was to enter the bottleneck, infiltrate their society, and learn of their mysterious origin. Because even though the builders could identify the moment they appeared in the bottleneck, they couldn't find where or when they came from.

So much information, yet Abby felt like she had only discovered more questions. What did 'first dawn' mean? Was it her name? What were the watchers, and was she named after one?

Was her father Justin a stand-in? Was he really Justinius the Watcher? Was her father the telepath of the group of three that they called the Renegades? Was that why she kept hearing voices like the baby leviathan, the young priestess, Norgren? What was the bottleneck?

Abby shook her head. It was starting to hurt. She was getting a headache. Again, she heard the powerful feminine voice in her mind,

It has been thousands of years since I granted audience to one that was not one of my servants. You have earned three questions, Captain Abigail. Go now, before the pain becomes damage. Your mind is not ready for this, yet. Go, enjoy the feast in your honor. When you are ready, return, and I will give you three answers. Choose wisely.

The faint pain began to throb. Abby reached up and touched her nose. There was blood on her fingertips. She looked back up and saw that Dawn had risen and walked back toward her cave.

The small floating liquid manta ray swam down in tiny spiraling circles and landed in Abby's outstretched hand. She heard Dawn's voice, one last time as she disappeared back into her cave,

A gift, to repay the incredible gift that you brought home to me.

Abby looked down at the amazing thing in her hand. She could barely feel its touch. It was like being kissed by mist. She saw the crystal lattice-work ring more clearly, surrounded by the thin liquid glowing manta ray shape,

What do I do with you?

As if in response, she saw the liquid manta ray shape being rapidly drawn into the gaps in the crystal lattice of the ring. The whole outer body was sucked into the ring. Now she had a glowing crystal bracelet in her hand about the size of a saucer.

Abby held it up in her fingers and stared at it. She put it on her left wrist and watched in amazement as it slowly shrank down to a perfect fit. Her eyes were wide with wonder at this amazing gift. It was incredible.

She couldn't even begin to imagine what type of science made it possible or what it was made of. Abby thought about taking it off and it immediately grew back to its original size. She made a joyful squeak of a laugh.

When she thought about the manta ray coming back, the liquid flowed out of the gaps and the manta ray was sitting in her palm once more. Abby held it up and looked at it with a huge smile on her face. The word amazing didn't do it justice.

She looked up, past the glowing little ray, and saw the young priestess sitting cross-legged on her rug, grinning at her like a happy kid. Strange little girl was a great actress. Queenly and regal one minute, then goofy kid the next.

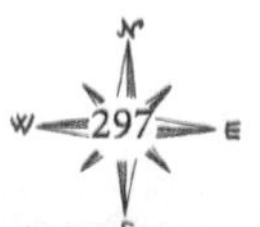

Abby smiled back a bit sheepishly. She had completely forgotten the other three people in the chamber.

She thought about the bracelet going back on her wrist and the liquid manta ray shape was immediately sucked back into the bracelet. She put it on her wrist and grinned broadly as it shrank back down. The light from the bracelet blinked off and immediately the torches started burning again.

Abby reached back and grabbed the torch behind her.

Shaking her head, she realized that the calm-inducing lethargy was rapidly wearing off. Sasha and Norgren woke up. Abby thought about Dawn being a powerful telepath. It made perfect sense that the bracelet would respond to mental commands.

She looked up at the smiling little priestess in her sparkling purple dress. She looked into the young girl's eyes and heard the soft tiny voice in her mind,

The goddess of the mountain has given this one a beautiful gift.

Abby just read her mind. She knew that was exactly what had just happened. She read the young girl's mind. It wasn't some fluke occurrence resulting from this strange world with its strong solar radiation that made most of the planet uninhabitable. It wasn't the proton bombardment that kept the night sky glowing with unending auroras.

It was her. She actually did it,

I can read people's minds.

Norgren leaned down and tapped Abby on the shoulder,

"You're going to explain what just happened here, right?"

Abby looked up and saw him standing there holding the second torch. He looked confused and irritated. She looked over at Sasha, brushing at some cave gunk on his clean white shirt. Abby looked back to the young priestess, now standing up.

Abby got up and looked at Norgren,

"Later, yes. For now, just act like this craziness is perfectly normal."

Norgren whispered back,

"Crazy has been the new normal since the moment I met you, Captain."

They followed the young priestess out of the cave and across the small lake to the beach where the shamans were waiting for them. The young girl headed for the path through the woods. The shamans walked with her, forming a circle around the little priestess.

Abby, Norgren, and Sasha followed behind them. Looking over, Abby noticed that Norgren was staring at her left wrist. He looked shocked, maybe, or very concerned. He was staring at where the crystal bracelet was hidden under the sleeve of her shirt. Abby grinned at him. He looked up at her with a raised eyebrow,

"Wha..."

He looked back down at her wrist. Abby laughed. Norgren shook his head,

"Still waiting for that explanation, Captain."

Abby gave him a sly grin,

"Later, let's just go enjoy our celebratory feast, eh?"

Sasha said,

"I'm just glad we're invited to enjoy the feast, and not BE the feast."

Abby smiled and Norgren chuckled. Norgren looked over at Sasha,

"You'd be safe, I don't think they eat delicate and fancy stuff here."

Abby laughed loudly while Sasha gave Norgren a scowl.

The priestess and four of her shamans moved forward out of sight as they reached the edge of the woods. The remaining two shamans came to a stop at a braided reed archway, decorated with streamers of flowers.

Abby elbowed Norgren,

"Sweet kid had them decorate the beach for us."

The shamans stood in the archway, waiting. Abby saw nothing but darkness beyond them. As Abby approached, the somber faced men took their torches and extinguished them in

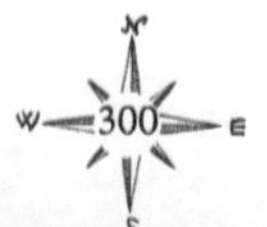

buckets next to the path. They waited in darkness for several minutes.

Looking up, Abby saw thick dark clouds overhead. Only faint traces of blue and green light could be seen above. A loud gong suddenly sounded from the beach ahead, startling her. Abby felt one of the shamans take her hand and lead her forward past the archway.

Six boats offshore launched dozens of screaming rockets into the sky. Booming explosions of colorful fire illuminated the beach brightly before her. Additional trails of sparkling screaming fire continued to rise into the sky and explode in a myriad of complex patterns and colors.

Abby saw the young high priestess standing atop a twenty-foot-tall tower, in her royal sparkling purple leviathan dress and glittering tiara. On the young girl's right, Abby saw the old bald man in his shimmering robes. On the priestess's left, she saw the young man who interpreted her complex hand gestures.

The explosions above and behind them, cast the structure below their feet in shadow. The fireworks shifted closer, lighting up a long platform closer and lower than the priestess. Across the long, wide platform, Abby saw twenty men in grass skirts with painted faces, thick heavily muscled bare chests, and fierce war-like scowls.

Drums began beating out a fierce deep rhythm. As one, the men on the platform raised their fists and shouted out a single unified battle cry. Fireworks continued to pound the sky as the drum pounding rhythm intensified.

The men on the platform broke into a perfectly synchronized chest beating, thigh slapping, back flipping, foot stomping war dance. Their feet pounding the platform with synchronized wood rattling steps matching the rhythm of the hammering drums.

Abby felt her heart racing at the sights and sounds before her. She was smiling from ear to ear. Colorful sparkling explosions accented the war dancing, drum beating performance.

Two long lines of torches suddenly ignited in rapid succession on each side of the dark open area in front of the platform. Abby saw six long, wide tables arrayed in front of the priestess and her dancers, filled with a hundred islanders.

As one, all of the islanders stood up and faced Captain Abigail of The Riptide Rider. As one, they broke into a thunderous standing ovation complete with shouts and cries in their strange, beautiful language.

She heard a chorus of praise and gratitude in her mind.

Abby couldn't stop herself from laughing as tears of joy rolled down her cheeks. She was completely emotionally overwhelmed. The loud, colorful complex display assembled before her was amazing to witness. The orchestration and performance in front of her was awe inspiring.

Fireworks rippled across the sky, bathing the beach in explosions of color. The battle-cry screaming dancer's, their feet stomping the platform, and the drum pounding rhythm vibrated through her body. A hundred islanders clapped and

cheered for her loudly.

All of it, in appreciation for bringing home their high priestess.

Norgren and Sasha looked at each other and nodded. They stepped away, off to each side, then turned and faced their captain. Smiling broadly, they joined in the standing ovation.

Tears streaming down her smiling face, Abby looked across the faces arrayed before her. She saw not the forced obedience of slaves, but genuine appreciation and joy. They wore the faces of people getting back something precious that was stolen from them.

Abby put a hand over her mouth and lowered the brim of her hat to hide her sobbing and the tears streaming down her cheeks. Norgren and Sasha stepped closer and patted her on the shoulders. The dancers stopped and replaced their costume scowls with genuine smiles, standing and clapping with the others.

Abby's shoulders were shaking from the emotions caused by the overwhelming display.

The priestess held up one small hand and the gong sounded loudly three times. The fireworks faded off, leaving the area lit only by the torches. The drums and applause went silent. Everyone stood quietly, looking toward Abby.

The priestess began making a series of hand gestures. The young man translated quietly and quickly to the old bald man. The old man lifted his head and loudly pronounced before

all,

"We, the Levash Tu'an, give thanks to the gods, for providing this deliverer. We give thanks to the one who came from the sky!"

He held out one hand toward Abby,

"She who defied the Syndicate, freed our people, and rescued our high priestess!"

A brief chaotic applause erupted from the islanders. The old man raised his hands and quieted the crowd,

"We salute you, Captain Abigail! We name you truest friend of the Levash Tu'an people! And we name you, most honored guest, for life!"

The old man leaned slightly forward and waved a hand slowly in front of him, gesturing to the tables and the crowd,

"Honor us now, with your presence. AND LET THE FEAST BEGIN!"

Everyone erupted into cheers and applause once more. Abby laughed and wiped the tears from her eyes. She looked up toward the high priestess. She saw the young girl smile and nod at her.

The priestess pointed toward the center of the large table closest to her. Abby saw that there was a section in the middle, on both sides, that was empty and reserved for them.

Abby made her way forward toward the far central table,

Sasha and Norgren following. Everyone she passed either shook her hand or patted her on the shoulder. There was a general chatter of conversation going on all around.

They reached the open seats in the center of the long table. Abby saw the priestess and her small entourage emerge from an opening in the curtain surrounding the platform. Abby waited for the young priestess to sit first, then took her seat. Sasha and Norgren took their places to each side, as did the old man and the young translator.

Everyone else took their seats. Abby heard more cheering and joyful shouts amid the sounds of feasting. She looked around at the tables overflowing with food. She saw large woven platters of various meats arranged on large leaves. She saw dozens of types of vegetables and fruits, breads and pastries, and countless desserts.

Abby could barely identify even half of the offered delights. She tried a couple bites of as many things as she could. She smiled happily at all the laughter and joy around her. Even the priestess relaxed. Several times she gestured out comments and jokes that the young man translated, and the old man spoke for her.

Abby leaned toward the old man,

"Why doesn't the high priestess speak for herself?"

The old man translated her question to the priestess, but he responded without needing her prompting,

"The high priestess has a holy voice that is reserved only

for the gods. Those of us lucky enough to be present when she speaks are honored to overhear her words to the gods."

Abby gestured to the high priestess,

"I've only heard her sing, not speak."

The old man translated her words for the young priestess. The young girl gestured, the young man translated, and the old man nodded his understanding. He looked back at Abby,

"On your ship, you heard the language of the gods of the deep, our protectors and guardians of the oceans. Their language does not sound like the language of the people, it sounds to us like singing."

He pointed to his bald head,

"The true language of the gods can be heard only by the mind. Speaking the true language of the gods, like the high priestess, is incredibly rare."

Abby looked at the young girl, understanding,

He's talking about telepathy.

The high priestess nodded, yes. She gestured, the young man translated, and the old man said,

"The high priestess says that you, Captain Abigail, also hear and speak the language of the gods. You proved this, when you heard her say, brother."

Abby nodded. Norgren and Sasha both turned and looked at Abby curiously. She quickly gestured to the young man,

"Is he, her brother?"

The old man nodded,

"Every priestess is paired with a family member who is trained to translate the hand speech of the priestess for the people."

The young priestess gestured, the young man translated, and the old man spoke,

"There are five tribes among the twelve Levash Tu'an Islands. Priestess Leilani is the only one, of twenty young priestess's, who speaks the language of the gods. She is currently trying to teach three others, that we are hopeful can learn."

The gesture, translate, speaking process continued,

"The high priestess says that this ability is passed down only from mothers, and only to daughters. It used to be passed on to one girl in three. But those who can speak the language are growing more rare."

Abby nodded at the old man, listening. While thinking about the big picture,

Their true language of the gods is telepathy. Does the bioengineered telepath in the mountain have something to do with all of this. Dawn herself said she had been around these people for thousands of years.

The old man's face turned beet red at the next translation. He turned and looked at the young girl with raised eyebrows and wide eyes, shocked. She nodded vehemently for him to continue. He looked back with a very red face,

"Priestess Leilani says that mothers who can pass on their gift, are rare and precious. She asks if any of the young men you see, would be suitable husbands for you to provide children to the Levash Tu'an people?"

Abby choked on a bite of something like an apple. After a moment of panic and choking, she coughed up the bite and took several deep breaths. Her eyes were wide with shock. Sasha looked appalled and offended. Norgren blinked several times, then started laughing hysterically.

Abby recovered and took a deep calming breath. She reminded herself that these islander people just had strange cultural differences. She laughed briefly, then looked directly at Leilani and shook her head, no. Leilani frowned.

Some time later, after more conversation and too much food, the feast began to wind down. Abby stood up, stretched, and looked at the old man,

"Would it be considered acceptable manners, to excuse ourselves for the night and return to our ship to rest?"

The old man translated the question. The young high priestess smiled and stood up. Everyone grew quiet and turned toward them, watching. Leilani walked all the way around the table and stood in front of Abby. She looked over at the young man and gestured briefly.

The young man stood up on his chair and spoke loudly to the crowd, in the beautiful sounding language of the Levash Tu'an. Every single islander stood up from their chairs and turned to face away from them. Understanding, and respecting, they all looked away from the very young girl, who filled very big shoes, with a young girl's emotions.

The high priestess looked around carefully. Then she stepped close and gave Abby a fierce 'little sister to big sister' hug. Abby smiled and hugged her back, she leaned her head down close and concentrated her thoughts,

You're welcome kid. Welcome home.

Brought Up to Speed

Several hours later, Abby, Norgren, and Sasha were all lounging on the deck of The Rider. They laid back and relaxed on reclining beach chairs that Norgren found in a small storage room on the galley and crew quarters deck below.

They stared at the auroras high above in relative silence, broken only by the gentle waves against the hull gently rocking the ship. Norgren and Sasha had distant, thoughtful looks on their faces, absorbing everything that Abby just finished telling them.

She told them about finding The Rider in the woods behind her home. She told them about the journal, the letter to herself from her older self. She told them about meeting older versions of them. She told them about the recorded video message from the older Norgren.

She told them everything. She even described the events that transpired in the cave after they fell asleep.

No one spoke for some time. Abby was fine with that, after talking at great length explaining all the events of the past couple days. Thinking about it now, in hindsight, they were very eventful days. It was no surprise that she was still exhausted, even after her nap earlier that day.

Out of the blue, Abby heard Sasha's voice in her mind,

I can't believe I was abandoned in the ocean! What the hell?

Abby laughed loudly, then looked over at him,

"Hey, it was your idea! Frankly, it's better than what happened to Norgren. I'm pretty sure he's dead. OK?"

Norgren held up his hand with a 'Rock On' gesture,

"Blaze of glory baby."

Sasha leaned forward and glared at Abby,

"You're not going to be reading our minds all the time, are you?"

Abby shrugged,

"Don't know, can't control it."

Sasha made an irritated 'pfft' noise,

"Well, isn't THAT convenient!"

Norgren spoke very calmly,

"Dude, bottom line is this. The older us, who knew her, were willing to risk dying for her. The younger her, who didn't even know us, was willing to risk dying to defend us at the atoll. Then she risked her life again, to free a very small boatload of slaves that she also didn't know. That should tell you absolutely everything you need to know my friend."

Sasha thought about that for a second and then nodded,

"Yeah. Yeah, it does. Sorry Captain."

Abby reached over and put her hand on Sasha's shoulder for a moment,

"The question before us now, is what we ask Dawn. We have three questions, three answers. We each get to take one and think it over tonight. If you could only ask her one thing, what would it be?"

Norgren leaned forward and looked past Abby at Sasha,

"We, she says. We get. You see what I mean?"

Sasha nodded,

"I do."

Abby got up and stretched. She headed to her cabin,

"Wait here."

After Abby walked away, Norgren looked over at Sasha,

"How did older you disappear from the locked kitchen with the robot voice?"

Sasha raised his eyebrows and held his hands out to each side,

"I have no idea!"

Norgren sat back and nodded slowly,

"That means it's something I invent in the future. That's so cool."

Abby came walking back and tossed the small video recorder to Norgren. He caught it, then looked up at her. Abby pointed to it,

"That's the video recorder that older you gave me. The first button has the recording I told you about. The second button has a technical breakdown on The Rider's systems, upgrades, and some general thoughts from the previous engineer. The third button is something he recorded specifically for you, just in case I found you. You got something for me?"

Norgren looked from the recorder up to Abby and cocked his head in confusion. Abby tugged her earlobe expressively. Norgren sat up quickly,

"OH, RIGHT!"

He dug into his pocket and pulled out a small case. He opened it and offered her the case. Abby took it and looked inside. There was an assortment of various designs of earrings. She saw a tiny skull and crossbones. She grinned.

She took the pirate earring and put it on her ear, then she handed back the case. Walking back toward her cabin, she called out over her shoulder,

"I'm locking down the quarterdeck consoles and the cargo hold. Manually lock the hatch to the lower decks on your way down. I think we can rest easy here, no watch."

Both men said,

"Aye Captain."

Abby went into her cabin, barring the door behind her. She set the journal on her desk and ran her fingers across the leather cover. It looked like a simple journal, but it most definitely wasn't.

On impulse, she picked it up again and untied it. She opened it up and looked at the pages. Written in her handwriting, was everything that had happened except for the very beginning in her kitchen. Strangely, there was no mention of old Sasha and old Norgren.

It was just her, finding the ship, fixing the engine, and freeing it from the ground. That was odd. It told about her flying across the country in the night, landing in the ocean, and eventually jumping away. The journal didn't mention Norgren and Sasha until she rescued them from the Syndicate. It was like the journal didn't see their older selves at all.

She put it back down and hung up her hat, her weapons, and the thick leather vest. She got comfortable on her bed. The islands were protected all around by the leviathans. The islanders all loved them. She figured it was safe to relax.

Abby laid her head back and stared at the ceiling, turning her options over in her mind.

She could ask Dawn about her father, but she already knew the truth. She just didn't want to believe it. The kind and gentle man that she remembered, was not the whole story. The

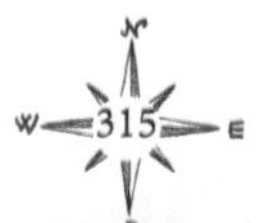

Imperial Operative, Justinius the Watcher, was her father. He was a telepath. He was the reason that she was a telepath.

Her father was one of the Imperial Renegades.

Abby turned onto her left side and looked across the cabin. Her eyes fell on the large aquarium with the chunk of toxop... something drone in it. She saw the rounded end of the loaf of bread sized chunk was at the top now. The broken off end pulled itself down into the sandy dirt and the water with long thin black roots.

She stared at it for several moments. Suddenly and strangely, she began to hear something like a voice in her mind. It sounded like a cartoon dwarf, humming some cheerful tune while he tapped away at an anvil with a small hammer.

Abby smiled. She focused harder and heard what sounded like a happy giddy child's voice, singing softly in the background,

Eat eat eat, drink drink drink.

Grow right up and learn to think.

Eat eat eat, drink drink drink.

Grow...

Abby laughed and turned to her other side. She reached for the crystal bracelet. The soft blue glow flared to life as it opened wider. She pulled it off her wrist. Up close, she saw the opposing spirals of crystal twist tighter and thinner as it opened wider. The technology had to be on par with The Rider,

if not even more advanced.

She set the crystal lattice band on the pillow next to her,

Keep me company?

The crystal bracelet leaked out the glowing blue liquid, but it didn't shape itself into a manta ray. The bracelet folded together on opposite sides. The two curves coming together and shifting and curving again as the liquid formed itself into a small cat with a crystal lattice spine.

Abby's eyes went wide, and she laughed,

"NO WAY!"

The softly glowing blue liquid cat stood up and stretched just like a normal cat would. It flicked its glowing tail back and forth, walked closer, and nudged her cheek with its soft head.

Abby scooped it up and laid on her back. She set the cat on her belly and looked down, watching it make little biscuit kneading motions on her shirt. She felt the faint sensation of the cat curling up on her stomach. She heard a purring sound that sent tiny vibrational ripples across its liquid surface.

Smiling happily, she closed her eyes.

Physically exhausted, she quickly drifted off. Somewhere on the edge between awake and asleep, Abby imagined she heard something like an airplane engine. She dismissed the thought with a chuckle. Her imagination was remembering the sound of airplanes.

She heard a distant splash. It was very faint and far, mostly drowned out by the creaking of her wooden ship and the waves slapping the sides. The next splash was louder and closer. Abby absently wondered if maybe the leviathans were fishing.

She imagined seeing a baby leviathan waving around a couple of tuna fish in its thick tentacles. The image of the baby leviathan in her mind flashed red for second, then stopped. At the very entrance to the world of dreams, Abby stopped and looked back toward the real.

With her eyes still closed, she saw a brief red glow again. Abby woke up and her eyes flickered open sluggishly. The liquid cat was in her face, pulsing back and forth from blue to bright red. Abby looked at it, confused,

What is going on?

She heard a single, loud, crashing, thump. Then a painful grunt, and a clattering tumbling rolling sound out on the deck. Faintly, in the distance, she heard screaming. Her eyes snapped wide open. She jumped up and grabbed her weapons, belting them onto her waist over her breeches.

She turned toward the door and froze as the latch and locking bar rattled violently,

Someone just landed on my ship and they're trying to get in my door.

Someone very large slammed into her door, she heard wood cracking. Her body jerked at the sound of the booming impact. It was something very heavy,

Islanders? That doesn't make sense. The splashing sounds, distant then closer.

Abby's eyes went wide with realization,

The plane engine! The Syndicate just dropped men from the air.

Abby reached for her sidearm, then looked at her feet. She thought about firing at someone on the deck of her ship. The explosion would blow a hole in the deck.

The rattling latch stopped, and the door shook with another heavy impact. She heard footsteps off to the side, rising up the port stairs. Then she heard loud thumping steps across the ceiling of her cabin,

They're up on the quarterdeck.

Still watching the door, she quickly thought,

In my hand! Back on my wrist!

She held out her open hand and glanced over her shoulder. The glowing cat was shifting in mid-air. Abby caught the crystal bracelet and slipped it onto her wrist. She squeezed her earring,

"We have intruders onboard! Main deck! Be careful!"

She heard whoever was on her quarterdeck pounding on the covered and locked control consoles. She had to get out there, get his attention, and distract him from damaging her ship.

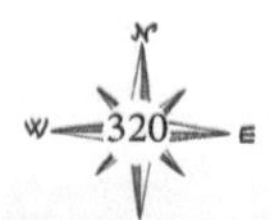

Abby quickly threw the locking bar, jerked the door open, and rushed outside, turning to look behind her. Up on the quarterdeck, glaring at the covered consoles, was a very big fish-man. He snapped his head up and hissed at her menacingly.

Something was wrong with him. Abby took a couple steps back. She wasn't an expert on fish-men, but she could tell there was something wrong with him. He had sores in numerous places on his body. There was blood coming from his nose. He reminded her of something out of a zombie movie.

Abby lowered her head slightly and narrowed her eyes as she drew her sword. She wasn't afraid. He didn't know it yet, but he was dealing with Captain Abigail. Abby had the muscle memory combat reflexes of a veteran pirate captain. She was going to gut this zombie fish-man, like a fish.

He put one hand on the rail and leapt over it, slamming down onto the deck in front of her. He looked at the young girl in front of him and sneered at her in derision. He walked closer.

Abby stood her ground, her left hand out to the side like a fencer. She kept her sword held close in front of her, pointed at the fish-man.

In her ear, she heard Norgren's groggy half-asleep voice,

"You says rudder board check? Daptin?"

Abby squeezed the earring and shouted,

"INTRUDERS! ON BOARD! NORGREN!"

The fish-man's face contorted at her calling for help. He

snarled and leapt forward, coming right at her. Abby thrust the sword forward, trying to pierce him through the heart. She missed, by several inches.

In that moment of panic, she felt the wind blowing through her hair. Her long hair that was unburdened by her hat. Her muscle-memory infused hat, that was hanging next to her door, inside her cabin.

Abby and the fish-man locked eyes for a split second, then both looked down at the blade hovering just inches from his chest. With a snarl, he slapped the sword right out of her hand as he stepped closer. His hand immediately swung back the other way, backhanding her so hard that she saw stars as she fell backward.

In mid-air, as Abby fell backward, she reached for her sidearm. She didn't get a good grip, but she did cock back the hammer. Her body hit the deck with a thud, knocking the wind out of her. Abby cried out in pain. Both from the brain rattling force of the backhand, and from landing hard on the deck.

Abby opened her eyes but saw only a haze of tears. She heard the fish-man laughing in a strange hissing gurgling way. Abby shook her head, trying to clear it. She blinked rapidly to clear her vision. She heard the fish-man moving closer.

Blinking again, Abby saw the fish-man standing above her with a large knife. He raised the blade over his head and grinned.

Abby slapped her hand on her sidearm and pulled the trigger.

The weapon fired the torpedo-like bullet between the fish-man's legs. It ricocheted off the deck, off her cabin, then shot up into the sky. Ugly pre-zombie fish-man stopped to look down at his legs as the missile shot between them.

They both heard it ignite and go screaming up into the air behind him. The fish-man leaned his head back and laughed, then he looked down at her with a cruel gaze. He snarled as he dropped down, the knife plunging toward her chest.

The missile did a quick loop and screamed back down, detonating above and behind the fish-man's head. The powerful explosion splattered Abby and the deck all around her with gooey, drippy, fish-man smoothie.

Norgren and Sasha burst out of the stairwell. Abby turned her head and opened one eye. She saw Norgren in boxer shorts and his old semi-grimy white T-shirt, with a hammer in one hand and a small blowtorch in the other.

She noticed that Sasha's blue pajamas had hundreds of little clown fish all over them. He had a frying pan. Both men were snarling like little bear cubs, waving their weapons menacingly.

Abby wiped fish-man goo from her eyes and face and glared at them. Norgren spotted her in the mess and ran over,

"Captain! Are you ok?"

Abby sat up and shook her head,

"No, not really. Apparently, without my hat, I kind of suck at using that sword."

Abby pointed off to the side. Norgren and Sasha looked and saw her sword lying twenty feet away. Norgren grimaced and scratched his beard,

"Well, maybe that's something we can work on, Captain. We'll um, find you a tutor."

Abby cocked her head, her white eyes surrounded by sushi shrapnel. Fish-man bits fell off her ear. She gave Norgren a stern look he couldn't quite read. Her eyes were fiercely undefinable. She flung her hands out to each side, slinging goo,

"Great! That's great! Maybe I can come back in time and try fighting this guy over again!"

Norgren grabbed Abby's hand and helped her to her feet,

"Sorry, Captain."

Abby took a deep breath and shook her head,

"No, you didn't do anything. I'm just covered in that thing's insides and I'm not really happy about it."

Sasha stepped up and started dabbing at her face with a small cloth. Abby stepped away, shaking her head,

"OH NO! You two get to clean that up!"

She pointed to the giant circle of blood and guts and other parts. It looked like someone made a horror movie version of a snow angel in the gore on the deck. She stalked toward her cabin,

"Hop to it, blowtorch and frying pan! Do we not have an armory or something?"

In the distance, they suddenly heard screaming coming from the island. All three of them froze and looked toward the island,

Oh no.

Abby felt a sudden sickening knot of fear in her gut,

"Priestess Lailani."

They heard gunfire coming from the island.

Abby looked back at the splattered fish-man, then she looked up into the sky. She suddenly realized why the fish-man looked like a zombie,

I have to get this off of me as fast as possible!

She turned and sprinted toward the starboard railing,

"NORGREN! GET US IN THE AIR! SASHA, LADDER!"

Abby jumped over the railing and splashed into the ocean. As she floated back up to the surface, she rubbed her face, arms, and body to get the fish man goo off of her.

She swam back toward the ship as the rope ladder came unrolling down the side. She heard the thrumming of the antigravity drives spinning up.

Climbing up the rope ladder, she saw Sasha waiting for

her. He had her sword. Abby took the sword and sheathed it. She checked her sidearm and headed toward her cabin. Norgren called down from the quarterdeck,

"What's the plan?"

Abby was furious,

"Start toward the beach and unpack your girlfriend."

Abby went into her cabin, dropped the weapon belt on the desk, and sighed loudly,

I'm just not meant to sleep.

She pulled on her boots and then the thick leather vest. She heard the cargo hold doors opening as she tied the weapon belt back on and tucked the journal in her belt.

Stopping briefly at her door, she grabbed her hat and pulled it snugly onto her head before heading back out.

Once out on deck, she climbed the stairs up to the quarterdeck. She glanced over and saw that the cargo doors were fully open, the gun turret was cranking its way up to the deck.

Abby relieved Norgren from the wheel. Norgren grinned and pointed at the guns. Abby nodded. She pushed the power levers up to twenty five percent and pulled back on the wheel, climbing higher. Abby looked around, where was Sasha? She squeezed her earring,

"Sasha, where are you?"

He sounded like he was breathing heavy from running,

"Just throwing on something more appropriate for battle than my pajamas, Captain!"

Abby chuckled and veered the ship off to the right, so she could bank back to the left to look down on the beach and the forest. Further down the beach from where they held the feast, Abby saw straw huts in the hundreds.

She saw larger structures in the forest, and a large separate compound that had a fence and a large wooden temple-like building. That had to be it. She pointed the ship in that direction.

Closing in on the temple, Abby saw a commotion amongst the huts. There were people fighting between some of the huts, close to the ocean. She heard and saw gunfire. She turned the ship, banking that direction,

This attack doesn't make any sense. How do they plan to get away?

Abby heard Norgren call out from the turret,

"Locked and loaded, Captain!"

Abby checked the scanner. She saw the Syndicate's escape plan. Six small fast boats were making a suicide rush for the beach. They must be thinking that once they had the priestess, the leviathan's wouldn't dare try to stop them from getting away. The boats were still pretty far out.

She looked down as she passed over the huts. There were a lot of bodies. The Rider's turret-mounted cannons and her

sidearm would both kill more islanders than bad guys.

The locals were just going to have to do their best to stop them. The Rider was just air support this time. There was no way to avoid it.

Abby pointed The Rider at the nearest inbound craft and pushed the levers to ninety percent forward power. Hurricane force winds slammed them hard from behind. The Rider was thrown forward out over the ocean.

She heard Sasha grunt in pain and then heard him tumble back down the stairs as the acceleration eased up. Sasha ran up the stairs, acting like nothing happened. He stepped up next to her and nodded crisply,

"Captain."

Abby glanced over. He had on black breeches, a white dress shirt, and a fancy black silk vest. She grinned, then nodded back,

"Looking good, steward."

They were approaching the first of the fast boats. Abby called out to Norgren, shouting loud enough for him to hear over the hurricane winds,

"GUNS, STARBOARD, FORWARD!"

She saw Norgren turn the turret to a point halfway between straight ahead and starboard. She banked left away from the fast boat, then banked right into a turn, pointing Norgren and his turret down towards the enemy. Abby eased

the power levers down to thirty percent, to give Norgren an easier time aiming.

She looked down and saw what looked like a cocaine smuggler's boat from the Florida coast. It was low in the water with a long thin profile. It was painted flat black and had two large propeller engines throwing up a huge rooster tail in its wake.

Abby shouted,

"FIRE AT WILL!"

Norgren shouted back,

"WHAT? WHO'S WILL?"

Abby shouted again,

"FIRE, FIRE, FIRE!"

The quad barrels of the anti-aircraft cannon roared to life. Abby held the ship's course steady, letting Norgren adjust his aim using the impacts of the shells on the surface of the water.

After a few seconds, he brought the stream of cannon fire across the boat and completely destroyed it. He stopped firing. There was nothing left but scattered burning debris.

Abby checked the scanner. The leviathans must have gotten two of the others. Only three remained. She banked The Rider toward the next fast mover and then leveled out and pushed the power levers back to ninety percent.

They closed on the next boat in just a couple of minutes. Abby shouted down to Norgren as she banked right, turning The Rider in closer to the island,

"GUNS, PORT, FORWARD!"

Norgren shifted the cannon turret to the other side of the ship, she banked hard left bringing Norgrens gun into close alignment. Abby heard the roar of the cannons and saw the fire blazing from the barrels before she even had a chance to tell him to fire.

Captain Watcher raised an eyebrow and looked down at Norgren fiercely.

She turned back toward the island and checked the scanner. The last two boats were getting closer. She set an intercept course that would put her in between them and the island and punched the levers forward to just shy of max power.

Abby glanced back at the rear of the ship briefly,

Good to know, the afterburners only engage at max power.

As the boats closed in on the beach, they also got closer together. Abby turned into a left bank and opened her mouth to shout the order. Again, Norgren fired before she got the words out of her mouth.

Captain Watcher growled with irritation. She cut thrust and let The Rider coast as Norgren strafed the guns across the last two boats, completely destroying them in just seconds.

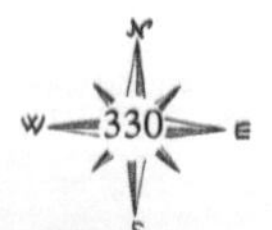

Captain Watcher banked right, shouting at Norgren,

"GUNS, STARBOARD, AND HOLD!"

The turret spun toward starboard as she banked toward the beach. They saw two men and a child down on the sand. As she brought The Rider in lower and closer, circling around them, she saw that one of the men had a short rifle and the other had the young priestess.

They were both fish-men. The young priestess was in a light sleeping gown.

Captain Watcher cut thrust to full stop once they had circled all the way back around and were over water again.

Both fish-men were still staring at the smoking wreckage of their only chance of escape. Most of the village was crowding up about a hundred feet away. They had torches and sticks and rocks and hatred in their eyes.

Captain Watcher walked over and put one foot up on the rail and shouted down at them,

"SURRENDER OR SUFFER!"

Sasha followed her to the rail,

"Don't you mean, or die, Captain?"

Abby shook her head, no,

"They're already dead Sasha, from radiation. They came in by air, high up, out of range of the leviathans."

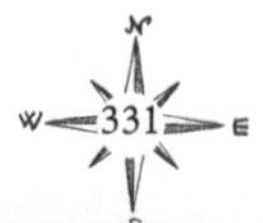

The two fish-men looked at each other. The first one threw down his rifle. The other released the priestess. She ran back toward the rest of the villagers. Abby walked back to the controls as the villagers descended on the two, soon to be dead, fish-men.

Abby took The Rider back out away from the beach to slightly deeper water. She set her down and dropped anchor.

Once they were anchored and Norgren's girlfriend was stored back below deck, Captain Watcher walked down and met with her crew. She had unfinished business.

Sasha and Norgren were both smiling. Captain Watcher wasn't. She looked at them with a serious expression and stared fiercely until their smiles faded. Sasha started to say something, but she held up a hand and he stopped.

Captain Watcher looked from one man to the other, her voice cold,

"Just who's running this show, eh?"

She pointed at Sasha, her voice getting louder,

"Is it you?"

She pointed at Norgren, and shouted angrily,

"Or is it you? You think you're in command here?!?"

Abby reached up and jerked the hat off her head. She tossed it in the direction of her cabin door. When she looked back, both men were staring at her nervously with wide eyes.

Abby closed her eyes and shook her head,

"I'm sorry. Autonomic Motor Neurogenesis seems to have some side effects."

She walked closer to them, and spoke calmly,

"She's not wrong though. This is uncomfortable, but necessary. Normally, I would do this in private. But, in this case I think it's best in the long run, that you both hear me now."

Both of them stared at her, waiting. Abby looked at Sasha,

"Sasha, if I tell you... No, that's not the right word. If I order you to act, and that action results in harm to one of us or damage to the ship. Who is at fault?"

Sasha raised an eyebrow and thought about it,

"Did I do something wrong, Captain?"

Abby shook her head,

"No, you didn't. Humor me please, just answer the question."

Sasha looked down at the deck,

"If I screw something up, it's my own fault, Captain."

She grabbed his upper arm, gently,

"Wrong, Sasha! Wrong..."

She looked them both in the eyes, for emphasis. First Norgren, then she turned back to Sasha,

"The fault would be mine. I was the one who ordered you to do it."

Both of them gave her an odd look, uncertain and confused. She let go of Sasha's arm and turned to Norgren,

"The last three boats you destroyed, you did so of your own accord. That can't ever happen again."

Norgren's face showed that he understood now. He looked guilty, like she caught him with his hand in the cookie jar. To his credit, he thought about his response before speaking and didn't try to excuse his actions. He understood and accepted, nodding,

"It won't happen again, Captain."

Abby nodded, but she wanted to make sure they understood,

"The decision to take a life, can never be easy or first. If killing becomes easy, or our first response, we've become the bad guys. Now, if one of you needs to kill to defend yourself, don't wait for me!"

Abby pointed at the deck,

"But here, onboard The Rider and working as a crew, you don't pull the trigger until I give the order. The consequences of any action that I order, will and should fall solely on me, as Captain."

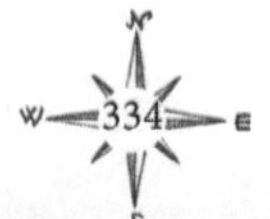

Norgren nodded and gave her a smile,

"Understood, Captain."

Sasha held up both hands, a tear in his eye, his voice high-pitched,

"Wait! He screwed up? Why am I getting THE TALK?"

Abby shook her head and closed her eyes. Norgren laughed and headed to the forward stairwell, he called back to Abby,

"I found something below that you're going to want, Captain. I'll be right back."

Abby opened her eyes and looked at Sasha. He was staring at her like she had deliberately offended him. She looked him in the eyes and concentrated. She tried to listen. She heard his voice in her mind,

WELL? Is she going to apologize or what?

Abby laughed loudly. She laughed so hard she had to bend forward and put her hands on her thighs. Sasha made a frustrated exhaling huffing type of noise and turned to walk away,

"Well, I never! The nerve!"

Abby laughed even harder. She heard Sasha talking to himself as he headed toward the stairwell,

"I work and I work, and what do I get? I get yelled at

because of that trigger happy grease monkey!"

Unexpected Gift

The Imperial Battleship, The Archon, spent two years of real time making the ninety-one jumps required to reach their destination. Each jump through time required the crew to wait five to six days for the behemoth battleship-sized time portal generator to recharge.

Ninety-one full power jumps, to move the enormous mass of The Archon three hundred million years into the past.

The arduous journey was vastly more complex than just jumping backward through time. The Emperor also sent The Archon as far away from the core timeline as it's generator could reach. Skirting the very edges of the interdimensional riptides to the extreme outer limits of dimensional fracturing.

The power required to push The Archon away from the core is the reason she spent two years in transit. The farther back in time, the farther apart dimensional fracturing expanded, making their journey exponentially longer.

~ ~

The first concept taught in the Divine Church of Imperial Trans-Dimensional Physics, is dimensional fracturing. It means that the number of dimensions connected by a single point in

time, increases as one moves through time.

The vast majority of freshman scholars, just beginning their holy journey of understanding, were shocked to learn that their assumptions were backwards. Fractures expanded backward into the past. Timelines didn't branch out as time moved forward.

All of the assumptions about free will and human decisions being responsible for branches in time were immediately dispelled. Leading to the primary truths being sought out by the Divine Church. What caused the timeline to fracture? Why did it expand backward through time? And most importantly of all, was it a natural phenomenon or deliberately caused?

~ ~

The Emperor himself, a god in the eyes of his subjects, gave the order to send The Archon on its mission. He also hand selected its commander, Warlord Acolyte Tristenius Barius Voss.

Battleships were special among the vast number of ships in the Imperial fleet. It was common knowledge that the Emperor personally boarded each battleship after its construction. His Divine Person walked the halls to the bridge and touched the chair of the commanding officer with his own hand. He blessed the man who would sit in that chair with his Divine Authority.

~ ~

Tristenius shifted uncomfortably in his chair. Tapping his fingers on the armrest, he watched his three subcommanders impatiently. Arrayed before him, on the slightly lower second tier, they watched their screens dispassionately. Giving Tristenius no indication of how close they were to reaching their destination,

Just one more jump...

After two painfully long years, the commander of The Archon was tired of staring over the back of their heads. The men in front of him sat lower, an obvious but unspoken nuance of all Imperial warship design. The effort to physically turn and lift their heads to look up, was a reminder of one's place as subordinate.

Tristenius looked beyond his sub-commanders. In front of them, on an even lower tier, he looked across the line of twelve junior command officers. They were the men responsible for direct physical control and oversight of the various systems and crew divisions on the battleship. Frustratingly, each one of them were calmly monitoring the various systems and waiting patiently.

Tristenius somehow sensed it. Maybe he subconsciously noticed a tiny indicator on one of the many displays arrayed before him, he didn't know or care. He just knew it was time. He stood from his chair just seconds before the junior officer turned and relayed the update from engineering.

Tristenius took an excited step forward as his subcommander turned to relay the information to him. High Seeker Maximus Volt, subcommander of navigation, opened his

mouth to speak. Tristenius cut him off,

"Engage the jump drive!"

The men of his command crew twitched in surprise at the vehemence and urgency in their commander's order. Several looked at each other briefly in confusion. It passed quickly with smiles and nods of understanding. The commander was just as ready to end their long journey as they were.

With the faintest hint of a smile, Maximus nodded curtly,

"Aye Commander."

Maximus turned back, standing from his seat also. He looked to the junior officer with the same passion as his commander,

"Engage the jump drive!"

Both of the other subcommanders stood, smiling at each other and joining in the excitement growing among the crew of the bridge. Everyone was ready for this moment.

The Archon's sub-light engines roared to life at maximum thrust, pushing the behemoth up to jump speed. The ridiculous amount of power required to open a portal large enough for the battleship, could only be maintained for a few seconds. The ship had to be moving forward at a high enough speed to pass through nearly instantaneously.

The A.I. that handled nanosecond-timed operations triggered the jump the instant the battleship hit jump speed.

The time portal generator surged to life, ripping a hole in the fabric of space directly in front of the ship.

The men of the bridge crew stared through the large forward venturi screen. They watched a stadium-sized ball of lightning appear. The ball of electrical energy instantly expanded into a ring of fire and lightning a quarter-mile wide. The Archon shot through the portal like a 360-billion-ton bullet.

The Archon emerged from the massive ring of electricity and fire to the calm and professional applause of the bridge crew. They just finished their last jump and arrived at their target space-time destination. Tristenius sat back down, letting out a long sigh,

Finally...

Tristenius looked around, thankful for the momentary feeling of accomplishment among his men. He knew it would pass quickly as the enormity of the next phase settled into their minds.

The Archon's mind-numbingly monotonous mission was to determine the plausibility of planetary orbital engineering over millions of years. It involved planting artificial gravity well generators in specific locations around the sun to modify the orbits of the planets over time.

The inane testing process was estimated to take thirty-five years to complete, then another two years to get home.

Warlord Acolyte Tristenius Barius Voss just finished the

first two years of his four decades of punishment. Sitting back in his command seat of Divine Authority, he watched his crew thoughtfully,

That's what this mission is, it's punishment. That fact will quickly become a certainty in the eyes of my crew, if it isn't already.

That's what Tristenius had to look forward to. Four decades of knowing that every single man onboard his ship was laughing at him behind his back. Laughing at him, while hating him, for being assigned to join his mission of penance.

It was punishment not just for losing his last battleship in combat with the Renegade known as Nero, but also for surviving the encounter. At the very least, if he had died in glorious combat, he would have been immortalized in the Imperial histories with his former rank of Divine Warlord.

Maximus nodded at the junior officer and turned to look up at Tristenius with a smile on his face,

"Scanners indicate we have arrived at our destination, Warlord."

Tristenius was grateful for the officers on the bridge. They gave him the grace of not adding the 'Acolyte' derogatory to his rank. Sparing him a daily reminder of his demotion. All of them referred to him simply as, Warlord, or Warlord Tristenius.

In hindsight, Tristenius spent the last two years treating his bridge crew with ever growing respect and gratitude for that one small gesture alone. It was humbling. Perhaps the

Emperor, in his divine wisdom, had foreseen this dynamic
playing out.

Tristenius stood and graced Maximus by returning his
smile,

"Most welcome news, Maximus. Pass the word to
the entire crew. Tonight, we indulge in a decadent feast to
celebrate the end of the long journey and the beginning of our
even longer toil."

Maximus nodded,

"Aye Commander."

Turning back to his station, Maximus touched the screen
icon for ship-wide broadcast. He conveyed the proclamation
of celebration to the rest of the ship, again drawing a subdued
celebratory applause from the men of the bridge.

Tristenius sighed with acceptance. It was time to get
started. They would start by deploying reconnaissance drones
to build a map of the system, accurate down to the nanometer.
He opened his mouth to give the order to launch the drones,
but he was interrupted by his subcommander over combat and
emergency operations.

Warlord Novice Gaius Pain, at center station directly in
front of Tristenius, was his second in command. Gaius sounded
surprised, but calm and professional,

"Warlord Tristenius, my punisher is reporting a TL-18
emergency beacon in system. Its backup power appears to be
failing, no detectable transmission. It is just now, this very

moment, beginning to fall into the Earth's gravity well."

Tristenius's brow furrowed in surprise and confusion,

Tech level 18 is Imperial technology! That's one of our beacons! It makes no sense. This fragment was chosen for the very reason that nothing will ever develop here...

In this timeline, by random chance, the Earth was directly in the destructive path of a pulsar that periodically sterilized the entire system. It was no danger to the Archon with her shields, but it made this timeline perfect for their research. There was no reason for the missile to be here.

Tristenius sat back down and issued orders,

"Launch drones immediately to recover that beacon! I want its memory. Warlord Pain, do we have time before it falls?"

Gaius conversed briefly with the junior officer, then looked back at Tristenius,

"It will be close Warlord. I can have the punisher direct beam hack the beacons memory."

Tristenius nodded,

"Do it."

The commander looked off to the side for a moment, his mind racing,

The odds of us jumping into this lifeless fragment and finding that

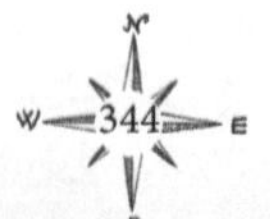

beacon are astronomical. The added variable of discovering it in the final moments before it burned up in the Earths atmosphere make it incalculable. Random chance is simply impossible. Somehow, the Emperor knew! The Emperor sent us here under the guise of a pointless mission of punishment, knowing we would find the beacon. There is no other possibility, this must be the real reason for our mission!

Warlord Pain turned toward him, obviously excited but maintaining a calm voice,

"Hack successful, Warlord. Beacon data downloaded."

Tristenius stood and called out to The Archon's A.I. operating system,

"Serenity, what are we looking at?"

The Archon's artificial intelligence operating system had the same sweet feminine voice that all Imperial ships employed. Serenity said,

"Repeating last recorded ship-wide broadcast from the Imperial cruiser, The Cronos, under the command of High Seeker Yano Vain."

The A.I.'s voice from The Cronos sounded identical to Serenity,

"Emergency Alert. Renegade Watcher detected. Launching emergency disaster beacon."

Serenity continued,

"Beacon data indicates that facial recognition of the

former Watcher Darius Moen triggered the alert and the emergency launch of the beacon. Two seconds after launch, the missile's flight path was interrupted. It appeared here, in this fragment, and settled into stable orbit around the Earth as programmed."

Tristenius gripped the armrests of his chair. Darius Moen, the Renegade, Nero. The one who single-handedly destroyed his last ship. Nero sent the beacon here to hide it from discovery. Tristenius felt his heart racing. His mind was spinning. Somehow, through his divine wisdom, the Emperor was giving him a chance at redemption.

Tristenius said,

"Serenity, tell me we salvaged its point of origin navigational data."

Serenity said,

"We have precise navigational data Warlord Tristenius. Missile originated from the core timeline, twelve millennia pre-bottleneck, just before the very beginnings of the Machine Wars."

Tristenius leaned forward, resting his chin on his fist. This was unexpected. This was extremely dangerous. The core timeline meant the actual builder line, his ancestors. It was the only timeline that went on into the future beyond the bottleneck. One day leading to the culture that would become known as the builders who would invent time travel and one day become the empire he served.

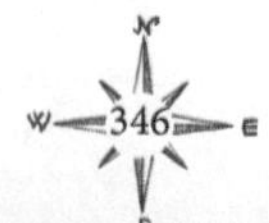

Any mistake impacting the builder line would be catastrophic.

No one knew why dimensional fracturing went backwards from the bottleneck, spreading out into history. But there was a rumored theory among high-ranking Imperial commanders. That something in the bottleneck prevented the fracturing from spreading forward into the future and ripping apart all of time.

Tristenius looked up at his bridge crew. Every single eye was on him. Every face as serious as the grave. Tristenius stood and met their gaze,

"Broadcast ship wide."

He took a deep breath before continuing,

"Fellow warriors of the empire, we have a rare chance at redemption and glory. The Emperor, in his divine wisdom, sent us to this remote fracture, millions of years in the past under the guise of a pointless mission. Against all probability, we found a lost imperial beacon, containing the exact temporal coordinates that will lead us to the Renegade Watcher known as Nero."

Tristenius paused to let the gravity of his words sink in,

"There is no doubt that this is our true mission. Two years to travel, two years to plan to be there when Nero arrives. We are going to surprise Nero and take him into custody. We are going to drag him home to face justice for his crimes. That is all for now."

Tristenius walked around behind his command chair and gestured for Warlord Pain and High Seeker Maximus to join him. Once his second and third in command approached, Tristenius spoke in a low tone,

"The two of you will join me in the chapel of tactics and planning. Task two security teams to bring the prisoners up from the vault of penance."

Gaius nodded, unphased. Maximus's eyes widened just slightly, but he gave no other indication of his feelings. Tristenius continued,

"It can't be coincidence that we were set upon by their ship, The Waylayer. It can't be coincidence that we were able to pull two survivors, a mage, and a telepath, from all that wreckage at a time when we are going to need both."

Tristenius put a hand on each man's shoulder and added,

"I know in my heart that all of this is being divinely orchestrated by the Emperor. Warlord Pain, you have interrogated our prisoners, yes? What have you learned?"

Gaius Pain made a sour expression,

"I have not learned as much as I would like, for the amount of effort invested, Warlord. From the albino human telepath, we've got nothing. Not a single word. The dark-skinned mage, however, she has been slightly more cooperative. She calls herself Vierna, she's a rare subterranean aberration of the race of elves. All of them are filthy abominations."

Pain made a disgusted face and continued,

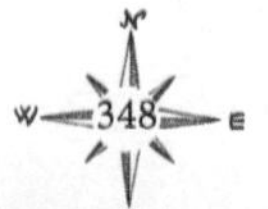

"Anyway, this Vierna creature eventually responded to our vigorous and repeated application of the Lashes of Wisdom upon her flesh. From her, we learned the albino telepath was the captain of The Waylayer. Answers to the name, Snow. She is the one we really need to crack, if we want to learn anything about how they found us along our journey."

Tristenius nodded gravely, looking off toward the forward Venturi screen,

"Perhaps helping us capture the Renegade and earning their unconditional freedom and release from custody will be more appealing than spending the rest of their miserable existence in a vault of penance."

Tristenius extended the two men the ultimate gesture of respect from a superior. He addressed them by their full titles and all of their names,

"Warlord Novice Gaius Pain, High Seeker Maximus Volt, see to the arrangements. I will meet you in the chapel. Thank you, warriors, may the Emperor's light shine upon you."

Both men bowed deeply in gratitude. When they rose, their faces were beaming with pride and purpose.

Once they left the bridge, Tristenius approached his remaining subcommander. High Seeker Cornelius Zion. With the immediate turn around and abandonment of the mission, Cornelius was likely feeling useless, his science background no longer needed.

Tristenius put a hand on his shoulder and leaned close,

"Cornelius, I have great need of you. On our journey, back to the future, I will need Pain and Volt attending to other things."

The High Seeker looked up at his commander,

"Warlord, I am ready to serve."

Tristenius nodded,

"I will need you to take the majority of the responsibility of getting us to where we need to be. For the bulk of the journey home, the bridge will be yours to command."

Cornelius smiled and nodded,

"I am honored, Warlord. I will not fail you."

Tristenius stood up, satisfied. Now the man had purpose. Tristenius made his way to the chapel of tactics and planning along a meandering route through the ship.

He looked into the eyes of the men onboard, weighing them, gauging their minds and feelings. He saw something new. He saw morale. He saw new life, new purpose. Finding the beacon changed everything.

Warlord Tristenius made his way to the chapel. He would confront the pirates who attacked his ship and recruit them to his cause. He was going to catch Nero. Then he was going to find out what prize had been so great as to draw Nero from hiding and make him risk traveling to the core timeline.

The Mission

Abby stood on the quarterdeck watching the scanner, when Norgren came back up from below. He walked up with a smile on his face, holding a long narrow case. Abby looked at him and raised an eyebrow. He opened the case and showed her the contents.

Smiling broadly, she reached in and took out the telescope. After looking at it for a few moments, she looked up at him,

"Thank you, Norgren. I love it."

He bobbed his head happily, grinning,

"Knew you would, Captain."

He turned away to head back down and looked back at her,

"We going to try to turn in, again? Salvage some of this night?"

Abby nodded,

"We are, with one minor adjustment. I'll take first watch."

Norgren laughed and held out a thumbs up as he walked away. Abby checked the scanner again. It was set to long range. Still nothing,

Syndicate fliers aren't sneaking up on me again. Be foolish to try it twice.

She looked toward the beach and saw some fires near the huts. Abby raised the telescope and looked toward the fires. She saw islanders standing around the fires holding their hands towards the sky.

Abby put down the telescope and whispered solemnly,

"I'm so sorry."

She knew what they were doing. The islanders lost a lot of family and friends, and they were mourning their loss. Abby looked at the scanner again and did a double take. She saw a small signature of a craft very close. She shifted to short range and realized it was something coming toward her from the island.

Abby switched the scanner back to long range, then stepped over to the rail and used her new telescope. It took her a minute to find it. It was one of their low dual canoe-based boats, with a platform on it. The sail was tied up, and the boat was being pushed by two men with long poles. She saw the old bald man sitting in the center.

She shook her head and wondered,

For the love of GOD! Now what?!?

It took them about ten minutes to get out to her. Abby waited by the railing, watching them approach. When they pulled alongside, the old man stood up and braced himself against the narrow mast. He called up to her,

"It is good that I caught you awake, Captain Abigail. I bring a message from our high priestess. If I may?"

Abby nodded,

"Yes, please."

"The high priestess Lailani has formally requested that you join her in the mountain temple at dawn."

Abby closed her eyes and made the faintest whimper. She opened her eyes and looked down at him,

"At dawn? Like a few hours from now? Can't wait."

Shaking her head,

That's why most of this world's dead. It's not the radiation, nobody gets any sleep here.

The old man waved goodbye and had the men with him return him to shore. Abby leaned her head back and groaned. She was so tired that she could barely keep her eyes open. She walked back up the stairs to the quarterdeck to check the scanner.

There was a steaming cappuccino waiting for her on the console. She looked around, but Sasha was nowhere to be seen,

How did he do that?

Abby picked up her pirate flag decorated cup and sipped the hot sweet coffee with its milky foamy sweet topping. She purred happily in appreciation and smiled,

An extra ration of rum for the steward.

About an hour later, Norgren came back up from below deck. He walked toward the quarterdeck and saw Abby by the scanner. She was leaning forward with her elbows on the console, propping her eyes open with her fingertips. Norgren chuckled and walked a little louder. By the time he got to the top of the stairs, she was standing upright blinking a little more than normal.

As soon as Norgren stepped away from the stairs, Abby went down them,

"No time for chit chat. I have to meet with that heartless tyrannical brat Lailani at dawn. Night Norgren."

Norgren just laughed and checked the scanner before checking other systems, making notes, writing down ideas for changes and modifications. He pulled the access cover to the console's inner workings and tested some connections and tweaked some settings.

Abby didn't bother with anything else. She dropped the journal and the weapon belt on her desk and plopped down on the bed, lowering the hat over her eyes. She was out like a light.

It felt like the second she closed her eyes. Sasha was suddenly calling her name from over by her desk. She groaned at him from under her hat,

"Noooooooo..."

She heard him chuckle,

"Combat shower, Captain. You can stand up and take it, or you can wear it."

Abby pushed her hat up and glared at him. Sasha stood by her desk, holding up her pirate cup. He grinned at her over the steam rising from her cappuccino. Abby narrowed her eyes at him,

"One of these days, that cup's not going to save you."

Sasha laughed and set the cup down. He headed for the door,

"But who would do your laundry?"

Abby threw her hat at the door as Sasha went out of it. She dropped the thick heavy leather vest on her bed and staggered over to her desk. Her body felt slow and heavy with exhaustion.

She stared at the bowl of water for a moment,

Lailani, you little brat. I saved your ungrateful hide out there.

Abby leaned forward and plunged her whole face into the freezing liquid. After a few seconds she stood up straight, eyes wide from shock, shaking her head,

"My god that's COLD!"

Her eyes were open now, but she splashed a few more handfuls of freezing water on her face and rubbed her cheeks for good measure. Abby stood there staring at the washcloth on the side of the bowl, trying to remember the last time she had an actual shower.

After a moment, she laughed and just shook her head before getting her gear on.

Norgren and Sasha were up on the quarterdeck, watching the islander boat approaching from the beach. Abby trudged heavily up the stairs and looked at them expectantly,

"Times up gentlemen. What are we asking Dawn?"

Norgren turned toward her,

"Tech is only as good as the operator's understanding. I've got my hands full learning everything involved with all the notes and walkthroughs left by my older self about The Rider. I recommend you ask her how that personal time portal generator around your neck works, before one day you accidentally just vanish, and we never see you again."

Abby nodded,

"That's good. I hadn't thought of that. Sasha?"

Sasha put his hands flat together and touched his lips to his fingertips. He gave her a very serious look. Finally, he held out both hands toward her,

"Ok, Captain. I have given this a lot of thought. I think the absolute most important thing to find out right now is whether or not my older self survived the ocean and made it to…"

Abby cut him off before he could finish,

"BOO… LAME!"

Norgren looked at Sasha like he was crazy,

"DUDE! How's the little mind reader woman supposed to know that?"

Sasha gave them both a hurt puppy type of glare. He looked like he was going to start crying. Sniffing and blinking, he squeaked out in his high-pitched voice,

"What if I'm not ok?"

Abby checked the scanner, shaking her head. Still nothing, even at long range. Turning toward Sasha, she saw him put his face in his hands and start sobbing gently. She put her hand on his shoulder,

"Listen. If I can't think of anything else, I'll think about asking her what she knows about your older self."

Sasha mumbled out, from behind his hands,

"Thank you, Captain."

Norgren looked at her and raised an eyebrow questioningly. Abby looked back at Norgren with wide eyes

and vehemently shook her head, NO. Norgren grinned and nodded. Abby walked over to the starboard stair and called back to Norgren,

"Eyes on the scanner until I return. If you see anything at all, you get her in the air and come get me."

She stopped with her foot on the first step and furrowed her brow and thought about it for a second. Abby turned back and looked at Norgren,

"On that note. While I'm gone, I need you to come up with a way we can pick up and drop off while The Rider is airborne. In case we're in a situation where we can't park The Rider in water at that moment."

Norgren nodded,

"The Rider's previous engineer, an obvious genius and extremely handsome man, already made one Captain. I'll show you when you get back. Good luck."

Abby gave him a thumbs up, then headed down the stairs to meet the islander boat.

On the way to the shore, she couldn't help but notice that the men pushing the poles and taking the boat to shore were both dancers from the stage performance. Both were big and tall and covered in muscles. They kept smiling at her and giving her weird looks every time she looked back at them.

Abby just laughed,

Nice try, Lailani.

Once they arrived at the beach, there were two more
of the big hulking dancers. All four of them carried torches to
guide her along the path to the lake and the cave that led into
the mountain. Abby crossed the lake and looked back.

Her four escorts sat down and planted their torches into
the sand. They placed their hands on their knees and watched
with reverent and dispassionate faces. Abby took off her crystal
bracelet and held it on her open palm,

Guide me in.

With the glowing air-swimming manta leading the way,
Abby followed it into the magma chamber. Waiting for her,
was the young priestess. There were only two square rugs in
front of the small empty wooden throne this time. Abby took a
seat on the unoccupied carpet and waited.

Before she took three seated breaths, a green light
preceded Dawn into the room. She had a new green manta ray.
Dawn took her place on the small wooden throne and smiled at
Abby. Above them, their green and blue glowing mantas circled
each other near the ceiling. It gave the room a strange rotating
sensation.

The young high priestess bowed her head to the floor.
Dawn looked from her to Abby and spoke out loud. Dawn had a
surprisingly sweet soft voice,

"Have you brought questions for me?"

Abby touched her necklace with the eight-sided crystal,

"How does this work? No, wait! I mean, how do I make

this work, or avoid accidently making it work?"

Dawn laughed,

"Sweet girl, I'm not an evil genie. If you wish for ultimate wealth, I won't drop ten tons of gold on your head and crush you to death. I'll consider it one question. For starters, the individual field generator is the most advanced device the builder race created, right before their end."

Dawn connected to Abby's mind telepathically, creating an image in Abby's mind as she continued,

"How it works is simple. The instant that it activates, it creates a twenty-foot diameter nullification sphere around the user and anyone else in range, centered on the generator."

Abby saw a small floating image in between her and Dawn, like a hologram. In the image, she saw a tiny figure standing in an open plain. The tiny featureless figure waved at her. Abby laughed.

Suddenly, a globe of energy appeared over the figure. The energy field looked about twenty feet wide, with the lower part extending about four or five feet into the ground,

"It also creates a point-to-point interdimensional link to an identical sphere at the target location and time."

The image extended off to the side. Abby saw another sphere of energy farther away, next to a short fence,

"All at once, in a single instantaneous moment, it swaps one sphere and everything in it with the other sphere.

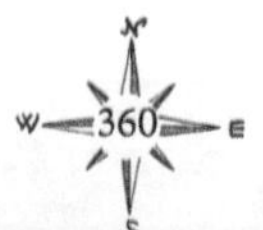

Transporting the traveler to the target location and moving anything in the target location back to where the user came from."

In the image, Abby saw the little figure appear in the sphere by the fence and a section of fence appeared where he was standing in the beginning. Both energy fields disappeared, then the image disappeared entirely. Dawn smiled, asking,

"Simple enough?"

Abby nodded,

"It basically swaps where you are, for where you're going?"

Dawn nodded, then looked down at Leilani who was still bowing forward with her face near the floor. Dawn spoke in the beautifully strange islander tongue. The very young girl sat up, got comfortable, and smiled gratefully. Dawn looked back at Abby and continued,

"As for how you make it work, that is also simple, technically. You will it, to activate. If you want it to work, and you try to make it to work, it will. The bad news? Imperial operatives go through years and years of training, learning how to control the time portal generators."

The mental hologram image reappeared. Abby saw a forest. Dawn continued,

"A first-time user, with no training, is more likely to end up looking at a dinosaur or being eaten by one, than actually going where they want to go."

In the forest, Abby saw the little figure appear in a fleeting sphere of light. The figure stood there looking around, before a Tyrannosaurus Rex came out of the trees and ate him. Again, Abby laughed as the image disappeared. Dawn smiled and continued,

"Learning how to control one takes a lot of time and training. Or it takes a lot of very dangerous practice. So, I'd be very careful, or very desperate, before you use that one you have."

Abby nodded gravely,

"I'd lose my ship. I'd lose my crew. Spend years learning how to try to find them again."

Dawn nodded, yes. Abby asked,

"Why are you here? You said it's been a thousand years since you spoke to someone who wasn't one of your priestess's. I'm guessing you haven't even left this mountain. You have the means to escape this world."

Abby pointed at her necklace,

"So, why are you here?"

Dawn narrowed her eyes just slightly,

"If I were an evil genie, I'd count that as two. You asked it twice."

Abby gave her a raised eyebrow. Dawn smiled,

"I can't leave. When I jumped into the bottleneck, I was very careful. I kept myself hidden while I searched for the mysterious arrivals in the core timeline. When I finally found them, I tried to infiltrate their secretive society. They lived hidden away from the rest of the world, in a nearly inaccessible chasm in a very dangerous forest.

Dawn spread her hands helplessly,

"Long story short, they knew immediately that I wasn't one of them, they knew everything. Who I was, where I came from, everything. They did several things to my mind, I'm not entirely sure what because they also messed with my memory."

The muscular little woman tapped the side of her head,

"As a group, they overpowered me easily. After they messed with my mind, they forced me, telepathically, to use my generator one last time. So, I ended up here and because of whatever they did, my field generator is lost to me. I can't use it anymore. I have tried a thousand times."

Abby listened carefully to every word. For several minutes, she sat there and thought about everything Dawn said. Abby shook her head slowly,

"I have one question left. But now I'm torn. You said, the individual field generator is the most advanced device the builder race created, right before their end. What end? What happened to them and why? But I also want to know about the bottleneck. What is it, when is it? How do I get there? Why is it so important? Will I find my father there? What can you tell me about it? I only have one question left, but now I have ten

times as many questions."

Dawn looked at the young priestess and smiled at her. Lailani suddenly laid down on her carpet and immediately fell asleep. Dawn looked back toward Abby,

"Can't risk her hearing what we're thinking. Captain Abigail Watcher let's recap two small points. One, I can't leave this world. Two, I've been trapped here for thousands of years."

Dawn leaned forward and looked deeply into Abby's eyes,

"So, hypothetically, let's say the Captain of the time travelling ship, The Riptide Rider, just happened to meet someone trapped on a dying world. I wonder, just what could that captain offer, in exchange for all the answers to all of her questions."

Abby smiled slyly,

"That's why you answered my first two questions so thoroughly. In fact, that's why you offered me three questions in the first place. You gave me enough general information to make me want a lot more specific information, didn't you?"

Dawn smiled,

"You're very sharp for a young woman your age. Did you know that?"

Abby reached down and idly ran her thumb across the key to the jump drive as she stared into Dawn's eyes, considering...

Warlock, Nero, and Alvarez.

The crew of the returning reconnaissance frigate appeared to be brainwashed or drugged. Insisting to port authorities that they were all just flower petals floating in the fishbowl Zen-garden of an invisible giant alien. This was both highly disturbing and completely unprecedented.

The supervisor over this area of the port, Scion Ptolemy Craw, instructed his men to do their best to contain the situation while he went for help.

Unfortunately, Ptolemy only had five men working the dock and all security and containment doors just went on the fritz. Everything unlocked and opened moments after the frigate was securely docked.

A dozen members of the twenty-man frigate crew were already running around the dock area leaping and dancing and wandering away from the facility. They couldn't be allowed to get past the stone castle walls surrounding the port compound.

The distraught dock supervisor tried to call for help, but the entire communication system suddenly went down. It was like gremlins had suddenly infested all of their systems.

Ptolemy ran across the castle courtyard toward the

port overseer's office in the main building. He needed help. He needed more men. He ran up the stone stairwell franticly, wide-eyed with panic. Nothing like this had ever happened before.

~ ~

It wasn't an ordinary military frigate that unexpectedly showed up at his docks with a mentally unstable crew. This was a clandestine reconnaissance vessel, a spy boat, an assassin transport. These men were Naval intelligence, covert operators.

The Imperial Navy Frigate, The Woodsman, jumped itself back to the core and docked at its home port on autopilot, navigating under emergency computer control.

The port authorities, Ptolemy's men, tried to question the first few crew members to wander off the frigate. The idiots wouldn't stop laughing. They believed everything around them was just a hallucination or a dream.

~ ~

Ptolemy burst through the thick iron-bound wooden door at the top of the stairwell. At the end of the hall, he saw the overseer's personal guard reflexively drop his hand to his sidearm. The dock supervisor shook his head and ran for the overseer's office. He held out one hand toward the guard, Janus, who Ptolemy knew recognized him,

"Don't shoot!"

~ ~

The overseer of the entire port facility, Warlord Regent

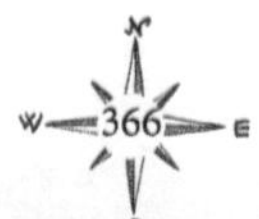

Marius Tiberius Quan already knew that something was very wrong with the crew of the unscheduled frigate. He tossed the non-functioning communicator onto his desk and sat down on the smooth stone sill of his office window.

Looking down, he watched the crew of The Woodsman wandering randomly around the courtyard below. One of Marius's eyebrows rose slightly. He made a soft noise that was half surprise and half amusement.

One of the strangely behaving crewmen down in the courtyard just splashed his way through the large but shallow decorative fountain. Now he was hugging the alabaster female statue in the center like it was his long-lost love.

Marius touched the contact point on the back of his left hand, under the skin. He felt the rapid pulsing and humming vibration in his head, from the mental connection to his bodyguard. The Warlord Regent sent a burst of thoughts,

An unscheduled frigate has docked without clearance or warning.

Something is very wrong with the crew of The Woodsman.

Our communication system just stopped working.

We have high value detainees in lockup awaiting pickup.

Be on high alert.

Marius quickly released the contact point on the back of his hand. The quantum link was very useful and gave him a great sense of security. But the act of linking his human mind to his bodyguard's A.I. neural network was uncomfortable at best.

The overseer reached back to his desk behind him and picked up a small ceramic cup of steaming chino. He casually sipped on the bitter, sweet liquid as he watched the strange antics of the men in the courtyard below.

His office door opened behind him. Marius heard the voice of his personal guard, Valkyrie Janus, try to announce the rapidly approaching supervisor. The same supervisor that Marius just watched running across the courtyard a few minutes before.

"Warlord Regent, the…"

Ptolemy frantically shoved his way past Janus, interrupting him. The supervisor started babbling incoherently about flower petals and invisible giant aliens. He was obviously in full panic over the situation unfolding down at the small highly restricted dock.

The same dock that was restricted to Naval intelligence use only. The very same dock, that Ptolemy was supposed to be down there supervising over.

Marius wasn't in the mood for incoherent babble. He held his right hand out and made a fist. He pulled his fist back in a quick jerking motion. Marius's tungsten-plated bodyguard leapt away from the corner near the door.

The extremely dense Synth-life robot landed in front of Ptolemy, sending a small earthquake of vibration through the thick stone floor. It grabbed the frantic port supervisor under the arms and lifted him off the floor, gently shaking him like a flabby snow globe.

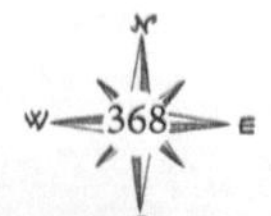

Still standing in the doorway, Valkyrie Janus watched the Warlord's bodyguard curiously. The robot had a bored but pleasant expression on his face, as if it were cordially asking about the weather. Ptolemy's pudgy little feet kicked uselessly below him.

Janus knew that the lifeless bodyguard wouldn't do any real harm to Ptolemy. There was no logical reason that the A.I.-driven Synth would even remotely consider the unarmed and balding dock supervisor any kind of threat.

Janus shook his head at poor Ptolemy and looked over at his boss sitting on the windowsill. Marius nodded at him and made a subtle dismissive gesture. The Valkyrie nodded respectfully and left the room, closing the door behind him.

Marius looked out the window. Several crew members from the Woodsman were on their knees worshipping the alabaster statue in the fountain. He shook his head and looked back at Scion Ptolemy Craw,

"Let him down."

The Synth lowered Ptolemy's feet to the floor. The pudgy supervisor took a deep breath and let it out slowly. He was slightly unsteady on his feet after the turbulent ride in the robot's arms. The lifeless bodyguard stared at him with a creepy pleasant smile as it moved slightly away.

Marius turned back to the window,

"Why are you up here, and not down there?"

Ptolemy swallowed, glanced at the Synth, then turned to

Marius,

"Warlord Regent, Sir, I need more men. The crew of the Woodsman are out of their minds and wandering randomly through the compound. These aren't just drunken sailors. These are incredibly dangerous men, and completely bonkers at the moment. Forgive me, but communications are down. I didn't know what to do, I had to come up."

Marius turned away from the window and nodded,

"You need men, and I need answers..."

Marius gestured at the door,

"Get Janus for me."

Ptolemy opened the door and leaned out. A moment later, Valkyrie Janus stepped inside the office. Marius looked at him and gestured toward Ptolemy,

"The supervisor here needs our help. Gather some of the other Valkyries and assist the port authorities with their manpower shortage. The Emperor's Light be upon you, Janus. Go."

Janus bowed and left immediately. Ptolemy smiled,

"Thank you, Warlord Regent. I'll get back to my duties."

Marius pressed the contact point on the back of his left hand. His Synth bodyguard moved quickly to the door and slammed it closed. Ptolemy, startled, turned to look at the sound, then turned back to the overseer,

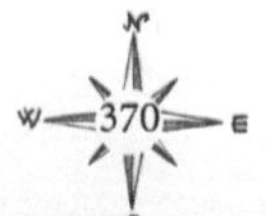

"I don't understand, Warlord..."

Ptolemy felt the Synth grab ahold of him. It had one hand on each side of his head. The overseer's voice came from the lifeless Synth,

"I told you I need information, and I don't have time to play twenty questions."

The emotionless automaton generated a surgical electromagnetic field between its hands. The field created a crude but effective neural connection to the supervisor's memories.

The connection let Marius download everything that Ptolemy saw, heard, or even thought. Everything from the moment the frigate showed up on their scopes, to right now.

- The Imperial Navy Frigate, The Woodsman -

The inspection team completed a comprehensive search of the ship. They cleared out and rounded up the rest of the wandering crew, handing them over to the Valkyries. After the ship was cleared, team leader Harbinger Titus Vino stood watch at the main hatch.

His engineering team were the only ones left onboard. They downloaded the computer archives and finished shutting down the ships systems. The Woodsman was going to be mothballed and towed to the main shipyard for storage. There the ship would wait for an Imperial detachment to do a more thorough investigation by both psychic and mage detectives.

Titus's engineering team passed through the airlock and gave him the thumbs up on their way off the ship. He smiled and nodded, reminding them to drop off the ship's memory data at the holy archives immediately. Titus stood just inside the airlock and called out to the ship's A.I. operating system,

"Cassiopeia?"

The sweet and gentle female voice didn't sound right,

"Harpy, ginger, tie, tie, tie, us. Ruder! On ridge! Urgency!"

Harbinger Titus Vino looked up at the speaker in the airlock curiously and raised an eyebrow. That was extremely odd. A.I.'s didn't have bad days. Perhaps his engineering team had inadvertently caused some kind of unforeseeable problem.

Titus tried one more time,

"Cassiopeia, confirm ship-wide shut down. Dry dock storage protocol, if you please."

The A.I. sounded even worse,

"Bee, nano, damn, AGE, shut, shut, up. No, no, no, no, forage, toto-calls, peas. Ruder! On ridge! Urgency!"

Titus rolled his eyes. If he couldn't get the A.I. to complete the shutdown, he'd have to manually finish the computer procedures. That could take days. Titus locked the outer airlock door and headed for the bridge. Might as well at least try just turning it off and back on again.

A panel in the ceiling lifted slightly then slid to the side, revealing a recessed computer maintenance area above. An odd-looking man dropped down out of the ceiling. He landed on his combat boot covered feet, brushed his hands on his camouflage pants, and grinned broadly,

"We're in, people. Imperial dock, in the core! Gotta immortalize this."

Alvarez pulled a yo-yo-cam from his pocket and tossed it out in front of him, then quickly posed for the picture. The small round camera flew about six feet through the air and snapped a picture of Alvarez. A picture of him standing on the bridge of The Woodsman, in his black tank top, grinning like an idiot under his red mohawk.

The yo-yo-cam suddenly reversed course, as if it hit an invisible wall and bounced back to Alvarez's hand. He tucked it in his pocket as the ships A.I., Cassiopeia, started talking through the bridge speakers,

"Dew, won't, get, get, get, a way!"

Alvarez looked up at the computer's communication processing module in the ceiling. The one he just uploaded a nanite virus into. He winked at the glitchy A.I.,

"We'll see about that, luv."

Alvarez walked over to the navigator's station control panel and knelt down on one knee. He held up his hand and made a fist. A ten-inch silvery spike slid out from between his second and third knuckles. Alvarez punched the spike into the control board and grinned as Cassiopeia protested,

"No, no, peas, no more, nano, dis, rup, rup, rup... mean... man..."

The A.I.'s voice faded to static as Alavarez injected more nanites into her system. He retracted the omni-link, stood up, and raised both fists into the air in victory,

"YEAH, MOTHER... Oh, uh, hi."

Alvarez slowly lowered his hands and smiled sheepishly at Harbinger Titus Vino, who was standing in the entry hatch with his mouth hanging open.

Titus stared at the strange intruder with wide disbelieving eyes. After a few seconds of stunned surprise, Titus

reached for the emergency alarm mounted on the side of the hatchway...

Alvarez mentally shifted cybernetic gears, slamming his body processes into overdrive.

His hardwired combat reflexes triggered a nanotech boost to his neural processes and throughout his entire nervous system. Custom grown bio-ware muscles, tritanium mesh bone wrap, and graphene tendon connections allowed him to move faster than most people could blink.

Alvarez grabbed the support railing on the console that was in between him and the Harbinger. He hopped up as he pulled against the railing, vaulting himself over the console. The force and speed of the movement bent the railing with a time-distorted warbling screeching noise.

Launching himself forward, he bent his knees and planted both feet in Titus's chest. Alvarez kicked out and launched the Harbinger through the hatch and down the main hall. Thirty feet away, Titus slammed into the rear bulkhead and collapsed unconscious to the deck.

After kicking the Harbinger off the bridge, Alvarez landed on his feet and stood there vibrating from the boost affects. He shifted his vision to electromagnetic scanning mode and watched his glowing nanites spread throughout the wiring and computer systems all over the bridge.

His nanites eradicated the last few traces of Cassiopeia. Alvarez grinned,

"Bye, bye."

~ Port Overseer's office ~

Marius dismissed the woozy dock supervisor to return to his duties. He could now scan through the man's memories and look for any clues that Ptolemy might have missed. Marius set his chino cup on the desk and looked down at the courtyard.

Harbinger Titus was heading toward the building from the dock. Mothballing procedures must be complete. Something was odd though. The overseer felt a chill run down his spine.

Marius recognized Titus from his holy vestments and the unique red Harbinger rank insignia emblazoned on the shoulders of his white robes. Titus had his prayer hood pulled up over his head. He was leaning forward, and his hands were clasped before his face. It looked like the man was praying to the Emperor while he walked.

He shook his head at the Harbinger's odd behavior. He didn't have time to puzzle it out. Marius had to focus on searching the dock supervisor's memories for clues or signs of things that were out of place. He might get lucky and notice anyone acting strange that the supervisor might have missed.

Alvarez entered the main structure of the port. He reached under his white robe and pulled out an emergency mineshaft sealer. A small glass ball with a nitrogen sensitive catalyzer, designed to rapidly seal mining tunnels. He opened

the door at the bottom of the stairwell and threw the mine sealer against the back wall.

The glass shattered and the catalyzing agent reacted with the nitrogen in the air, filling the entire stairwell with a rapidly hardening mist. In minutes, the mist would become a dense goo that would harden into an impassable rock-like material.

Alvarez continued through the building toward the Vaults of Penance several floors down. He had to rescue Warlock and Nero, before they were transported to the Emperor's Palace for execution. Most of the Empire's clandestine operatives were already dead.

Warlock, Nero, and Alvarez were the last Watchers still breathing.

What Dreams May Come

Abby looked down at Lailani's sleeping body,

"What about them? What happens to your followers, if you bail?"

Dawn knocked on the wooden armrest of her little throne,

"Grand scheme of things? I think eventually Lailani will probably want a larger throne, once she reaches her full height."

Abby nodded casually,

"Who will Lailani sit on the throne and lead, now that you've somehow driven the telepathic ability out of her people?"

Dawn sat back and stared at Abby curiously,

"What would make you suspect that I had anything to do with that?"

Abby pointed at her,

"You did. How many of the mysterious arrivals in the bottleneck, did it take to overpower you?"

Abby cocked her head and looked up toward the ceiling, thinking back. She looked back at Dawn,

"If I remember right, you said, 'In a group, they easily overpowered me.', right? Individual power is nullified by numbers? After what they did to you, there's no way you would risk that happening again, right?"

Dawn slowly smiled and nodded,

"You just might be a little too sharp, for a young woman your age."

Captain Watcher shifted on her carpet, smiling calmly and pleasantly. Dawn's eyebrows went up and she smiled nervously,

"Easy Captain, you're in no danger from me. Controlling the local population was purely about my safety and is easily reversed."

Dawn chuckled nervously, and added,

"Besides, if you fired that in here, you'd likely drop the ceiling and kill all three of us."

Captain Watcher moved her right hand out from beside her thigh, holding her sidearm. She stood up and stepped backward toward the entrance to the cave,

"I need to think about it."

Dawn nodded,

"Take as much time as you need."

Captain Watcher held her left hand out, and the glowing blue manta ray landed. She turned and headed out through the cave, slapping her sidearm onto the plate. THUNK. She held the glowing manta ray until she was out of the cave, then slid the crystal bracelet onto her wrist.

The men waiting outside the cave escorted her back to the beach and rowed her back out to The Rider. Abby shook her head and laughed at the grinning dancers. She waved goodbye, then climbed up the ladder onto the deck.

Norgren smiled down at her from the quarterdeck,

"Welcome back, Captain."

Abby pulled her hat off, closed her eyes, then leaned her head back feeling the sun on her face,

"I'm so tired Norgren. I want you to fire the cannons on anyone who approaches this ship in the next twenty-four hours."

Norgren laughed as he checked the scanner, then he stepped over and sat down on the top of the stairs,

"Get some sleep, me and Sasha can hold down the fort."

Abby turned toward him and looked him in the eyes,

"The telepath living in the mountain, wants us to take her with us when we leave."

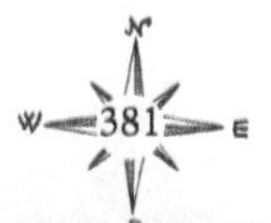

Norgren's eyes went wide,

"What about her people?"

Abby laughed,

"That's what I said!"

Norgren shook his head, then looked off toward the bow. Abby turned her head and saw Sasha just outside the hatch to the forward stairwell. Grinning, he gave them a thumbs up. She gave him a curiously raised eyebrow and looked back at Norgren.

Norgren nodded at Sasha, then looked at Abby,

"We set you up a surprise down by the galley, Captain."

She looked at him suspiciously, eyes narrowed. Norgren laughed, then gestured toward the stairwell,

"Trust me, Captain, you'll love it. And frankly, you need it."

Abby made her way down the stairwell and walked past the Galley toward Sasha. Her grinning steward was standing in front of a door, waiting for her. Abby cocked her head slightly and spread her hands,

"Are you guys kicking me out of my cabin?"

Sasha laughed and shook his head, no. He stepped to the side of the door and held up a hand, pointing out the new sign on the door. It read: Captain Abigail Only,

"Norgren remodeled one of the extra crew quarters!"

Abby scrunched up her face, looking confused,

"You made me a backup cabin?"

Sasha laughed, then reached out and pushed the door open. Abby looked inside and saw ceramic tile covering the walls and floor. Curious, she walked in and suddenly smiled from ear to ear.

Norgren had converted the room into a huge private bathroom, complete with garden tub and walk-in shower. Abby walked back out in the hall and hugged Sasha,

"Tell Norgren I've officially decided to keep him too."

She went back in and closed the door as Sasha walked away laughing.

An Hour Later

Standing on the quarterdeck, Sasha watched the scanner while Norgren cleaned and oiled the cannon turret. Abby walked past them smiling like she was on cloud nine, carrying her vest and her weapon belt over one arm. They both grinned as she went by, then they went back to work.

In her cabin, Abby saw a plate of food waiting on her desk. She squeezed her earring,

"Are you two competing for captain's favorite?"

She heard them both start laughing outside her cabin.

Abby hung her vest on the stand, hung her weapon belt next to it, and sat down to eat.

She got about halfway through her plate of fish, cheese, nuts, and something like a blueberry muffin, when she suddenly glanced over at the aquarium. Her eyes widened and she laughed, almost choking on a piece of muffin.

The spiny black toxop-whatever thing looked like a small black desert cactus with two bent arms pointing up toward the ceiling. Abby swallowed the muffin then laughed loudly.

In a very short time, the captain of The Riptide Rider curled up in bed and closed her eyes, quickly falling asleep. She finally got some real rest, since the start of all this madness, and fell deep into a dream...

~~~~~

Abby's eyes flickered open briefly. It was dark. She heard Sheriff Baker breathing heavily. Her body was jostling gently back and forth as he carried her through the woods. She heard leaves crunching underfoot and branches snapping. A woman's voice came from the sheriff's radio,

"Chopper is inbound, Sheriff. You should reach the clearing just over Benton Ridge. Adams is there now, waving a flare for the pilot."

The sheriff's response was muffled and faded out...

Abby heard the helicopter blades and felt the heavy gravity sensation of the medivac lifting off. There was a mask
~~~~~

over her face, and she heard a gas hissing sound in her ear. Her vision was just a blur. She heard a woman's voice very close to her,

"Patient is a fifteen-year-old female, with possible traumatic brain injury. Heavy bleeding and lacerations in both the parietal and occipital areas of the skull..."

~~~~~

Abby sat up in bed breathing heavily and panicking. She reached up and felt the back of her head. The Rider was rocking gently beneath her as she looked around her cabin. She sighed and shook off the lingering adrenaline from the dream.

With fresh clothes and boots, leather vest, belt and weapons, Abby pulled on her black three corner hat and stepped out of her cabin. She smiled and squinted at the morning sun,

How long was I asleep?

Norgren called down from the quarterdeck,

"We were starting to worry, Captain."

Abby stretched her back and headed up the stairs. She found a tray waiting on one of the consoles. On one side was an empty plate with some crumbs and an empty cup. On the other side was a plate with bacon, some unknown fruit in a wooden bowl, and her beautiful pirate mug with white foamy topped cappuccino.

She grabbed her cup as she squeezed her earring,

~~~~~

"Sasha, you're getting a raise."

Norgren was on his back, head and shoulders under part of the control console. She heard him chuckle. Sasha's voice came over the earring,

"You're going to start paying us? That's welcome news, Captain!"

Abby laughed and sipped on her cappuccino. It was cold, but still delicious. Looking down at Norgren,

"What's going on down there?"

"Only the best upgrade The Rider's ever seen. Back channel called it, Slipstream. I just finished adding the last components and teaching The Rider how to do it."

With a sip of cappuccino and a raised eyebrow,

"I'm sorry, back channel?"

Norgren chuckled,

"Remember that little video recorder you gave me? Turns out, after I removed the back panel, I found another screen and another button. Private channel recorded by my predecessors, with secret running updates on various secret modifications and whatnot. Running consensus is that it's best for everyone if we don't talk about it."

Abby nodded,

"So, code 'back channel' means, don't ask?"

"HA! Exactly!"

She laughed and shook her head,

"Duly noted. Where's Sasha?"

"Rounding up resupply on the island, foodstuffs, other basics. You know you slept almost twenty-four hours?"

"Wow... I guess I was tired."

Norgren chuckled again,

"Well, I'm glad you got some rest. Cause we'll be ready to test the upgrades in a couple hours. Unless you want to stay here a while. Islanders did say you were basically welcome to stay indefinitely."

Abby turned away from the island and stared out toward the open ocean. Several minutes went by and Norgren slid out from under the console. He watched her for a moment, then slid back under the console,

"What's on your mind, Captain?"

She set down her cup and ate a few bites of bacon,

"We're leaving."

"You're the boss."

Another strip of bacon later,

"How much longer to complete the upgrade?"

"Upgrades Captain, plural. Almost done, another hour to double check everything, two tops."

Abby smiled,

"Nice."

She squeezed her earring,

"You moving in with one of those islander girls or what? What's taking so long, steward?"

"I have a name, you know!"

Abby and Norgren both laughed.

~ ~

An hour later, Abby saw the large islander boat heading out toward The Rider,

"Looks like Sasha is planning to fill up the cargo hold."

Norgren looked over and grunted something like a laugh. Abby watched the islander boat for a moment, then cocked her head to the side,

"You know what? I haven't even been down there. What's in the cargo hold?"

"Other than all the junk we brought from the atoll, just a bunch of unmarked barrels and crates."

She looked down at Norgren next to her. He was on one knee adjusting the new 'combat maneuvers' stabilizing brace

behind her. It was a padded backrest that flipped up from behind the pilot station.

For one of Norgren's upgrades he replaced the camouflage mode toggle behind the wheel arm with a three-way switch. Center position was now normal operation. Flipping it down put The Rider into camouflage mode. Flipping it up, activated the new combat maneuvering mode.

It wasn't as dramatic as Norgren made it sound, but Abby was excited to test it out. If everything actually worked right, the quarterdeck would emit a field that held their feet to the deck. Additionally, a stabilizing brace would rise up behind whoever was manning the wheel, giving the pilot additional support.

Norgren stood up,

"How's that feel?"

Abby grabbed the wheel and leaned back on the padded support against the small of her back. She reached out to the controls to each side and bounced back against the support a few times,

"Feels perfect, comfortable, very solid."

Norgren reset the stabilizer and locked it down. He got up, wiped his hands on his coveralls, and tucked his tools away in his belt,

"I'm going to finish up below deck, then I'll double check everything."

Abby nodded and went down to the gate in the railing, waiting on the islander boat. She saw the old bald man in his shimmering robes standing next to Lailani, both were smiling at her. Lailani broke her 'High Priestess' act, enough to wave. Abby laughed.

She saw Sasha standing by a large pile of crates, barrels, and canvas sacks, checking things against a list.

The men working the poles secured the boat to The Rider then seemed to just freeze. Lailani and the old man both did the same. Something was wrong. Abby started to jump over to their boat when she suddenly heard Dawn's voice in her mind,

Have you made your decision, Captain?

Abby stopped and smiled,

You're doing this.

Of course.

She saw Sasha across the islander boat looking around confused, Abby thought,

You'll give the islanders back whatever you took away?

Already done.

Alright, you can come with us, but I want answers.

Sasha waved at her and spread his hands, looking confused. Abby held up a finger toward him, signaling wait.

From one of the small tent-like structures in the middle of the islander boat, a very thick, short, hooded figure emerged and walked toward Abby. Sasha stared with wide eyes.

Dawn stepped up to the railing,

Permission to come aboard, Captain?

Abby chuckled and nodded,

Permission granted.

I'm going to go below for now.

Dawn stepped aboard and headed to the bow, disappearing into the forward stairwell. Abby looked at Sasha and put a finger to her lips. Confused, with wide eyes, Sasha slowly nodded.

All of the islanders woke up. The old bald man held up a hand in greeting,

"If you wish it, our men can help load supplies, Captain Abigail Watcher."

Sasha spread out the cargo net on the islander boat, while Abby setup the boom.

Slipstream

Abby secured the cargo hold doors, trotted down the stairs, and walked back to the gate in the railing. Not even pretending to be the reserved 'High Priestess' anymore, Lailani came over and gave Abby a hug with tears in her eyes. Abby hugged her back and concentrated, thinking,

I'll miss you too, kid.

The crew of The Riptide Rider bid farewell to the islanders.

Abby climbed the stairs and took her place at the wheel. Sasha took his place on her left, Norgren at the auxiliary control console on her right. Excited to be under way once again, Abby activated the antigravity drives.

Closing her eyes, she took a moment and listened to the gentle thrumming of the drives. She felt the vibration through the deck and a soft breeze sneaking under the sides of her hat.

Abby opened her eyes and dialed up the lift power. As The Rider cleared the water, she extended the lower masts and unfurled the sails. Turning away from the islands, Abby slowly pushed the power levers up to fifty percent, climbing at a gentle angle. The wind sent them faster and faster across the

open ocean, toward much deeper waters.

Glancing to each side, she saw Norgren smiling and Sasha fretting nervously. Abby smiled broadly, turning her head back toward Norgren,

"How's it work?"

"Slipstream, Captain?"

Abby nodded. Norgren pointed to some new controls on the console,

"We can activate it while airborne, but the risk wouldn't be worth it unless it was seriously dire straits. Slipstream is designed for stealth. We sail forward on the water, engage the cloaking system, and activate the slipstream. It's a new hybrid process of the jump drive and The Rider's primary engine working together."

Norgren pointed to an indicator on the console,

"Theoretically, once we get the green light here..."

Norgren pointed to the small golden jump drive activation key hanging from her journal,

"...you activate the jump drive, and the rest is automatic. You just have to pilot her through the vortex."

Abby furrowed her brow,

"Vortex?"

Norgren held up both hands, palms down,

"Easy Captain, I'm getting there."

Sasha piped in,

"No, no, no! Don't go easy, Captain! You make him explain! This sounds crazy to me! A vortex? What on Earth is a vortex? And why would any sane person pilot a ship through one?"

Abby laughed and nodded for Norgren to continue. Norgren rolled his eyes at Sasha's minor panic attack,

"Ok, like I was saying, we get up to speed and activate the cloaking process. That will generate a huge fog bank around the ship. Then, you activate the slipstream. That will create a vortex in the water in front of the ship. The vortex will suck in the fog and mask both our leaving and our arrival at the destination."

Norgren moved his hand forward and dipped it down like he was demonstrating a truck driving through a large gulley or ditch,

"We should get the green light on the panel as soon as The Rider tips her bow into the vortex and begins a diagonal dive into the channel under the surface of the ocean. You hit the jump drive key as soon as she begins her descent, and the jump drive opens a portal under the water."

Norgren looked over at her and made eye contact,

"That's how we hide from the Empire's sensors, Captain.

The Rider passes through the time portal underwater, masking our wake. She emerges in an ascending vortex channel at her destination. You slam the power levers forward and we push up out of the channel. We'll be covered by the fog that's been generated by the cloaking system and gets pulled through the vortex ahead of us. It's that simple."

Sasha scoffed and mumbled something less than optimistic. Abby reached for the controls and pushed The Rider into a steep dive,

"Might as well test it!"

Both Norgren and Sasha started to freak out as Abby laughed and leveled out the ship,

"I'm kidding."

Abby slowed The Rider and stowed the lower sails, then retracted the lower masts. She eased the ship into the water,

"Is there an optimum speed? Or power setting?"

Norgren nodded,

"It's just a calculated guess mind you. But we should be pushing ahead at twenty-five percent power, activate cloak and slipstream. Soon as we tip into the vortex, activate the jump drive. Soon as we pass through the portal, push power higher for the climb, then cut thrust once we clear the vortex on the other side."

Abby set The Rider sailing forward at twenty-five percent power. She looked over at Norgren,

"Why exactly did we need this slipstream upgrade?"

Norgren looked at the deck for a moment. When he looked up, he met her gaze,

"We're not The Rider's second crew, Captain. We're her fifth, and every single one of them were caught by the Empire trying to get through the bottleneck into the future beyond it. We need every aspect of stealth we can acquire."

Abby looked forward and nodded,

"Where do we go from here? We're definitely not ready for the bottleneck yet. What's the point anyway? Why were they trying to get past the bottleneck?"

Sasha spoke softly,

"We could go see if I survived jumping into the ocean..."

Norgren and Abby laughed. Norgren said,

"We should start by trying to round up the rest of the original crew, Captain."

Abby nodded,

"Sounds good. I'm guessing you know about them from the..."

"Back channel, yeah."

Abby nodded,

"So, where to? How do we find them? For that matter,

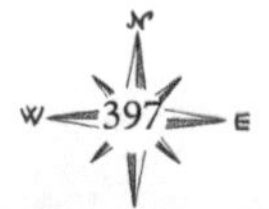

what about our guest below deck? Is Dawn part of the crew?"

Norgren shook his head,

"She was never mentioned as part of the crew by any of the others before us. Apparently, crew isn't always exactly the same. But there are a few that have been crew every time."

"Ok, where to? And how?"

Norgren held up a small digital viewer with a picture of a young man on it,

"From what I understand, you gotta keep the image in your mind. Concentrate on his face while you think about him being a former member of the crew. The Rider should be able to zero-in on him with that, based on her previous experience. The Rider has a lot of prior knowledge we can tap into if we do it right."

Abby cocked her head,

"The Rider has knowledge?"

"That's right. Hundreds of years of experience under her belt. Somewhere around seventy or eighty years just under your command, Captain."

Abby's eyes went wide. She knew there were previous Captain Abigails, but still, wow,

"Alright, hold that image up. Let me see it."

Norgren held up the viewer. Abby focused on the image,

Alright girl, he's been crew before, we need to find him again...

Abby reached over and activated the cloaking system. When she did, down in the engine room, the emergency venting system shunted water, fire, and air in precise ratios to the overpressure vents. Dense fog began pouring out of The Rider in every direction.

Very quickly, the entire area around The Rider was completely engulfed in fog. Everything around them was obscured, with visibility inside the fog reduced to just thirty or forty feet. From the quarterdeck, they could just barely make out the forward stairwell.

Sasha whimpered and gripped the railing. Abby and Norgren looked at each other and grinned. Abby reached for the console, flipped open the safety cover, and pushed the button, activating the slipstream.

A powerful electromagnetic whine and a chugging humming low frequency warble began emanating from below deck. They heard the ocean water ahead of the ship begin roaring and rushing louder and louder.

In the back of her mind, Abby thought she heard the faint sound of helicopter blades.

All around, the fog began moving forward, sucked into the vortex that they could not yet see. Norgren shouted over the noise,

"WE CAN STILL ABORT, CAPTAIN!"

Abby shook her head,

"NO! WE'RE GOING!"

Norgren grabbed the railing. The sound of churning and rushing water grew louder. Abby reached forward and flipped the switch up, activating the combat maneuver setting. The fog rushed forward around them, beginning to drop at the edge of their vision.

Norgren tried one last time,

"LAST CHANCE TO ABORT, CAPTAIN! ONCE THE RIDER ENTERS THE VORTEX, WE'RE COMMITTED!"

It was hard to hear him over the steadily growing whine of the jump drive powering up, along with the roar of The Rider's engine at full power. Abby imagined it in her mind. The heart of The Rider, the magnetar powered engine that normally pushed the wind forward to accelerate the ship, glowing brightly in the engine room below.

Norgren's upgrades added a new function that allowed the elementally fueled magical engine to churn the ocean waters ahead of them into a massive vortex that The Rider was about to drop into.

Again, she heard the faint sound of helicopter blades, and hissing gas. It made no sense. She shook it off. Abby leaned back against the support and braced her feet. She focused her mind on the picture of the young man that Norgren showed her,

We're counting on you, girl.

She held the wheel in one hand and grabbed the jump

drive key in the other,

"WE'RE COMMITTED! WE'RE GOING! HOLD FAST!"

The ocean in front of The Rider dropped away. The waters spun rapidly, swirling before the ship in a massive spiral that dropped into the ocean at a steep angle. The bow and the front ends of the antigravity drives were visible as The Rider moved past the edge.

Instinctively, Abby began to turn the wheel into the swirl, to keep the ship pointed forward. Norgren's mind rapidly ran through all the possible outcomes of trying to steer the ship manually through the vortex.

He reached out, grabbing and stopping the wheel, shouting just barely louder than the roar of the churning maelstrom,

"NO! KEEP HER UP WITH THE DRIVES..."

Abby's hand rapidly moved across the controls.

"PULL BACK JUST ENOUGH TO KEEP HER BOW OUT OF THE CHURN..."

She pulled back on the wheel as The Rider began to tilt forward over the edge.

"USE THE DRIFT TO KEEP HER CENTERED, GLIDE ACROSS THE SURFACE!"

Abby's mind raced with his last-minute instructions,

Antigravity drives, adjust pitch bow up, center with drift, glide the surface, OH MY GOD WE'RE GOING TO DIE!

The Rider's center of gravity passed the edge of the vortex. The ship fell forward, slamming into the churning, rushing waters at a forty-five-degree angle, rapidly accelerating forward.

Abby quickly pulled back on the wheel, lifting the bow as the rotation of the vortex began to turn the ship. Without looking down, she adjusted the lift control, pulling The Rider back up out of the waters that were pulling her to the side. She moved her hand and shifted the drift. She tweaked the wheel.

The Riptide Rider plunged downward into the vortex at a terrifying angle, pointed slightly to the side, riding the rotating tunnel of ocean water like a giant, fat surfboard.

Norgren shouted,

"ACTIVATE THE JUMP DRIVE BEFORE THE VORTEX COLLAPSES!"

Abby's hands were busy working the wheel, adjusting the antigravity lift power, and controlling the drift all at once to keep The Rider stable.

Sasha screamed like a little girl, then froze. His eyes squeezed shut, mouth open wide in mid-scream. The sudden silence had a soft ringing background.

Abby's attention was suddenly drawn to a single drop of water, falling incredibly slowly in front of her nose. The vortex was barely moving, her body was frozen in the moment, but her

mind was moving at the speed of light.

She felt a sweet subtle humming vibration coming from the time traveling device hanging on a silver chain around her neck.

She heard multiple phantom voices in the back of her mind, she couldn't make out what they were saying. Then she heard a woman's voice close to her ear, helicopter blades beating softly in the background,

"You can do this sweetheart. You have to hold on for me. You have to be brave for me."

Abby reached out toward the ship with her thoughts. She spoke to The Riptide Rider with her mind,

JUMP GIRL! JUMP!

Time rocketed back to full speed. The Rider's time portal generator discharged with an explosive electromagnetic pulse that flashed forward through the vortex. An electrical flash in front of the ship opened into a wide ring of lightning and fire, covering the width of the vortex before them.

The Rider passed through the portal at the bottom curve of the churning tunnel of ocean water, with both the engine and Sasha screaming at maximum volume. The waters roaring all around them. Norgren shouted,

"CLIMB, CAPTAIN! FULL POWER CLIMB!"

The exit vortex now rose up before them. Swirling fog rushed forward in a spinning tornado around the ship.

Abby pulled the wheel back hard and slammed the levers to maximum power. The Rider's nose pushed into the rising waters, swamping the deck with ocean water.

Terror and adrenaline shot through them all as the ship began to slide forward into the rising wall of water, dragging against the bow and pulling her nose down.

Insanely, Abby heard her mom's voice, high-pitched and strained with desperation,

"Don't you dare die on me, Abigail Josephine Watcher! Don't you dare!"

Abby narrowed her eyes, gritted her teeth and held the wheel back at maximum lift,

Come on girl, don't let us down.

Abby felt a powerful forward push as the afterburners engaged. The Rider's bow lifted free. The ship leaned back at a frighteningly steep angle, pushing rapidly forward, bouncing and rocketing upward through the rapidly shrinking vortex.

Norgren shouted,

"WE'RE LOSING HER!"

The Rider roared forward and upward, water sprayed across the deck as the upper masts began digging into water at the top of the shrinking tunnel. Abby held the power levers firmly at max,

"DEEP BREATH! HOLD FAST!"

The vortex collapsed on them. The ocean engulfed the ship. The Rider exploded onto the surface. Her nose pointed halfway up, toward the sky. Abby immediately pulled back on the power levers and the ship stopped rising, hanging frozen in the air for a torturously long second.

The Rider's front end started coming down and accelerated very rapidly. She slammed down onto the water with a massive splash and the sound of groaning and cracking wood. The impact shocked and vibrated all three of their bodies, painfully.

Thick, dense fog swirled ominously around them in the sudden silence. A large-sounding, unidentifiable creature roared somewhere high above, far off in the distance.

Sasha sighed and dropped unconscious to the deck. Abby turned her head to look at Sasha and heard Norgren collapse on her other side.

Eyes wide with sudden apprehension, Captain Watcher whispered ominously in her scratchy harsh voice,

"Betrayed we are lads."

Abby felt her mind go heavy and her eyes started to close. Thinking fast in her final moment, she reached forward and grabbed for the three-way switch behind the wheel arm. She tried to flip it all the way down, but only got it to center position before her strength failed completely.

Without the maneuvering support, Abby fell backward onto the deck and into the loving embrace of the darkness.

Shadow Puppets

Abby's eyes were already closed. But they suddenly, reflexively, squeezed even tighter as she became consciously aware of the painfully bright light surrounding her. The smell of blood and vomit and antiseptic filled her nose. She heard organized chaos all around.

She felt people touching her. Someone was moving her arm. Another was touching her neck. A woman spoke softly,

"She's regaining consciousness, doctor."

She heard a louder voice that sounded vaguely similar to Norgren,

"We're losing her! John, another 10CC's."

She heard her mom's voice, high-pitched and strained with desperation. She was distant and moving further away. Like Kat was somewhere behind the doctors and nurses surrounding her in the bright emergency room,

"Don't you dare die on me, Abigail Josephine Watcher! Don't you dare!"

Someone said something about her blood type being

confirmed.

She heard Sheriff Baker's voice,

"Come on, Kat! Come with me! You can't be here now!"

Abby heard machines beeping and gas hissing. A baby cried out somewhere nearby. The doctor shouted,

"Nurse, get that IV in now!"

Things began to fade away again as she felt her body being moved and pulled. The last thing she heard was that same doctor's voice,

"We need to get control of this bleeding before she crashes..."

About the Author

Damien M. Cross

Adam Seif Photography

Damien M. Cross is a Christian, husband, father, and cat dad. He has six amazing children, and three beloved cats, who currently live in the Midwest. Damien served in the United States Marine Corps, has worked private security for some global level elites, and dabbled in the field of law enforcement. His hope in writing is to get people to think for themselves about the reality of the world around them. And consider what kind of world they want to build for their children to live in. His hobbies include making mead like a Viking.